The Bridegroom

"Jin's new collection of short stories . . . shows he could teach some native-born writers a few things about the beauty of spare prose and the power of a few well-chosen words." — *USA Today*

"For his revelations about ordinary life in the hinterlands of China . . . Ha Jin commands attention. For his mastery of the literary craft in English, he merits awe." — *San Francisco Examiner & Chronicle*

"Amusing. . . . Realistic. . . . Rarely has China seemed less exotic and more accessible. . . . The stories have the air of fables."
— *Los Angeles Times*

"Ha Jin achieves a novella-like compression of narrative power and a Tolstoyan wide-angle empathy. . . . As a chronicler of the craziness of post–Cultural Revolution China, he's an Ishmael, a singular eyewitness telling us of a dazzling tragedy."
— *Milwaukee Journal Sentinel*

"A finely nuanced collection of stories whose vivid portraits and pungent details bring into sharp relief the realities of modern-day China." — *Elle*

"The 12 stories in *The Bridegroom* . . . lay bare the ironies of tyranny in all its forms. . . . Part of the pleasure of this collection . . . lies in its revelation of an unknown world. . . . [Ha Jin's] eye for detail, his great storytelling talent . . . suffuse his work."
— *The New York Times Book Review*

"[A] vivid picture . . . of Chinese society in the era just after the Cultural Revolution." — *Chicago Tribune*

"Brilliant. . . . Delightful. . . . Ha Jin's customs, ideology and landscapes might be of an Eastern persuasion, but his narratives communicate universally. Without being didactic or condescending, these stories often resemble modern fables. . . . With humor, wit, clarity and poise, Ha Jin brings us another amalgamation of efficiently gorgeous tales, while weaving emotional insights from the East and West inextricably throughout."
— *Star Tribune* (Minneapolis)

"Opens the door to a world that is at once forbidding . . . and highly recognizable. The settings may be unfamiliar, but the characters are driven by universal emotions. . . . Ha Jin's spare prose, subtle wit, and surprising plot twists make for a read that is both quick and memorable." — *Entertainment Weekly*

"A collection of edgy, twisted stories. . . . *The Bridegroom* stands squarely among the world's best literature of oppression."
— *The Boston Globe*

"*The Bridegroom* . . . continues the standard of excellence [Ha Jin's] set for himself. . . . Jin consciously strips his prose of modern references and aspires to the kind of timelessness Chekhov achieved in his stories." — *The Oregonian*

"The real charm of *The Bridegroom* . . . comes from the realization that [Ha Jin's] characters . . . are stuck in lives very much like ours."
—*The Washington Post Book World*

"Beautifully understated short stories of life in contemporary China. Some of them are likely to break your heart." —*People*

HA JIN
The Bridegroom

Ha Jin left his native China in 1985 to attend Brandeis University. He is the author of three books of poetry; two previous collections of stories, *Under the Red Flag,* which won the Flannery O'Connor Award for Short Fiction, and *Ocean of Words,* which won the PEN/Hemingway Award; and two novels, *In the Pond* and *Waiting,* which won both the National Book Award and the PEN/Faulkner Award. He lives in Atlanta.

INTERNATIONAL

The Bridegroom

STORIES

Ha Jin

VINTAGE INTERNATIONAL

VINTAGE BOOKS

A DIVISION OF RANDOM HOUSE, INC.

NEW YORK

FIRST VINTAGE INTERNATIONAL EDITION, SEPTEMBER 2001

The stories in this collection have been previously published, sometimes in slightly
different form, in the following: "Saboteur" has appeared in *The Antioch Review;*
reprinted in *The Best American Short Stories* (1997); • "Alive" in *AGNI;* • "In the
Kindergarten" in *Five Points;* reprinted in *The Best American Short Stories* (1999);
• "A Tiger-Fighter Is Hard to Find" in *The Oxford American;* • "Broken" in
Columbia; • "The Bridegroom" in *Harper's;* reprinted in *The Best American
Short Stories* (2000); • "An Entrepreneur's Story" in *Witness;* • "Flame"
in *Missouri Review;* • "A Bad Joke" in *Manoa;* • "An Official Reply"
in *Shenandoah;* • "The Woman from New York" in *The Boston Book
Review;* • "After Cowboy Chicken Came to Town" in *TriQuarterly;*
reprinted in *The Best American Short Stories* (2001).

The Library of Congress has cataloged the Pantheon edition as follows:
Jin, Ha, 1956–
The bridegroom : stories / Ha Jin.
p. cm.
ISBN 0-375-42067-3
Contents: Saboteur—Flame—In the kindergarten—A tiger-fighter is hard to find—
Broken—The bridegroom—An entrepreneur's story—Alive—A bad joke—
An official reply—The woman from New York—
After Cowboy Chicken came to town.
1. China—Social life and customs—1976—Fiction. I. Title.
PS3560.16 Q54 2000
813'.54—dc21 00-028405
CIP

Vintage ISBN: 0-375-72493-1

Book design by Maura Fadden Rosenthal/mspaceny

www.vintagebooks.com

Printed in the United States of America
10 9 8 7 6 5 4 3 2 1

To Lisha

Contents

The Bridegroom

Saboteur

Mr. Chiu and his bride were having lunch in the square before Muji Train Station. On the table between them were two bottles of soda spewing out brown foam and two paper boxes of rice and sautéed cucumber and pork. "Let's eat," he said to her, and broke the connected ends of the chopsticks. He picked up a slice of streaky pork and put it into his mouth. As he was chewing, a few crinkles appeared on his thin jaw.

To his right, at another table, two railroad policemen were drinking tea and laughing; it seemed that the stout, middle-aged man was telling a joke to his young comrade, who was tall and of athletic build. Now and again they would steal a glance at Mr. Chiu's table.

The air smelled of rotten melon. A few flies kept buzzing

above the couple's lunch. Hundreds of people were rushing around to get on the platform or to catch buses to downtown. Food and fruit vendors were crying for customers in lazy voices. About a dozen young women, representing the local hotels, held up placards which displayed the daily prices and words as large as a palm, like FREE MEALS, AIR-CONDITIONING, and ON THE RIVER. In the center of the square stood a concrete statue of Chairman Mao, at whose feet peasants were napping, their backs on the warm granite and their faces toward the sunny sky. A flock of pigeons perched on the Chairman's raised hand and forearm.

The rice and cucumber tasted good, and Mr. Chiu was eating unhurriedly. His sallow face showed exhaustion. He was glad that the honeymoon was finally over and that he and his bride were heading back for Harbin. During the two weeks' vacation, he had been worried about his liver, because three months ago he had suffered from acute hepatitis; he was afraid he might have a relapse. But he had had no severe symptoms, despite his liver being still big and tender. On the whole he was pleased with his health, which could endure even the strain of a honeymoon; indeed, he was on the course of recovery. He looked at his bride, who took off her wire glasses, kneading the root of her nose with her fingertips. Beads of sweat coated her pale cheeks.

"Are you all right, sweetheart?" he asked.

"I have a headache. I didn't sleep well last night."

"Take an aspirin, will you?"

"It's not that serious. Tomorrow is Sunday and I can sleep in. Don't worry."

As they were talking, the stout policeman at the next table stood up and threw a bowl of tea in their direction. Both Mr. Chiu's and his bride's sandals were wet instantly.

"Hooligan!" she said in a low voice.

Mr. Chiu got to his feet and said out loud, "Comrade Police-man, why did you do this?" He stretched out his right foot to show the wet sandal.

"Do what?" the stout man asked huskily, glaring at Mr. Chiu while the young fellow was whistling.

"See, you dumped tea on our feet."

"You're lying. You wet your shoes yourself."

"Comrade Policeman, your duty is to keep order, but you purposely tortured us common citizens. Why violate the law you are supposed to enforce?" As Mr. Chiu was speaking, dozens of people began gathering around.

With a wave of his hand, the man said to the young fellow, "Let's get hold of him!"

They grabbed Mr. Chiu and clamped handcuffs around his wrists. He cried, "You can't do this to me. This is utterly unreasonable."

"Shut up!" The man pulled out his pistol. "You can use your tongue at our headquarters."

The young fellow added, "You're a saboteur, you know that? You're disrupting public order."

The bride was too petrified to say anything coherent. She was a recent college graduate, had majored in fine arts, and had never seen the police make an arrest. All she could say was, "Oh, please, please!"

The policemen were pulling Mr. Chiu, but he refused to go with them, holding the corner of the table and shouting, "We have a train to catch. We already bought the tickets."

The stout man punched him in the chest. "Shut up. Let your ticket expire." With the pistol butt he chopped Mr. Chiu's hands, which at once released the table. Together the two men were dragging him away to the police station.

Realizing he had to go with them, Mr. Chiu turned his head

and shouted to his bride, "Don't wait for me here. Take the train. If I'm not back by tomorrow morning, send someone over to get me out."

She nodded, covering her sobbing mouth with her palm.

After removing his belt, they locked Mr. Chiu into a cell in the back of the Railroad Police Station. The single window in the room was blocked by six steel bars; it faced a spacious yard, in which stood a few pines. Beyond the trees, two swings hung from an iron frame, swaying gently in the breeze. Somewhere in the building a cleaver was chopping rhythmically. There must be a kitchen upstairs, Mr. Chiu thought.

He was too exhausted to worry about what they would do to him, so he lay down on the narrow bed and shut his eyes. He wasn't afraid. The Cultural Revolution was over already, and recently the Party had been propagating the idea that all citizens were equal before the law. The police ought to be a law-abiding model for common people. As long as he remained coolheaded and reasoned with them, they probably wouldn't harm him.

Late in the afternoon he was taken to the Interrogation Bureau on the second floor. On his way there, in the stairwell, he ran into the middle-aged policeman who had manhandled him. The man grinned, rolling his bulgy eyes and pointing his fingers at him as if firing a pistol. Egg of a tortoise! Mr. Chiu cursed mentally.

The moment he sat down in the office, he burped, his palm shielding his mouth. In front of him, across a long desk, sat the chief of the bureau and a donkey-faced man. On the glass desktop was a folder containing information on his case. He felt it bizarre that in just a matter of hours they had accumulated a small pile of writing about him. On second thought he began to wonder whether they had kept a file on him all the time. How could this have happened? He lived and worked in Harbin, more than three hundred miles away, and this was his first time in Muji City.

The chief of the bureau was a thin, bald man who looked serene and intelligent. His slim hands handled the written pages in the folder in the manner of a lecturing scholar. To Mr. Chiu's left sat a young scribe, with a clipboard on his knee and a black fountain pen in his hand.

"Your name?" the chief asked, apparently reading out the question from a form.

"Chiu Maguang."

"Age?"

"Thirty-four."

"Profession?"

"Lecturer."

"Work unit?"

"Harbin University."

"Political status?"

"Communist Party member."

The chief put down the paper and began to speak. "Your crime is sabotage, although it hasn't induced serious consequences yet. Because you are a Party member, you should be punished more. You have failed to be a model for the masses and you—"

"Excuse me, sir," Mr. Chiu cut him off.

"What?"

"I didn't do anything. Your men are the saboteurs of our social order. They threw hot tea on my feet and on my wife's feet. Logically speaking, you should criticize them, if not punish them."

"That statement is groundless. You have no witness. Why should I believe you?" the chief said matter-of-factly.

"This is my evidence." He raised his right hand. "Your man hit my fingers with a pistol."

"That doesn't prove how your feet got wet. Besides, you could have hurt your fingers yourself."

"But I am telling the truth!" Anger flared up in Mr. Chiu. "Your police station owes me an apology. My train ticket has expired, my new leather sandals are ruined, and I am late for a conference in the provincial capital. You must compensate me for the damage and losses. Don't mistake me for a common citizen who would tremble when you sneeze. I'm a scholar, a philosopher, and an expert in dialectical materialism. If necessary, we will argue about this in *The Northeastern Daily,* or we will go to the highest People's Court in Beijing. Tell me, what's your name?" He got carried away with his harangue, which was by no means trivial and had worked to his advantage on numerous occasions.

"Stop bluffing us," the donkey-faced man broke in. "We have seen a lot of your kind. We can easily prove you are guilty. Here are some of the statements given by eyewitnesses." He pushed a few sheets of paper toward Mr. Chiu.

Mr. Chiu was dazed to see the different handwritings, which all stated that he had shouted in the square to attract attention and refused to obey the police. One of the witnesses had identified herself as a purchasing agent from a shipyard in Shanghai. Something stirred in Mr. Chiu's stomach, a pain rising to his rib. He gave out a faint moan.

"Now you have to admit you are guilty," the chief said. "Although it's a serious crime, we won't punish you severely, provided you write out a self-criticism and promise that you won't disrupt the public order again. In other words, your release will depend on your attitude toward this crime."

"You're daydreaming," Mr. Chiu cried. "I won't write a word, because I'm innocent. I demand that you provide me with a letter of apology so I can explain to my university why I'm late."

Both the interrogators smiled contemptuously. "Well, we've never done that," said the chief, taking a puff at his cigarette.

"Then make this a precedent."

"That's unnecessary. We are pretty certain that you will comply with our wishes." The chief blew a column of smoke toward Mr. Chiu's face.

At the tilt of the chief's head, two guards stepped forward and grabbed the criminal by the arms. Mr. Chiu meanwhile went on saying, "I shall report you to the Provincial Administration. You'll have to pay for this! You are worse than the Japanese military police."

They dragged him out of the room.

After dinner, which consisted of a bowl of millet porridge, a corn bun, and a piece of pickled turnip, Mr. Chiu began to have a fever, shaking with a chill and sweating profusely. He knew that the fire of anger had gotten into his liver and that he was probably having a relapse. No medicine was available, because his briefcase had been left with his bride. At home it would have been time for him to sit in front of their color TV, drinking jasmine tea and watching the evening news. It was so lonesome in here. The orange bulb above the single bed was the only source of light, which enabled the guards to keep him under surveillance at night. A moment ago he had asked them for a newspaper or a magazine to read, but they turned him down.

Through the small opening on the door noises came in. It seemed that the police on duty were playing cards or chess in a nearby office; shouts and laughter could be heard now and then. Meanwhile, an accordion kept coughing from a remote corner in the building. Looking at the ballpoint and the letter paper left for him by the guards when they took him back from the Interrogation Bureau, Mr. Chiu remembered the old saying, "When a scholar runs into soldiers, the more he argues, the muddier his point becomes." How ridiculous this whole thing was. He ruffled his thick hair with his fingers.

He felt miserable, massaging his stomach continually. To tell the truth, he was more upset than frightened, because he would have to catch up with his work once he was back home—a paper that was due at the printers next week, and two dozen books he ought to read for the courses he was going to teach in the fall.

A human shadow flitted across the opening. Mr. Chiu rushed to the door and shouted through the hole, "Comrade Guard, Comrade Guard!"

"What do you want?" a voice rasped.

"I want you to inform your leaders that I'm very sick. I have heart disease and hepatitis. I may die here if you keep me like this without medication."

"No leader is on duty on the weekend. You have to wait till Monday."

"What? You mean I'll stay in here tomorrow?"

"Yes."

"Your station will be held responsible if anything happens to me."

"We know that. Take it easy, you won't die."

It seemed illogical that Mr. Chiu slept quite well that night, though the light above his head had been on all the time and the straw mattress was hard and infested with fleas. He was afraid of ticks, mosquitoes, cockroaches—any kind of insect but fleas and bedbugs. Once, in the countryside, where his school's faculty and staff had helped the peasants harvest crops for a week, his colleagues had joked about his flesh, which they said must have tasted nonhuman to fleas. Except for him, they were all afflicted with hundreds of bites.

More amazing now, he didn't miss his bride a lot. He even enjoyed sleeping alone, perhaps because the honeymoon had tired him out and he needed more rest.

The backyard was quiet on Sunday morning. Pale sunlight streamed through the pine branches. A few sparrows were jumping on the ground, catching caterpillars and ladybugs. Holding the steel bars, Mr. Chiu inhaled the morning air, which smelled meaty. There must have been an eatery or a cooked-meat stand nearby. He reminded himself that he should take this detention with ease. A sentence that Chairman Mao had written to a hospitalized friend rose in his mind: "Since you are already in here, you may as well stay and make the best of it."

His desire for peace of mind originated in his fear that his hepatitis might get worse. He tried to remain unperturbed. However, he was sure that his liver was swelling up, since the fever still persisted. For a whole day he lay in bed, thinking about his paper on the nature of contradictions. Time and again he was overwhelmed by anger, cursing aloud, "A bunch of thugs!" He swore that once he was out, he would write an article about this experience. He had better find out some of the policemen's names.

It turned out to be a restful day for the most part; he was certain that his university would send somebody to his rescue. All he should do now was remain calm and wait patiently. Sooner or later the police would have to release him, although they had no idea that he might refuse to leave unless they wrote him an apology. Damn those hoodlums, they had ordered more than they could eat!

When he woke up on Monday morning, it was already light. Somewhere a man was moaning; the sound came from the backyard. After a long yawn, and kicking off the tattered blanket, Mr. Chiu climbed out of bed and went to the window. In the middle of the yard, a young man was fastened to a pine, his wrists handcuffed around the trunk from behind. He was wriggling and swearing loudly, but there was no sight of anyone else in the yard. He looked familiar to Mr. Chiu.

Mr. Chiu squinted his eyes to see who it was. To his astonishment, he recognized the man, who was Fenjin, a recent graduate from the Law Department at Harbin University. Two years ago Mr. Chiu had taught a course in Marxist materialism, in which Fenjin had enrolled. Now, how on earth had this young devil landed here?

Then it dawned on him that Fenjin must have been sent over by his bride. What a stupid woman! A bookworm, who only knew how to read foreign novels! He had expected that she would contact the school's Security Section, which would for sure send a cadre here. Fenjin held no official position; he merely worked in a private law firm that had just two lawyers; in fact, they had little business except for some detective work for men and women who suspected their spouses of having extramarital affairs. Mr. Chiu was overcome with a wave of nausea.

Should he call out to let his student know he was nearby? He decided not to, because he didn't know what had happened. Fenjin must have quarreled with the police to incur such a punishment. Yet this could never have occurred if Fenjin hadn't come to his rescue. So no matter what, Mr. Chiu had to do something. But what could he do?

It was going to be a scorcher. He could see purple steam shimmering and rising from the ground among the pines. Poor devil, he thought, as he raised a bowl of corn glue to his mouth, sipped, and took a bite of a piece of salted celery.

When a guard came to collect the bowl and the chopsticks, Mr. Chiu asked him what had happened to the man in the backyard. "He called our boss 'bandit,' " the guard said. "He claimed he was a lawyer or something. An arrogant son of a rabbit."

Now it was obvious to Mr. Chiu that he had to do something to help his rescuer. Before he could figure out a way, a scream broke out in the backyard. He rushed to the window and saw a tall policeman standing before Fenjin, an iron bucket on the ground. It was the same young fellow who had arrested Mr. Chiu in the square two days before. The man pinched Fenjin's nose, then raised his hand, which stayed in the air for a few seconds, then slapped the lawyer across the face. As Fenjin was groaning, the man lifted up the bucket and poured water on his head.

"This will keep you from getting sunstroke, boy. I'll give you some more every hour," the man said loudly.

Fenjin kept his eyes shut, yet his wry face showed that he was struggling to hold back from cursing the policeman, or, more likely, that he was sobbing in silence. He sneezed, then raised his face and shouted, "Let me go take a piss."

"Oh yeah?" the man bawled. "Pee in your pants."

Still Mr. Chiu didn't make any noise, gripping the steel bars with both hands, his fingers white. The policeman turned and glanced at the cell's window; his pistol, partly holstered, glittered in the sun. With a snort he spat his cigarette butt to the ground and stamped it into the dust.

Then the door opened and the guards motioned Mr. Chiu to come out. Again they took him upstairs to the Interrogation Bureau.

The same men were in the office, though this time the scribe was sitting there empty-handed. At the sight of Mr. Chiu the chief said, "Ah, here you are. Please be seated."

After Mr. Chiu sat down, the chief waved a white silk fan and said to him, "You may have seen your lawyer. He's a young man without manners, so our director had him taught a crash course in the backyard."

"It's illegal to do that. Aren't you afraid to appear in a newspaper?"

"No, we are not, not even on TV. What else can you do? We are not afraid of any story you make up. We call it fiction. What we do care about is that you cooperate with us. That is to say, you must admit your crime."

"What if I refuse to cooperate?"

"Then your lawyer will continue his education in the sunshine."

A swoon swayed Mr. Chiu, and he held the arms of the chair to steady himself. A numb pain stung him in the upper stomach and nauseated him, and his head was throbbing. He was sure that the hepatitis was finally attacking him. Anger was flaming up in his chest; his throat was tight and clogged.

The chief resumed, "As a matter of fact, you don't even have to write out your self-criticism. We have your crime described clearly here. All we need is your signature."

Holding back his rage, Mr. Chiu said, "Let me look at that."

With a smirk the donkey-faced man handed him a sheet, which carried these words:

> I hereby admit that on July 13 I disrupted public order at Muji Train Station, and that I refused to listen to reason when the railroad police issued their warning. Thus I myself am responsible for my arrest. After two days' detention, I have realized the reactionary nature of my crime. From now on, I shall continue to educate myself with all my effort and shall never commit this kind of crime again.

A voice started screaming in Mr. Chiu's ears, "Lie, lie!" But he shook his head and forced the voice away. He asked the chief, "If I sign this, will you release both my lawyer and me?"

"Of course, we'll do that." The chief was drumming his fingers on the blue folder—their file on him.

Mr. Chiu signed his name and put his thumbprint under his signature.

"Now you are free to go," the chief said with a smile, and handed him a piece of paper to wipe his thumb with.

Mr. Chiu was so sick that he couldn't stand up from the chair at first try. Then he doubled his effort and rose to his feet. He staggered out of the building to meet his lawyer in the backyard, having forgotten to ask for his belt back. In his chest he felt as though there were a bomb. If he were able to, he would have razed the entire police station and eliminated all their families. Though he knew he could do nothing like that, he made up his mind to do something.

"I'm sorry about this torture, Fenjin," Mr. Chiu said when they met.

"It doesn't matter. They are savages." The lawyer brushed a patch of dirt off his jacket with trembling fingers. Water was still dribbling from the bottoms of his trouser legs.

"Let's go now," the teacher said.

The moment they came out of the police station, Mr. Chiu caught sight of a tea stand. He grabbed Fenjin's arm and walked over to the old woman at the table. "Two bowls of black tea," he said and handed her a one-yuan note.

After the first bowl, they each had another one. Then they set out for the train station. But before they walked fifty yards, Mr. Chiu insisted on eating a bowl of tree-ear soup at a food stand. Fenjin agreed. He told his teacher, "You mustn't treat me like a guest."

"No, I want to eat something myself."

As if dying of hunger, Mr. Chiu dragged his lawyer from restaurant to restaurant near the police station, but at each place he ordered no more than two bowls of food. Fenjin wondered why his teacher wouldn't stay at one place and eat his fill.

Mr. Chiu bought noodles, wonton, eight-grain porridge, and chicken soup, respectively, at four restaurants. While eating, he kept saying through his teeth, "If only I could kill all the bastards!" At the last place he merely took a few sips of the soup without tasting the chicken cubes and mushrooms.

Fenjin was baffled by his teacher, who looked ferocious and muttered to himself mysteriously, and whose jaundiced face was covered with dark puckers. For the first time Fenjin thought of Mr. Chiu as an ugly man.

Within a month over eight hundred people contracted acute hepatitis in Muji. Six died of the disease, including two children. Nobody knew how the epidemic had started.

Alive

Liya's letter threw her parents into a quandary. She informed them that she had been admitted by Sunrise Agricultural School in Antu County, to specialize in veterinary medicine. They didn't mind her pursuing that profession. What worried them was that with a diploma from such a school she might remain in the countryside for good, as an educated peasant.

For three days her father, Tong Guhan, didn't know what to write back to her. He wished she could have returned to Muji City. If he could have found her a job here, he would tell her to forget about the agricultural school. On the other hand, the admission promised better employment and could take her away from the chicken farm where she had worked for three years.

Should he tell her to go to the school? Or should he let her wait for an opportunity to come back home? He was torn by the dilemma.

"Dad, why don't you apply for a new apartment?" his son, Yaning, asked at lunch.

"It's not the right time yet," said Guhan. "Don't worry about that. If everything works out all right, we should have another apartment soon."

"I can wait, but I don't know how long Meili can wait." Yaning dropped his bowl on the table with a thump, his face twitching. He and Meili couldn't marry because there was no housing available, though they had been engaged for four years.

His mother, Jian, put in, "Yaning, be patient. Tell her to just wait a few months. When your father becomes the vice director, he'll ask for a new apartment. They'll give us one for sure." She peeled a green leaf off a lettuce, dipped it into the fried soy paste, and put it into her broad mouth.

"I don't know." Guhan sighed, twisting his mustache with his fingers, and his close-set eyes squinted at Yaning.

He was sympathetic to his son, whose facial tic made it harder for him to keep a fiancée. If their one-room apartment were larger, he would have let the young couple marry and move in, but there was no extra space for them. An ideal solution would be for him to get another apartment, one of those built recently near East Cannery, where he led the Packing Section; then he could give this old apartment to Yaning, whose work unit, a bookstore, was too small to own any residential housing. What prevented Guhan from applying for an apartment now was that he might be promoted to vice director of the cannery, and any selfish act at this moment might cause animosity among the staff and workers and upset his promotion. His superiors had already assured him that he was the strongest candidate for the position because he had a college degree.

Tong Guhan was a simple man, not very interested in power. But recently he realized that if he were the vice director, he could have moved into a new apartment long ago and said to his son, "Prepare for the wedding!" and he could also have written to his daughter, "Forget veterinary medicine and come back home. I'll get you a residence card and find you a good job here." Obviously the solutions to both problems depended on whether his promotion would materialize in time. These days he became anxious. Every morning, when watering the violets, cannas, roses, and cyclamen in his tiny backyard, he'd pray in silence that today he'd be officially notified of the promotion.

It was a sunny day. Buildings, trees, electrical poles, and kiosks were still wet with rainwater; the night before, a thunder shower had poured on the city. The blue trolley-bus Guhan was taking to work was full of passengers, wobbling along River Boulevard like a boat sailing through a harbor. The sunlight slanted in through the trolley's windows, shining on people's faces and the backs of the imitation-leather seats. Guhan let both arms, thin and swarthy, remain basking in the sun. He hoped the previous night's lightning had not damaged the ice-cabinets in his workshop.

On arrival at the cannery, he ran into Fei, a spindly young man who had recently joined the Party. "Good morning, Old Tong," Fei greeted him pleasantly, his round head tilted to one side. "Did you have a good bus ride?"

"It was all right," Guhan replied lukewarmly.

"Director Li wants to see you."

"About what?"

"I've no idea."

Guhan disliked Fei, who seemed too clever and oily. It was rumored that Fei would lead the Packing Section if Guhan left for his new position. The warmth Fei exuded made Guhan feel that the young man couldn't wait to take over.

He went to Director Li's office in the back of the factory building. At the sight of him, Li poured him a cup of green tea from a tall thermos bottle and said, "Old Tong, Secretary Liu and I want you to take a trip to Taifu City."

"What for?"

"To get our money from the coal mine." Li winked. His eyes were so big that some workers called him Director Ox-Eyes behind his back.

Guhan had heard of the debt. Knowing he had no choice, he said, "Of course I'll go."

"You'll represent our factory as our vice director. I hope they'll pay us this time, otherwise we won't be able to operate next year. The apartment building has gobbled up most of our funds."

"I'll try my best, Director Li." Guhan's face brightened at the mention of his new title.

"I wish you luck, Old Tong. Be stubborn with them." Li gave him a meaningful look and tapped his cigarette over the ashtray on the desk, revealing the stump of his third finger lost in the Korean War.

Guhan realized the trip was meant to test his ability as a factory leader. Two years ago the coal mine had bought twenty-four tons of canned food from East Cannery, but to date, though dunned every month, the mine hadn't paid a fen. Despite knowing it was a difficult mission, Guhan dared not show any reluctance in front of Li. He told himself, If they don't pay the debt this time, I won't come back. He believed the trip might either finalize or cancel his promotion.

That evening, after dinner, his wife sewed into his underwear a secret pocket in which he could carry cash and national food coupons. Unlike other women in the neighborhood, Jian had always been a housewife ever since they married. Guhan had never cursed or beaten her; for that he was respected by their neighbors.

Jian asked him repeatedly when he'd be back, saying she'd miss him, but he couldn't give her a definite date. He said, "Don't worry. I can take care of myself. I'll come back soon."

One morning in late July, after an eleven-hour train ride, Guhan arrived at Taifu. That very afternoon he went to the coal mine, but found only a few clerks in the office building. An accident, a cave-in, had occurred in a tunnel, and all the leaders had gone to the scene.

The next morning he again went to the office building, which was a two-story manor, constructed of black bricks and red tiles, its doors and windows painted sky blue. On both sides of the front entrance stood a few sunflowers, heavy-headed, soaked with dew, and facing southeast. Several bumblebees were humming among the yellow, toothed petals, darting about. Guhan nodded at the guard, who remembered him. He went up the iron stairs that led to the main office. Manager Ren, a stout man with a double chin, received him. He had heard of Guhan's previous visit, and after an exchange of greetings, he said they'd wire the money to East Cannery soon.

"How soon?" Guhan asked, taking a puff of a Winter Jasmine cigarette while his other hand fingered his lighter.

"In a week or so."

"Manager Ren, could you give me a written statement confirming that? Otherwise I won't be able to go back."

Ren shook his head and sighed. "We really don't have a set date. Sorry, I cannot give you a written statement, Director Tong."

"You see, we'll go bankrupt if you don't pay us soon. We owe a construction company thirty thousand yuan, but our coffers are empty. They're going to sue us if we don't pay them within a month."

"Well, fact is I can't decide this matter by myself. We'll have a meeting to discuss it."

"All right, in that case I'll wait here, at the inn. When will you let me know your decision?"

"Why don't you go back to Muji? We'll send you an official letter in a couple of days."

"I was instructed not to return without the money."

Guhan was prepared for the difficulty, so he was not deterred by Ren's equivocal responses. Before leaving, he told the manager that he would have to come back the next day. Ren grimaced, scratching the back of his ear.

The following afternoon Guhan went to the mine's office building again, but Manager Ren was out visiting the injured workers at the hospital. He left Ren a note, begging him to cherish the friendship between the mine and the cannery and clear up the debt without further delay.

With heavy legs, he returned to Anti-Imperialism Inn. The inn was a pleasant place, compared with the drab surroundings—hillsides spotted with the dark mouths of tunnels, coal piles here and there accompanied by the skeletons of cranes and conveyers, and trains crawling about like giant caterpillars. It consisted of four brick houses that formed a large courtyard, in which there was a small well topped with a winch. A dozen apple trees stood on both sides of the path that divided the yard in half. A few small cages, made of cornstalks, containing grasshoppers and cicadas, hung under the eaves of the northern house. Two or three pieces of radish greens were stuck into each cage—food for the insects, which, when evening settled in, would start chirring. Their metallic chirrups would continue until midnight.

Guhan caught Manager Ren the next day. This time Ren told him frankly that the mine didn't have the cash to square the account, so they decided to pay the cannery with coal instead. "The best anthracite, at a twenty-percent discount," Ren said, fanning his face with a large clipboard, as if both parties had already agreed to the settlement.

This was absolutely unacceptable to Guhan. The cannery didn't need so much anthracite. Besides, how could they transport the coal to Muji? Railroad wagons, rationed by the state, were unavailable. Even if they managed to ship the coal back, there would be no place in the cannery to store the six hundred tons. So, Guhan resolutely refused the offer. Frustrated, he threatened that his factory would sue the mine.

Manager Ren replied helplessly, "What else can I say? Even if you beat me to death, I can't come up with any cash. You can't squeeze any fat out of a skeleton. We just had a terrible accident, you know that, and all our savings have gone to the medical bills."

Go bankrupt! Guhan said mentally.

That night he wrote to his daughter, telling her to accept the admission to the agricultural school. By now he had become uncertain whether he'd be promoted to vice director, since it was unlikely he could fulfill his mission. He should at least let Liya get off the chicken farm; as for her return to the city, there might be some opportunity in the future.

It was sultry that evening. A few drops of rain fell; stars were unusually bright, piercing the thin mist in the sky. Despite the heat, Guhan went to bed early, having drunk three cups of sweet-potato liquor at dinner. His two roommates were with other tenants in the courtyard, where they were watching the well, which had somehow begun spouting water. A narrow ditch had been dug to drain the yellowish stream out into the street. Before Guhan went to sleep, some startled horses broke into neighing outside the inn and galloped away toward the railroad in the south. Many tenants went out to have a look, but Guhan was too tired to get up. Soon he fell asleep.

At about four o'clock the next morning, suddenly the room started trembling and jolting. A male voice yelled in the corridor,

"Earthquake!" Guhan opened his eyes and saw the beds colliding—one of his roommates was flung up, crashed into the wall, and dropped on the cement floor. Instantly the man ceased making noise. Guhan jumped up and rushed toward the window, but the floor was shifting back and forth like a sieve; his legs were twisting as though shocked by electricity, and he was thrown down. He managed to sit up, then the room began swaying like a boat caught in a storm. Things crashed against one another while the roof was crackling. The ceiling fan fell to the floor, and thermos bottles, lamps, coat trees, chairs, and tables were flying about. Unable to get up, he tried crawling to the window. A jolt from below shot him upward and tossed him out of the room. With a crash he landed in a puddle, covered with bits of glass. Meanwhile, a chimney tumbled down the roof and crashed to the ground; a large brick hit his left wrist and smashed his Seagull watch. "Ow!" he yelled, holding his broken wrist, and rolled toward one of the apple trees, which all seemed to be capering about, their branches sweeping the ground right and left like brooms. It was bright everywhere as if in daylight; colorful flashes streaked across the sky, which turned now red, now pink, now blue, now silver, now saffron, now green. A long orange ribbon blazed in the air as though a set of power lines had caught fire. Around him were dust, explosions, screams, the rumble of collapsing houses and buildings. A roar, like that made by a thousand old oxen together, was rising from underground.

When he finally managed to get to his feet by holding the trunk of an apple tree with his right arm, all the houses around were leveled. Streets disappeared, covered by rubble. The landscape had widened in every direction, and here and there more trees emerged. From beneath the ruins came muffled groans and cries. Somewhere a man yelled, "Help! Ah, help me!"

A little girl, who had also been thrown out of a house,

shrieked, "Mom! Save my mom!" Her small hand was clawing toward the debris.

Apples dropped about Guhan, whose arm was still around the trunk of the tree. In the east, jets of muddy water were shooting into the air, about twenty feet high, and fireballs broke out like bombs in places. A gust of wind tossed over an intense smell of methane, as though the air itself were burning and exploding.

Guhan, wearing only his underwear, remained motionless, as in a trance; his upper body was so thin that all his ribs were visible. He tried to shout, but no sound came out of his mouth. The aftershocks shook the ground continually, so he dared not let go of the tree.

Soon he collapsed, feeling as though he were engulfed by darkness, sinking deep into the sea.

Toward midafternoon some soldiers arrived. They wrapped Guhan in a blanket and dragged him away. After a medic bandaged up his wrist and let him drink some water from a canteen, a young officer asked Guhan, "Can you help us distribute canned food?"

"Oh, help!" he screamed.

"Can you join us in the rescue?"

"Help! Save me!"

"He's out of his mind. Take him away," the officer said.

A soldier led Guhan to a crowd of children and lightly injured adults. Twenty minutes later they were put into three Nanjing trucks, which were going to a suburban area where help was available. On the way, all the adults were speechless, though time and again someone broke into sobs. A few children kept crying for their parents who had disappeared.

The sight of the destruction overwhelmed everyone. All the houses and buildings in view had collapsed; there was only a concrete smokestack standing upright like a gigantic gun pointing to the sky. An apartment building had fallen and rolled all the way down a slope and broken to pieces at the bank of a brook. Another building was cut in half, in one of its rooms a white sheet and a line of colorful washing still flapping lazily. Here and there were cracks on the ground, some of which were too broad for the trucks to cross, so the soldiers filled them up with rocks and wooden poles. Now and then they came on a flooded crater caused by a caved-in mine tunnel. At the roadside near a cemetery, a tractor, together with its trailer, was almost buried by earth and pebbles, as though a mouth had opened from underneath to eat it but was unable to swallow the whole thing. Beyond the tractor, more than half of the gravestones had toppled over in the graveyard.

When the trucks passed a column of green ambulances that were heading for the city and were loaded with soldiers gripping shovels, picks, and broad banners, two helicopters emerged in the sky. One of them went on announcing, "All citizens must abide by the law and help one another. Any looter caught will be executed on the spot." Beyond the helicopters a plane was banking away and dropping boxes of food and bundles of blankets to the citizens, who were working in groups to rescue the survivors trapped in the ruins.

"What's your name?" an army doctor asked Guhan two days later in a field hospital.

"Apple," he answered.

"Where are you from?"

"Apple."

"Where is your work unit?"

"Orchard."

"What orchard?"

"Apple."

"How old are you?"

"Apple."

The doctor sighed, shaking his head, and said to a nurse, "Amnesia. Let's hope he'll get his memory back soon."

A brief checkup showed that except for a broken wrist Guhan was physically well, though he had lost his mind, unable to remember anything before the earthquake. Because he had nothing but some cash and national food coupons on him—in his underwear—it was impossible to ascertain who he was. Among the refugees there was a small group of unidentifiables. One man remembered his name as Wenyao but couldn't recall his surname or where he came from; several children had lost their parents and couldn't tell where their homes had been.

Guhan was given a name, Sweet Apple, and was assigned to collect trash at the field hospital. Every morning he held a short shovel or a wicker basket and walked about the camp with Wenyao. Together they picked up scraps of paper, rags, broken bowls and bottles, animal and human feces. They then burned the garbage in a pit. Guhan didn't enjoy the job, but he had no idea what else he could do. Everybody was too busy and too tense to complain. The medical staff worked around the clock, and the kitchen served free meals day and night. Group after group of injured people came and then left. Those who hadn't been identified stayed, doing chores to earn their meals at the hospital, which remained the same—two dozen tents encircled by a barbed-wire fence.

Because of his carefree state and unlimited access to food, Guhan gained weight rapidly. A month later, when trees began shedding leaves and the millet fields nearby turned yellow waiting to be gathered in, he was no longer a skeletal man. Now he looked healthy and a little robust, his ribs covered with a thick layer of fat, and he wore the large-sized uniform. His wrist had healed. Still, he looked like a half-wit and would smile at every woman he met.

The hospital was ordered to return to Yingkou City before winter came. Guhan heard that bulldozers had finished digging collective graves and burying corpses in Taifu, and that airplanes had sprayed enough insecticide over the city to wipe out the swarming flies and mosquitoes. Now construction workers moved in to replace the soldiers. Before the hospital withdrew, Guhan, along with the other unidentifiable ones, was handed over to the Administration of Taifu City.

There were too many homeless people for the city to take care of, especially the elderly and the orphans. As winter was coming, it became difficult for the citizens to continue to share tents and shacks. Most of them had been living in small groups, each of which consisted of several broken families. By October, many people had left Taifu to stay with relatives in other provinces; yet the quarter-million people who remained had to be accommodated properly. At the moment, most of the construction teams were busy building huts for schools, so that children would have temporary classrooms to study in during the winter. After that, more huts had to be set up for stores, restaurants, banks, inns, bathhouses, police stations. And although the residential housing did not take priority, it was crucial for the city's stability. Therefore the newly formed City Administration encouraged people to work in teams to construct shacks for themselves for the winter, using the bricks, rocks, and wood left in the ruins, in addition to the building materials donated by other provinces. The Construction Bureau provided a few shacks as models, which were low-pitched and cozy inside and had roofs made of straw, reed mats, and tar paper. In mid-October forty thousand soldiers were sent in to help the civilians build residential shacks.

Meanwhile, another movement was also under way, which was called Form New Families. The authorities urged the thirty thousand people who had lost their spouses in the earthquake to marry again, as a way to promote social order and provide havens for homeless children and old people. The temporary orphanages and old-folks homes simply couldn't take in so many of them. Soon a slogan began circulating among the survivors: "We must live on!" It not only silenced the voices against the family-forming movement but also helped bring around some of those who had made up their minds not to remarry. As soon as the residential shacks were built, branches of the Party, the Youth League, and the Union all set about matchmaking for the people who had lost their spouses. This undertaking proceeded nicely. Every weekend some group weddings would take place, at each of which more than a dozen new families were established—candies, dried dates and persimmons, roasted peanuts and sunflower seeds, and fresh fruits were supplied in washbasins. Every one of these families comprised at least three members, usually from three homes.

Since this was an emergency measure, love wasn't always taken into account; so long as a couple didn't dislike each other, a marriage certificate would be issued to them. People ought to help one another in such a situation. Also, these were men and women who were accustomed to family life and needed it badly; in their hearts there was the natural longing for such a union. We all know how miserable loneliness can be. Besides, there were two great incentives to an immediate marriage: the city promised to grant the newlyweds priority for housing when the apartment buildings were completed the next summer, and they would have an advantage over others for job assignments as well. Therefore thousands of people signed up for the family-forming movement. As long as you were healthy and normal, you were entitled to a spouse and a child or two, sometimes even to an old mother or father.

Already over fifty, Guhan no longer had strong sexual desires, but he was persuaded to help others and entered his name for a family. He looked like a normal man now, working as a clerk in the city's waterworks, because his handwriting looked handsome and he could do sums. But it wasn't a permanent job. Nobody knew who he was, and the authorities wouldn't run the risk of employing a man with an unclear background. So he was on piecework, copying bills and numbers.

His bride-to-be, Liu Shan, was a small woman in her late thirties who had lost her husband and two daughters. When they met in an office in the Civil Bureau's cottage, she didn't ask Guhan any questions but just gave him a look. Her oval face was soft and smooth; her slight figure reminded him of a bullet, prob- ably because she had sloping shoulders and wore quilted trousers.

"Do you agree to marry him?" an old woman cadre asked Liu Shan the next afternoon when the couple met in the office again. The bride-to-be nodded without a word.

Turning to Guhan, the official asked, "How about you?"

He gave her a big smile. She said, "You think you're lucky, huh? Look how young and how pretty she is."

He smiled again, and that settled it. With a flurry of writing she filled in a red glossy certificate for them. "Love and respect each other," she said solemnly, revealing two broken teeth. "Com- rade Sweet Apple and Comrade Liu Shan, may you remain a de- voted couple to the end of your lives."

Compared with other men, Guhan wasn't a bad choice; he looked gentle, strong, and well educated. To him, Shan was a fine woman. She worked as an accountant in a department store, so she must know how to manage money in a household; her voice was so quiet that she must have an even temper; her hands, small and slim, looked dexterous; her earlobes were thick, which was a sign of wealth. In a word, she seemed full of the makings of a good wife. The couple were assigned a new shack and a four-

year-old boy named Mo, who would bring them an additional
twenty-four yuan a month.

The wedding took place the next Saturday inside a large tent
across the street from the Civil Bureau. Twenty-one couples,
most of whom were middle-aged, became husbands and wives
officially that evening. At the mouth of the tent two strings of
firecrackers exploded; then the names of the brides and grooms
were announced inside the tent. After a round of drums, pipes,
gongs, and horns, together the couples sang "Even My Parents
Are Not as Dear as the Party and Chairman Mao" and "Our
Gratitude to the People's Army." Then a vice mayor, a spare man
in steel-rimmed glasses, spoke briefly and gave them the city's
congratulations. After the speech, he presented to each couple the
gift of a rice pot and a kettle.

However, the wedding wasn't jolly and noisy, as weddings
should be. Most of the brides looked rather somber; a few grooms
stood motionless, their arms crossed before their chests, as though
they were spectators. Some of them didn't even touch the Great
Gate cigarettes passed to them on plates. The air was hazy, humming a little; a dozen balloons were wavering languidly. Only a
few children seemed in high spirits, seeing so many goodies on the
folding tables.

"Happy marriage!" the mayor said loudly to Shan.

Shan's hand trembled and she spilled her apple brandy. The
wine stained the cuff of the mayor's trouser leg and the head of
his leather boot.

Guhan stepped forward and grasped her arm, saying with a
smile, "Excuse us, Comrade Mayor. She has drunk too much."

"I understand," the leader replied unemotionally.

Hurriedly Guhan pulled his bride away. Among all the
grooms he seemed the happiest. Some people shot sidelong
glances at him.

Within just one hour, more than half of the couples had left.

The band was packing up. An old man at the tea stand mumbled, "This is shorter than a breakfast. My seat isn't warm yet."

When Guhan and Shan returned to their shack, Mo had fallen asleep in Guhan's arms. They took off the boy's khaki jacket and pants and put him into the brick bed, which had been heated by an old woman from the Street Committee of the neighborhood.

Guhan sat down on their only chair and looked at Shan, who was washing her face over a yellow basin in a corner. Steam issued from her head, and her chest bulged a little in a red woolen sweater. Quietly he got up and went over. His palm touched the small of her back, caressing her while his stomach tightened.

She knocked off his hand with the wet towel and turned around, her eyes dim and a few tears on her cheeks. "Don't touch me!" she cried.

"What happened?" he asked in surprise.

"I can't do it tonight."

"Do what?"

"You know."

"Why?"

"I can't."

"Come on, I've been waiting for such a long time." He grinned suggestively.

"I can't do it."

He kicked away the brand-new enamel chamber pot, which was a present from the Street Committee, and added, "Then why did you agree to get married?"

She turned to look at the sleeping boy, who didn't stir. Lowering her head, she burst out sobbing. That frightened Guhan. He embraced her shoulders with one arm and asked rather gently, "What's wrong, Shan? If you don't want to, I can wait. Don't be scared. I'm not a cruel man." He kissed her cheek and noticed

she had long eyelashes, which cast frail shadows on her lower
lids.

"I'm not scared," she moaned with her eyes shut. "I feel so
sad, can't shut my family out of my mind. I see him on your face.
Even your voice reminds me of his. Oh, how I miss them! I don't
even have a photo of them."

Guhan felt bad, but said, "There, now, don't cry so hard. I'll
help you get over it."

But her sobbing became unstoppable. She lay down on her
stomach beside the boy and buried her face in a pillow. He
wanted to console her some, but didn't know what to say. Having
sat in silence for a few minutes, he took off his clothes, climbed
into his camp bed, and covered himself with a quilt.

She wept into the small hours.

Before the wedding, Shan had asked Guhan several questions, none of which he could answer. He couldn't even tell her
his exact age, just saying, "I'm around fifty," or describe what his
former family was like. "Probably he goes by an alias," suggested
Aunt Tian, who lived next door. Never had he shown any trace
of grief over the loss of his family, whose other members, according to his words, had all vanished in the earthquake. More unusual, he always slept soundly, unlike other newlyweds who
would weep or wail for hours during the first few nights. Maybe
he hadn't lost anything or anybody and was actually a gainer.

From the first day, Mo regarded Guhan as his uncle, but he
called Shan mother. At night, he'd sleep with her, with his only
toy, a MIG-15 jet fighter, placed beside his pillow. He had dark
skin, his fat cheeks chapped. His hands and toes and heels were
swollen with chilblains. Every night, Shan would wash and rub
his hands and feet in warm chili water. The boy would whine
with pain, but he allowed her to work on them. Soon scabs
formed over Mo's sores, and Shan kept telling him not to pick

them so that they could heal quickly. By the official record, Mo's father had been a truck driver and his mother a spinner; both had worked in a textile mill.

At a good meal, the boy could eat almost as much as Guhan could. Naturally their grain rations were not enough, and they had to buy some corn flour, rice, and sorghum at tripled prices on the open market. Yet Shan always let Mo eat as much as he wanted. She was a good cook and could make four dishes with half a pound of pork; she was also skillful with needles, her hands often busy knitting something—a sock or a hat or a glove. As Guhan had expected, she turned out to be a dutiful wife and never complained about housework. He felt lucky to have married her, though he was unsure whether he loved her; sometimes he preferred to stay a little longer at the waterworks at the end of the day. Unlike other couples, who would quarrel and fight during their adapting period, Shan and Guhan were very compatible and had none of those problems that many of the newlyweds accused their spouses of having, such as shrieking and kicking in their dreams, abusing children or parents, grinding their teeth at night, sleepwalking, having a bloody nose, or a gluttonous appetite, or bad breath, or underarm odor. Guhan smoked and liked to drink a mug of wine or beer at dinner, but that was normal, as other men did the same.

As it got colder, the three of them would crowd into the brick bed, which they didn't have enough coal to heat. Every night they'd shiver together for an hour or two before falling asleep. Their only hot-water bottle was tucked under Mo's feet.

Guhan liked the boy a lot, but he soon thought of having his own baby. This was a once-in-a-lifetime opportunity: every new couple were allowed to have one child of their own. Evidently there would be a baby boom in the city the next summer, since so many women were already pregnant. To Guhan's dismay, Shan refused to go to the hospital and have the contraceptive ring taken out of her womb. She had just begun to feel comfortable in lovemaking, but she insisted she wasn't ready for a baby yet. "Be patient, sweetheart," she said to him one evening. "I'm still very weak. Next year we'll try."

"Next year I'll be an octogenarian," he replied peevishly.

"Come on, Apple, I still can't stop thinking of my kids." Her eyes turned red.

"All right, all right, don't think of them anymore. We have this baby with us, don't we?" He grabbed Mo and set him on his lap. The boy seemed to understand what they were talking about; he embraced Guhan's neck tightly. Outside, an icicle fell to the ground, and the wind was screaming.

Though Guhan didn't know his age exactly, he felt old, eager to prove he was still fertile. After a few fruitless attempts to persuade Shan to have the ring removed, he gave up, only hoping the policy on new babies wouldn't change soon. This frustration made him treat Mo more like a son. He would buy him spiced beans, hawthorn flakes, baked sweet potatoes, ice cream bricks, and walnuts. The boy enjoyed riding on his neck to stores and open-air theaters; at dinner the two often shared a mug of wine. At long last, in mid-December, when Guhan bought Mo a wind-up torpedo boat, the boy began to call him dad. Guhan was so happy that he promised to buy Mo a pile of firecrackers at the Spring Festival.

On the whole, they led a peaceful life. The temporary Street Committee voted them a model family in January.

A week before the Spring Festival, the city was decorated with colorful lanterns, scrolls, bunting, and red flags, though a lot of rubble remained uncleared. These days, train after train of relief goods poured into Taifu; as a result, the citizens were allocated more meat, fish, fruit, eggs, and branded cigarettes for the festival than in other years. There were even some fresh vegetables on the market, like cabbages, turnips, spinach, bamboo shoots, cucumbers, garlic stems. Every family was given a coupon for one bottle of wheat liquor, but there was no limit on draft beer and wine. The supply of hard candies and pastry was abundant, too.

On his way home one evening, Guhan caught a whiff of fragrance in the air—something very familiar, like that of leek dumplings. It was an unusual smell for late winter, when leeks were hard to come by. As the aroma entered his lungs, a domestic scene suddenly opened in his mind. He saw a cheerful family making dumplings at a table—a slender girl in a pink apron was grinding a chunk of dough with a rolling pin, a young man was kneading together the edges of a wrapper with his fingertips, and a middle-aged woman stirred the stuffing in a porcelain bowl with a pair of chopsticks. A dizzy feeling surged in him, and he got off his bicycle and squatted down on the snow-covered sidewalk. As he sniffed the fragrant air some more, the domestic picture grew clearer. He lit a cigarette and focused his mind on the scene. Gradually their talk became audible. A male voice, somewhat like his own, said, "It's time to heat water to boil the dumplings."

That voice shocked him, though he couldn't see himself in the scene. "No rush, Dad," the girl said, clapping her floury hands.

Again he was surprised. Did she talk to me? he asked himself. Yes, it seemed so. Why did she call me dad? Was I her father? Who were they? Why did the young man look like me? Who was the middle-aged woman? Were they my family? Did I really have a family? Where did this gathering take place? And how long ago?

By instinct he followed the leek scent, which came from a hut about a hundred yards to the east. As he was walking, a sign emerged above the door of the restaurant: TASTY DUMPLINGS. He hastened his steps toward the hut while his mind's eye still observed the family scene. "Dad, you should put these in neat rows," the young man said, lining up the dumplings. Those words shook Guhan and made him realize that the girl and the young man must have been his children. He froze, then turned a little, gripping the handlebars of his bicycle with both hands while his left shoulder leaned against the bole of a dried mulberry tree killed by the earthquake. A gust of cold wind passed by and made him sneeze and cough. As though the coughing had been meant to precipitate his recollection, picture after picture of his family came back to him—Yaning's tic fits, the garlic eggplant Jian had pickled, the handsome shoes she had made out of pasted rags stitched together with jute threads, Liya's sweet voice and thin braids, the tropical fish he had kept, as large as bats. He tried hard to control his emotions as he raised the door curtain and went into the restaurant.

He sat down in a corner and ordered half a pound of dumplings, which came in a white bowl with a blue rim. While he was eating, his memory was further revived and sharpened by the familiar taste of the stuffing, made of pork, leeks, cabbage, dried shrimp, ginger, sesame oil. Every bit of the memory became unmistakable now. He recalled that the family gathering had taken place on the Spring Festival's eve two years ago, when his daughter had returned from the chicken farm and spent the holiday season in Muji. Leeks hadn't been available in stores at the time, but he had obtained two pounds through the back door. He had done that mainly for Liya, because she, after a year in the countryside, had lost her appetite, grown emaciated, and suffered from low blood pressure. At his daughter's name—Liya—he was suddenly overcome with self-pity and began weeping and sniffling, his tears dribbling into the tiny vinegar plate. None of the diners or waitresses took the trouble to console him. They were used to such an occurrence; every day there were a few customers who wept in here, especially those who ate alone.

From the family his mind moved to the cannery. He remembered that he had been a section leader in the factory and that people had called him Old Tong. His name was Guhan, not Sweet Apple. He had held a respectable position, giving orders to forty-eight people, unlike at his current job, where he merely copied names and statistics. What's more, he had been liked by his workers, who had elected him an outstanding cadre every year. Oh, how he missed his wife and children. How warm and clean his home had been. How pretty those flowers he had grown in his yard. How he wanted to return to Muji and work in the cannery again.

When he finished eating, it became clear to him how he had been trapped in Taifu. What was to be done now? The question baffled him. He didn't love Shan very much, but he had grown quite attached to Mo, whom he often carried in his lap when he bicycled around. He thought of secretly taking Mo with him back to Muji, but on second thought he realized the police could easily track him down if he had the boy with him. Besides, Mo had almost become Shan's flesh and blood now; he shouldn't rob her of this sole solace. Should he tell Shan everything? Would she believe him? Or should he inform the authorities of his real name and identity? Would they allow him to leave without a thorough investigation? No, they wouldn't. They might demand that he be responsible and stay with Shan and Mo, at least for some months.

He walked all the way home, pushing the bicycle with one hand. As he was getting close to his shack, a miserable feeling again overwhelmed him. He crouched down and wiped his tear-stained face with handfuls of snow. He made up his mind to leave this hopeless place as soon as possible.

"Ah, there you are. How we were worried!" Shan said at the sight of him and rose to her feet.

"Daddy, I miss you," Mo cried, placing his plump hand on his chest, and expected to be carried up.

Guhan bent down, kissed the boy on the cheek, and turned to Shan. "I don't feel well," he said, then went to bed.

"Don't you want to eat dinner?" she asked. "I made twisted rolls, still warm on the stove."

"I ate already."

"Are you sick?" She came over and touched his forehead.

"I'm all right, just tired." He avoided looking at her. "I'll be fine tomorrow morning." He felt like weeping, but he contained himself.

Together she and Mo resumed reading a story about how a pair of young bunnies outsmarted a gray wolf. Guhan had just subscribed to the children's magazine *Tell Me a Story* for Mo. Two weeks ago Shan had begun teaching the boy how to read and do addition.

After midnight, when he was certain that Shan and Mo were fast asleep, Guhan got out of bed, left on the table the key to the bicycle and three ten-yuan notes—half his savings—and stuck into Mo's pocket a thick pack of firecrackers that he had forgotten to give the boy. He put on his army overcoat and sneaked out. In the howling wind he set off for the train station.

Crowds of passengers were waiting for buses in front of Muji Train Station. Many of them wore fur coats. Soon Guhan began shivering, his cotton-padded overcoat unable to keep out the cold. Fortunately, after just an hour's wait, he got on a bus bound for Victory District, where his home was. The bus was so packed that soon he felt warm.

When he arrived at his apartment, he was surprised to see that at the center of the door was a New Year picture, in which a fat baby boy was sleeping in a bean pod floating on a river. He stopped for a minute, wondering whether his family still lived in there.

Where else could they be? he thought. This is my home.

With a throbbing heart he knocked on the door. A moment later his son stepped out, rubbing his sleepy eyes. "Who are you looking for?" asked the young man, his left cheek twitching.

"Yaning, I—I'm your father!" Guhan moaned.

His son was taken aback, then looked at him closely. "Are you really my dad? He's very thin."

"Look at me!" He took off his felt hat; the morning sun flooded in through a window, glistening on his sweaty balding head, which sent up coils of steam. He said, "I gained some weight because I was sick after the earthquake and lost my memory for a while."

Yaning recognized him and rushed over; father and son embraced, sobbing. Meili, his daughter-in-law, came out, wearing dark-blue maternity trousers, and she joined them in weeping. His family had thought he was dead. The memorial service had been held five months before, after the cannery notified the Tongs that he had vanished in the earthquake.

"Where's your mother?" asked Guhan.

"She's at Uncle's," his son answered, then turned to Meili. "Go tell her Dad is back."

Meili put on a fur overcoat, then waddled away with her protruding belly to Gorki Street, where the uncle's family lived.

Because the Tongs had believed Guhan was dead and they had been afraid the cannery would take back their housing, Yaning and Meili had gotten married a week after the memorial meeting and moved into the apartment. At the same time, Jian— the "widow"—went to stay at her brother's, since she refused to sleep in the kitchen. Exhorted time and again by her friends and relatives, she had just begun looking for a man, a husband-to-be, so that she would again be able to live under her own roof someday.

The Tongs had made another decision that was sensible

under such circumstances. Instead of going to the agricultural school, Liya had returned to Muji City; the cannery hired her, filling the quota left by her father; now she worked as a quality inspector in the lab.

Hearing Guhan had come back alive, his wife almost passed out. She cried, stretching up her bony hand, "Lord of Heaven, why are you so cruel to us? Why didn't you let me know my old man was still alive? Or why didn't you kill me instead? Where can I hide my face?"

Initially, on leaving Taifu, Guhan had planned to give his family a joyful surprise, but their joy was mixed with confusion, shame, and sadness. At dinner that evening, Liya kept blaming herself for returning to the city, while Yaning was crestfallen, having no idea how to accommodate his parents now. However, Guhan had a large heart and assured his children that everything would be all right and that the cannery might provide him with new housing, because this mess had been caused by nature and nobody should be responsible for it. He told his family, "I've worked for them for over twenty years, so I belong to the cannery. When I'm alive, I am their man; when I'm dead, I am their ghost. They have to take me. Don't worry so much. It's good just to be alive."

But the next morning, when Guhan showed up at the cannery, he found his position already occupied by Fei, the young Party member; more surprising, there was a vice director now, who had been sent over by the city's Light Industry Bureau. Obviously Guhan was no longer needed here. Heavens, in just six months he had become an unwanted man, as though he were truly dead, back as a mere ghost.

His reappearance shocked the workers and staff. Some of them gathered around him, listening to his story and telling him how heartbrokenly they had wept at the memorial service. They told him that twenty large wreaths had been placed on both sides of his portrait and that his wife had cried so hard her limbs had cramped. Now, who could imagine he was still alive! A few people went on asking, "Are you really Old Tong?" Two even touched his knees to make sure he was corporeal.

Both Director Li and Secretary Niu sympathized with Guhan, but they said the cannery couldn't employ him anymore, for his daughter had taken the only quota available. They had managed to obtain the residence card for Liya mainly because they had named him a Revolutionary Martyr; otherwise the police would not have cooperated. As for additional housing now, it was out of the question. How could he think of such a thing when he no longer worked for the factory? If they had assigned him an apartment, how could they have appeased those employees in line for housing?

After a Party meeting, the leaders came up with a solution: they allowed Guhan to retire on a pension. He had no choice but to accept this offer. Since the Spring Festival was just two days away, his brother-in-law took him and his wife in. Yaning begged his parents to let him retain the apartment, saying they'd wreck his marriage if they drove his pregnant wife and himself out. So they allowed him to keep it; after the holiday, they'd have to search for housing for themselves.

Guhan became reticent and gloomy. He couldn't resist wondering whether he should have stayed with Shan and Mo in Taifu and let people here believe he had left this crowded world for good.

In the Kindergarten

Shaona kept her eyes shut, trying to sleep. Outside, the noonday sun was blazing, and bumblebees were droning in the shade of an elm. Time and again one of them would bump into the window's wire screen with a thud and then a louder buzz. Soon Teacher Shen's voice in the next room grew clearer.

"Oh please!" the teacher blubbered on the phone. "I'll pay you the money in three months. You've already helped me so much, why can't you help me out?"

Those words made Shaona fully awake. She moved her head closer to the wall and strained her ears to listen. The teacher begged, "Have mercy on me, Dr. Niu. I've an old mother at home. My mother and I have to live. . . . And you know, I lost so much blood, because of the baby, that I need to eat eggs to recuperate. I'm really broke now. Can you just give me another month?"

Shaona was puzzled, thinking how a baby could injure her teacher's health. Her grandmother used to say that babies were dug out from pumpkin fields in the countryside. Why did her teacher sound as though the baby had come out of her body? Why did she bleed for the baby?

Teacher Shen's voice turned desperate. "Please, don't tell anyone about the abortion! I'll try my best to pay you . . . very soon. I'll see if I can borrow some money from a friend."

What's an abortion? Shaona asked herself. Is it something that holds a baby? What does it look like? Must be very expensive.

Her teacher slammed the phone down, then cried, "Heaven help me!"

Shaona couldn't sleep anymore. She missed her parents so much that she began sobbing again. This was her second week in the kindergarten, and she was not used to sleeping alone yet. Her small iron bed was uncomfortable, in every way different from the large soft bed at home, which could hold her entire family. She couldn't help wondering if her parents would love her the same as before, because three weeks ago her mother had given her a baby brother. These days her father was so happy that he often chanted snatches of opera.

In the room seven other children were napping, one of them wheezing with a stuffy nose. Two large bronze moths, exhausted by the heat, were resting on the ceiling, their powdery wings flickering now and again. Shaona yawned sleepily, but still couldn't go to sleep.

At two-thirty the bell rang, and all the nappers got out of their beds. Teacher Shen gathered the whole class of five- and six-year-olds in the corridor. Then in two lines they set out for the turnip field behind the kindergarten. It was still hot. A steamboat went on blowing her horn in the north, and a pair of jet fighters were flying in the distant sky, drawing a long double curve. Shaona wondered how a pilot could fit inside those planes, which looked as small as pigeons. In the air lingered a sweetish odor of dichlorvos, which had been sprayed around the city to get rid of flies, fleas, mosquitoes. The children were excited, because seldom were they allowed to go out of the stone wall topped with shards of dark brown glass. Today, instead of playing games within the yard as the children of the other classes were doing, Teacher Shen was going to teach them how to gather purslanes. Few of them knew what a purslane looked like, but they were all eager to search for the herb.

On the way, their teacher turned around to face them, flourishing her narrow hand and saying, "Boys and girls, you'll eat sautéed purslanes this evening. It tastes great, different from anything you've ever had. Tell me, do you all want to have purslanes for dinner or not?"

"Yes! We do," a few voices cried.

The teacher smacked her lips. Her sunburned nose crinkled, a faint smile playing on her face. As she continued walking, the ends of her two braids, tied with green woolen strings, were stroking the baggy seat of her pants. She was a young woman, tall and angular, with crescent eyebrows. She used to sing a lot; her voice was fruity and clear. But recently she was quiet, her face rather pallid. It was said that she had divorced her husband the previous summer because he had been sentenced to thirteen years in prison for embezzlement.

When they arrived at the field, Teacher Shen plucked a purslane from between two turnip seedlings. She said to the children, who were standing in a horseshoe, "Look, its leaves are tiny, fleshy, and egg-shaped. It has reddish stems, different from regular veggies and grass. Sometimes it has small yellow flowers." She dropped the purslane into her duffel bag on the ground and went on, "Now, you each take charge of one row."

Following her orders, the children spread out along the edge of the field and then walked into the turnip seedlings.

Shaona lifted up the bottom of her checked skirt to form a basket before her stomach and set out to search. Purslanes weren't difficult to find among the turnips, whose greens were not yet larger than a palm. Pretty soon every one of the children gathered some purslanes.

"Don't stamp on the turnips!" Uncle Chang shouted at them from time to time. Sitting under an acacia, he was puffing away at a long pipe that had a brass bowl, his bald crown coated with beads of sweat. He was in charge of a few vegetable fields and the dilapidated pump house.

Shaona noticed Dabin, a rambunctious boy, sidling up to her, but she pretended she didn't see him. He nudged her and asked, "How many did you get?" He sniveled—two lines of dark mucus disappeared from his nostrils, then poked out again.

She lowered her skirt, showing him about a dozen purslanes.

He said with one eye shut, "You're no good. Look at mine." He held out his peaked cap, which was full.

She felt a little hurt, but kept quiet. He turned away to talk to other children, telling them that purslanes tasted awful. He claimed he had once eaten a bowl of purslane stew when he had diarrhea. He would never have touched that stuff if his parents hadn't forced him. "It tastes like crap, more bitter than sweet potato vines," he assured them.

"Not true," said Weilan, a scrawny girl. "Teacher Shen told us it tastes great."

"How can you know?"

"I just know it."

"You know your granny's fart!"

"Big asshole," Weilan said, and made a face at him, sticking out her tongue.

"Say that again, bitch!" He went up to her, grabbed her shoulder, pushed her to the ground, and kicked her buttocks. She burst out crying.

Their teacher came over and asked who had started the fight. Shaona pointed at Dabin. To her surprise, the teacher walked up to the boy and seized him by the ear, saying through her teeth, "You can't live for a day without making trouble. Come now, I'm going to give you a trouble-free place to stay." She was dragging him away.

"Ouch!" he cried with a rattling noise in his throat. "You're pulling my ear off."

"You'll have the other one left."

Passing Uncle Chang, Teacher Shen stopped to ask him to keep an eye on the children for a short while. Then she dragged Dabin back to the kindergarten.

Shaona's mouth fell open. The boy would be "jailed," and he might get even with her after he was released. On the second floor of their building was a room, a kitchen used only for storage, in a corner of which sat three bedside cupboards. Sometimes a troublesome boy would be locked in one of them for hours. Once in a while his teacher might forget to let him out in time, so that he had to go without lunch or dinner.

About ten minutes later, Teacher Shen returned, panting hard as though she had just finished a sprint. She counted the children to make sure nobody was missing.

Shaona soon forgot Dabin, immersed in looking for more purslanes. For most of the children this was real work. Few of them had ever tasted anything they had gathered themselves, so they were searching diligently. Whenever their little skirts or caps were full, they went over to unload the purslanes into the duffel bag, from which their teacher was busy picking out grass and other kinds of herbs mixed into the purslanes. The children were amazed that in just one and a half hours the bag was filled up, and that they had almost combed the entire field. Their teacher kept reminding them of a proverb they had learned lately—"Many hands provide great strength."

When they had searched the field, they were lined up hand in hand behind the pump house, ready to return to the kindergarten. But before leaving, for some reason their teacher gave several handfuls of purslanes to Uncle Chang. With grudging eyes they watched her drop almost a third of their harvest into the old man's wicker basket, but none of them made a peep. The old man went on smiling at the young woman, saying, "All right, enough, enough. Keep the rest for yourself." As he was speaking, spittle was emitted through his gapped teeth.

Shaona's mind was racing, and she couldn't wait for dinner. She thought, If purslane tastes real good, I'll pick some for Mom and Dad. She knew a place in the kindergarten—inside the deserted pigsty—where she had seen a few purslanes.

To her dismay, dinner was similar to other days': corn glue, steamed sweet potatoes, and sautéed radishes. There wasn't even a purslane leaf on the table. Every one of her classmates looked upset. Not knowing what to say, some children were noisily stirring the corn glue with spoons. Shaona wanted to cry, but she controlled herself. She remembered seeing her teacher leave for home with the bulging duffel clasped on the carrier of her bicycle. At that moment Shaona had thought the green bag must have contained laundry or something, because it was so full. Now she understood, their teacher took their harvest home.

Shaona liked sweet potato, but she didn't eat much. Anger and gas filled her stomach. Despite their sullen faces and disappointed hearts, none of the children mentioned purslanes. Everyone looked rather dejected, except for Dabin. He had kept glaring at Shaona ever since he was let out of the cupboard for dinner. She knew he was going to take his revenge. What should she do?

In the dusk, when the children were playing in the yard, Shaona caught sight of Dabin. She called and beckoned to him. He came over and grunted, "What's up, little tattletale?"

"Dabin, would you like to have these?" In her palm were two long peanuts. Her father had given her six of them when she was coming back to the kindergarten two days ago.

"Huh!" he exclaimed with pursed lips, "I never saw a peanut with four seeds in it." He snatched them from her hand and without another word cracked one. His eyes glittered and his mouth twitched like a rabbit's while he was chewing the roasted kernels.

Within a few seconds he finished the peanuts off, then he asked, "Do you have more?"

"Uh-uh." She shook her head, her slant eyes fixed on the ground.

He touched her sweater pocket, which was empty. She had hidden the other four peanuts in her socks. He said, "You must be nice to me from now on. Remember to save lots of goodies for me, got it?"

She nodded without looking at him.

Standing below a slide, she watched him running off on his bowlegs to join the boys who were hurling paper bombers and imitating explosions. Behind the cypress hedge, near the closed front gate, a couple of children were playing hide-and-seek, their white clothes flickering and their ecstatic cries ringing in the twilight.

That night Shaona didn't sleep well. She was still scared of the dark room. One of her roommates, Aili, snored without stopping. An owl or a hawk went on hooting like an old man's coughing. A steam hammer in the shipyard on the riverbank pounded metal now and then. Unable to sleep, Shaona ate a peanut, though the rules didn't allow her to eat anything after she had brushed her teeth for bed. She took care to hide the shells under her pillow. How she missed her mother's warm, soft belly; again she cried quietly.

It rained the next morning, but the clouds began lifting after nine o'clock, so the children were allowed to go out and play. In the middle of the yard stood a miniature merry-go-round, sky blue and nine feet across. A ring of boys were sitting on it, revolving and yelling happily. Dabin and Luwen, who was squint-eyed, were among them, firing wooden carbines at treetops, people, birds, smokestacks, and anything that came into sight. They were shouting out "rat-a-tat" as if the spinning platform were a tank turret. Shaona dared not go take a spin. The previous week she had ridden on that thing and had been spun giddy and was sick for two days.

So instead, she played court with a bunch of girls. They elected her the queen, saying she looked the most handsome among them. With four maids waiting on her, she had to sit on the wet ground all the time. Weilan and Aili were her amazons, each holding a whittled branch for a lance. The girls wished they could have made a strong boy the king, but only Dun was willing to join them. He was a mousy boy, and most of the girls could beat him easily. He should have been a courtier rather than the ruler. Soon Shaona couldn't stand playing queen anymore, because she felt silly calling him "Your Majesty" and hated having to obey his orders. She begged other girls to replace her, but none of them would. She got up from the ground, shouting, "I quit!" To keep the court from disintegrating, Aili agreed to be a vice queen.

Because of the soggy ground, many of the children found their clothes soiled by lunchtime. Teacher Shen was angry, especially with those who had played mud pies. She said that if they were not careful about their clothes, she wouldn't let them go out in the afternoon. "None of you is a good child," she declared. "You all want to create more work for me."

After lunch, while the children were napping, Teacher Shen collected their clothes to scrub off the mud stains. She was unhappy because she couldn't take a nap.

Too exhausted to miss her parents, Shaona fell asleep the moment her head touched her pillow. She slept an hour and a half. When she woke up, she was pleased to find her sweater and skirt clean, without a speck of mud. But as her hand slotted into the sweater pocket she was surprised—the three peanuts were gone. She removed the terry-cloth coverlet and rummaged through her bedding, but couldn't find any trace of them; even the shells under her pillow had disappeared. Heartbroken, she couldn't stop her tears, knowing her teacher must have confiscated the peanuts.

The sun came out in the afternoon, and the ground in the yard turned whitish. Again Teacher Shen led the twenty-four children out to the turnip field. On their way they sang the song "Red Flowers," which they had learned the week before:

> Red flowers are blooming everywhere.
> Clapping our hands, we sing
> And play a game in the square,
> All happy like blossoms of spring.

When they arrived at the field, Uncle Chang was not in view, but the water pump was snarling, tiny streams glinting here and there among the turnip rows.

The sight of the irrigation made their teacher hesitate for a moment, then she said loudly to the children, "We're going to gather more purslanes this afternoon. Aunt Chef couldn't cook those we got yesterday because we turned them in too late, but she'll cook them for us today. So everybody must be a good child and work hard. Understood?"

"Understood," they said almost in unison. Then they began to search among the turnips.

Although most of the children were as high-spirited as the day before, there weren't many purslanes left in the field, which was muddy and slippery. A number of them fell on their buttocks and had their clothes soiled. Their shoes were ringed with dark mud.

Yet the hollow of Shaona's skirt was soon filled with several puny purslanes, and some children had even dropped a load into the duffel, which began to swell little by little. Unlike the silly boys and girls who were still talking about what purslanes tasted like, Shaona was sulky the whole time, though she never stopped searching.

In front of her appeared a few tufts of wormwood, among which were some brownish rocks partly covered by dried grass. A swarm of small butterflies rested on the wormwood, flapping their white wings marked with black dots. Now and then one of them took off, flying sideways to land on a rock. Shaona went over to search through the grass; her motion set the butterflies in flight all at once like a flurry of snowflakes. Suddenly a wild rabbit jumped out, racing away toward a group of girls, who all saw it and broke out hollering. The animal, frightened by their voices, swerved and bolted away toward the back wall of the kindergarten. At the sight of the fleeing creature, Teacher Shen yelled, "Catch him! Don't let him run away!"

All at once several boys started chasing the rabbit, which turned out to have a crippled hind leg. Now their teacher was running after it too, motioning to the children ahead to intercept the animal. Her long braids swayed from side to side as she was dashing away. Within seconds all the children except Shaona joined the chase. The turnip field was being ruined, a lot of seedlings trampled and muddy water splashing from the running feet. Shrieks and laughter were rising from the west side of the field.

Shaona was not with them because she wanted to pee. Looking around, she saw nobody nearby, so she squatted down over the duffel, made sure to conceal her little bottom with her skirt, and peed on the purslanes inside the bag. But she dared not empty her bladder altogether; she stopped halfway, got up, and covered the wet purslanes with the dry ones she had gathered. Then with a kicking heart she ran away to join the chasers.

The rabbit had fled out of sight, but the children were still excited, boys huffing and puffing, and bragging about how close they had got to the animal. Dabin swore that his toes, peeping out of his open sandals, had touched that fluffy tail. Luwen said that the wild rabbit tasted much better than the domestic rabbit; a few children were listening to him describe how his uncle had shot a pair of wild rabbits in the mountain and how his aunt had cut them into pieces and stewed them with potato and carrot cubes. Their teacher stopped him from finishing his story. Without delay she assembled the children and led them out of the field, fearful that Uncle Chang would call her names on account of the trampled turnips.

Before dinner Shaona was worried for fear the chef might cook the soiled purslanes for them. To her relief, dinner turned out to be more of the usual. She was thrilled. For the first time in the kindergarten she ate a hearty meal—three sweet potatoes, two bowls of corn glue, and many spoonfuls of fried eggplant. The whole evening she was so excited that she joined the boys in playing soldier, carrying a water pistol, as though all of a sudden she had become a big girl. She felt that from now on she would not cry like a baby at night again.

A Tiger-Fighter Is Hard to Find

We were overwhelmed by a letter from the provincial governor's office. It praised our TV series *Wu Song Beat the Tiger*. The governor was impressed by the hero, who fought the tiger single-handedly and punched it to death. The letter read: "We ought to create more heroic characters of this kind as role models for the revolutionary masses to follow. You, writers and artists, are the engineers of the human soul. You have a noble task on your hands, which is to strengthen people's hearts and instill into them the spirit that fears neither heaven nor earth." But the last paragraph of the letter pointed out a weakness in the key episode, which was that the tiger looked fake and didn't present an authentic challenge to the hero. The governor wondered if we could improve this section, so that our province might send the series to Beijing before the end of the year.

That evening we had a meeting and decided to reshoot the tiger-fighting scene. Everybody was excited, because if the series was sent to the capital, it meant we'd compete for a national prize. We decided to let Wang Huping take the part of the hero again, since the governor had been impressed with him in the first version. He was more than happy to do it. Now the problem was the tiger. First, a real animal would cost a fortune. Second, how could we shoot a scene with such a dangerous animal?

With the governor's letter in hand, we obtained a grant from the Municipal Administration without difficulty. Four men were dispatched to Jilin Province to bring back a tiger just caught on Ever White Mountain. By law we were not allowed to acquire a protected animal, but we got papers that said we needed it for our city's zoo. A week later, the four men returned with a gorgeous Siberian tiger.

We all went to see the animal, which was being held in a cage in the backyard of our office building. It was a male, weighing over three hundred pounds. Its eyes glowed with a cold, brown light, and its scarlet tongue seemed wet with blood. What a thick coat it had, golden and glossy! Its black stripes would ripple whenever it shook its head or stretched its neck. I was amazed at how small its ears were, not much larger than a dog's. But it smelled awful, like ammonia.

We were told to feed it ten pounds of mutton a day. This was expensive, but if we wanted to keep it in good shape, we had no choice.

Wang Huping seemed a little unnerved by the tiger. Who wouldn't be? But Huping was a grand fellow: tall, muscular, straight-shouldered, and with dreamy eyes that would sparkle when he smiled. I would say he was the most handsome young man in our Muji City, just as his nickname, Prince, suggested. A girl told me that whenever he was nearby, her eyes would turn watery. Another girl said that whenever he spoke to her, her heart would pound and her face would burn with a tickle. I don't know if any of that was true.

A few days before the shooting, Director Yu, who used to be a lecturer at a cinema school in Shanghai, gave Huping a small book to read. It was *The Old Man and the Sea,* by an American author, whose name has just escaped me.

The director told Huping, "A man's not born to be defeated, not by a shark or a tiger."

"I understand," said Huping.

That was what I liked most about him. He wasn't just handsome, like a flowered pillowcase without solid stuff in it; he studied serious books and was learned, different from most of us, who merely read picture books and comics. If he didn't like a novel, he would say, "Well, this isn't literature." What's more, he was skilled in kung fu, particularly mantis boxing. One night last winter, he was on his way back to his dorm when four thugs stopped him and demanded he give them his wallet. He gave them a beating instead. He felled them with his bare hands and then dragged the ringleader to a nearby militia headquarters. For that, he got written about in the newspapers. Later, he was voted an outstanding actor.

The morning of the shooting was a little windy and overcast. Two Liberation trucks took us four miles out of the city, to the edge of an oak wood. We unloaded the tiger cage, mounted the camera on the tripod, and set up the scene by placing a few large rocks here and there and pulling out some tall grass to make the flattish ground more visible. A few people gathered around Huping and helped him with his costume and makeup. Near the cage stood two men, each toting a tranquilizer gun.

Director Yu was pacing back and forth behind the camera. A scene like this couldn't be repeated; we had to get everything right on the first take.

The medic took out a stout jar of White Flame and poured a full bowl of it. Without a word, Huping raised the liquor with both hands and drank it up in a long swallow. People watched him silently. He looked radiant in the shifting sunlight. A black mosquito landed on his jaw, but he didn't bother to slap at it.

When everything was ready, one man shot a tranquilizer dart into the tiger's rump. Holding his forefinger before Huping's face, Director Yu said in a high-pitched voice, "Try to get into the character. Remember, once you are in the scene, you are no longer Wang Huping. You are the hero, a true tiger-fighter, a killer."

"I'll remember that," Huping said, punching his left palm with his right fist. He wore high leather boots and a short cudgel slung across his back.

Director Yu's gaze swept through the crowd, and he asked loudly if everyone was ready. A few people nodded.

"Action!" he cried.

The door of the cage was lifted up. The tiger rushed out, vigorously shaking its body. It opened its mouth, and four long canine teeth glinted. It began walking in circles and sniffing at the ground while Huping, with firm steps, began to approach it. The animal roared and pranced, but our hero took the cudgel from his back and went forward resolutely. When he was within ten feet of the tiger, the snarling beast suddenly sprang at him, but with all his might Huping struck its head with his cudgel. The blow staggered the tiger a little, yet it came back and lunged at him again. Huping leaped aside and hit its flank. This blow sent the animal tumbling a few feet away. Huping followed it, striking its back and head. The tiger turned around with a menacing look. Then they were in a real melee.

With a crack the front half of the cudgel flew away. Huping dropped the remaining half, just as Wu Song does in the story. The beast rushed forward, reached for Huping's leg, and ripped his pants, then jumped up, snapping at his throat. Our hero knocked the animal aside with his fist, but its attack threw Huping off balance—he tottered and almost fell.

"Keep engaging it!" Director Yu shouted at him.

I stood behind a large elm, hugging my ribs.

"Closer, closer!" the director ordered the cameraman.

Huping kicked the tiger in the side. The animal reeled around and sprang at him again. Huping dodged the attack and punched the tiger's neck. Now the drug began taking effect; the tiger wobbled a little and fell to its haunches. It lurched to its feet, but after a few steps it collapsed. Our hero jumped on its back, punching its head with all his strength. The tiger, as if dead, no longer reacted to the beating, only its tail lashing the grass now and again. Still Huping pulled and pushed its huge head, forcing its lips and teeth to scrape the dirt.

"Cut!" Director Yu called, and walked over to Huping as two men helped him up from the unconscious animal. The director said, "I guess we didn't time it well. The tiger passed out too soon."

"I killed him! I'm the number-one tiger-fighter!" Huping shouted. With his fists balled at his flanks, he began laughing huskily and stamping his feet.

People ran up to him and tried to calm him down. But he wouldn't stop laughing. "I killed him! I killed him!" he yelled, his eyes ablaze.

The medic poured some water into the bowl and took out a sedative tablet. He made Huping take the medicine.

"Good wine, good wine!" Huping said after drinking the water. He wiped his lips with his forearm.

Then, to our astonishment, he burst out singing like a hero in a revolutionary model opera:

> *My spirit rushing toward the Milky Way,*
> *With my determination and bravery*
> *I shall eradicate every vermin from earth. . . .*

A young woman snickered. Two men clutched Huping's arms and dragged him away while he was babbling about plucking out the tiger's heart, liver, and lungs. They put him into the back of a truck.

"He's punch-drunk," said Secretary Feng. "Tough job—I don't blame him."

The tiger was lifted back into its cage. Director Yu wasn't happy about the botched scene. According to the classic story, which our audience would know well, the hero is supposed to ride the tiger for a while, bring it down, and punch its head hundreds of times until it breathes its last. The scene we had just shot missed the final struggle, so we would have to try again.

But Huping was in no condition to work. For the rest of the day he laughed or giggled at random. Whenever someone came into sight he'd shout, "Hey, I killed the tiger!" We worried about him, so we called in a pedicab and sent him to the hospital for a checkup.

The diagnosis was mild schizophrenia, and the doctor insisted that Huping be hospitalized.

What should we do about the fight scene? Get another tiger-fighter? Not so easy. Where on earth could we find a fellow as handsome and strapping as our Prince? We looked through a pile of movie and TV magazines in the hopes of finding someone who resembled him, but most of the young actors we saw were mere palefaced boys; few had the stature and spirit of a hero.

Somehow the prefecture's Propaganda Department heard about the governor's interest in our TV series. Its deputy director phoned, saying we should complete the revision as early as possible. It was already mid-September, and trees were dropping leaves. Soon frost and snow would change the color of the landscape and make it impossible to duplicate the setting.

Because it was unlikely that we would find a substitute for Huping, some people suggested using him again. Quite a few of us opposed this idea; those who supported it didn't seem to care that a man's life was at risk. In private, some of us—clerks, assistants, actors—complained about the classic novel that contains the tiger-fighting episode. Why would an author write such a difficult scene? It's impossible for any man to ride a tiger and then beat it to death bare-handed. The story is a pure fabrication that has misled readers for hundreds of years. It may have been easy for the writer to describe it on paper, but in reality, how could we create such a hero?

Full of anxiety, Director Yu suffered a case of inflamed eyes—they turned into curved slits between red, doughy lids. He'd wear sunglasses whenever he went out of the office building. He told us, "We must finish the scene! It's a once-in-a-lifetime opportunity!"

One night he even dreamed he himself wrestled the tiger to the ground, and his elbow inflicted a bruise on his wife's chest.

We were worried, too. Our company couldn't afford to feed the tiger for long; besides, we had no place to shelter it for the coming winter.

The following week, Secretary Feng held a staff meeting with us. We discussed the predicament at some length. Gradually it became clear that if we couldn't find a substitute, we might have to use Huping again. The proponents of this idea argued their position logically and convinced us, its opponents, that this was the only way to get the job done.

At the end of the meeting, Director Yu stressed that this time everything had to be accurately designed and calculated. The tranquilizer dart should carry a smaller dose so that the tiger would remain on its feet long enough for our hero to ride it a while. Also, we would have to be more careful not to let the beast hurt him.

To our relief, when the leaders broached the plan with Huping, he eagerly agreed to fight the tiger again. He said that he'd live up to their expectations and that he felt fine now, ready for work. "I'm a tiger-fighter," he declared. His voice was quite hoarse, and his eyes glittered.

"Yes, you are," agreed Secretary Feng. "All the provincial leaders are watching you, Huping. Try to do a good job this time."

"I shall."

So we trucked the tiger to the site the next morning. The weather happened to be similar to that of the previous time: a little overcast, the sun peeking through the gray clouds now and then. I identified the elm and the spot where the fight had taken place before. Huping sat on a boulder with a short cudgel across his naked back while the medic was massaging his shoulders. After a tranquilizer dart was shot into the tiger's thigh, Huping rose to his feet and downed a bowl of White Flame in two gulps.

Director Yu went over to give him instructions, saying, "Don't lose your head. When I shout, 'On the tiger!' you get on its back, ride it for a while, then bring it down. Until it stops moving, keep punching its head."

"All right." Huping nodded, his gaze fixed on the caged animal.

In the distance, on the hillside, a few cows were grazing, the west wind occasionally blowing their voices to us.

The tiger was let out. It pranced around, bursting with life. It opened its mouth threateningly. It began eyeing the distant cows.

"Roll the camera!" shouted Director Yu.

As Huping was approaching the tiger, it growled and rushed toward him. Our hero seemed stunned. He stopped and raised the cudgel, but the beast just pounced on him and pawed at his shoulder. With a heartrending cry, Huping dropped his weapon and ran toward us. The tiger followed, but having been caged for weeks, it couldn't run fast. We scattered in every direction, and even the camera crew deserted their equipment. Huping jumped, caught a limb of the elm, and climbed up the tree. The animal leaped and ripped off Huping's left boot, and instantly a patch of blood appeared on his white sock.

"Save me!" he yelled, climbing higher. The beast was pacing below the tree, snarling and roaring.

"Give it another shot!" Director Yu cried.

Another dart hit the tiger's shoulder. In no time it started tottering, moving zigzag under the elm.

We watched fearfully while Huping yelled for help. He was so piteous.

The tiger fell. Director Yu was outraged and couldn't help calling Huping names. Two men quietly carried the cage over to the motionless animal.

"Idiot!" Director Yu cursed.

The medic wiggled his fingers at Huping. "Come down now, let me dress your foot."

"No."

"The tiger's gone," a woman said to him.

"Help me!" he yelled.

"It can't hurt you anymore."

"Shoot him!"

No matter how many comforting words we used, he wouldn't

come down from the tree. He squatted up there, weeping like a small boy. The crotch of his pants was wet.

We couldn't wait for him like this forever. So Secretary Feng, his face puffy and glum, said to a man, "Give him a shot, not too strong."

From a range of five feet a dart was fired into Huping's right buttock.

"Ow!" he cried.

A few men assembled under the elm to catch him, but he didn't fall. As the drug began affecting him, he turned to embrace the tree trunk, descending slowly. A moment later the men grabbed his arms and legs and carried him away.

One of them said, "He's so hot. Must be running a fever."

"Phew! Smelly!" said another.

Now that our hero was gone, what could we do? At last it began to sink in that the tiger was too fierce for any man to tackle. Somebody suggested having the beast gelded so as to bring the animal closer to the human level. We gave a thought to that and even talked to a pig castrator, but he didn't trust tranquilizers and wouldn't do the job unless the tiger was tied up. Somehow the Choice Herb Store heard about our situation and sent an old pharmacist over to buy the tiger's testicles, which the man said were a sought-after remedy for impotence and premature ejaculation. In his words, "They give you a tiger's spirit and energy."

But finally realizing that the crux of our problem was the hero, not the tiger, we decided against castrating the animal. Without a man who physically resembled Huping, we could get nowhere, even with a tamed tiger. Then someone suggested that we find a tiger skin and have it worn by a man. In other words, shoot the last part of the scene with a fake animal. This seemed feasible, but I had my doubts. As the set clerk, whose job it is to make sure that all the details match those in the previous shooting, I thought that we couldn't possibly get a skin identical to the real tiger's. After I expressed my misgivings, people fell silent for a long time.

Finally Director Yu said, "Why don't we have the tiger put down and use its skin?"

"Maybe we should do that," agreed Old Min, who was also in the series, playing a bad official.

Secretary Feng was uncertain whether Huping could still fill his role. Director Yu assured him, saying, "That shouldn't be a problem. Is he still a man if he can't even fight a dead tiger?"

People cracked up.

Then it occurred to us that the tiger was a protected animal and that we might get into trouble with the law if we had it killed. Director Yu told us not to worry. He was going to talk with a friend of his in the Municipal Administration.

Old Min agreed to wear the tiger's skin and fight with Huping. He was good at this kind of horseplay.

Two days later, our plan was approved. So we had the tiger shot by a militiaman with a semiautomatic rifle. The man had been instructed not to damage the animal's head, so he aimed at its chest. He fired six shots into the tiger, but it simply refused to die—it sat on its haunches, panting, its tongue hanging out of the corner of its mouth while blood streamed down its front legs. Its eyes were half closed, as though it were sleepy. Even when it had finally fallen down, people waited for some time before opening the cage.

To stay clear of anybody who might be involved with the black market, we sold the whole carcass to the state-owned Red Arrow Pharmaceutical Factory for forty-eight hundred yuan, a little more than we had paid for the live tiger. But that same evening we got a call from the manager of the factory, who complained that one of the tiger's hind legs was missing. We assured him that when the carcass left our company, it was intact. Apparently en route someone had hacked off the leg to get a piece of tiger bone, which is a kind of treasure in Chinese medicine, often used to strengthen the physique, relieve rheumatic pains, and ease palpitations caused by fright. The factory refused to pay the full price unless we delivered the missing leg. But how on earth could we recover it? Secretary Feng haggled hard in vain, and they docked five hundred yuan from the original figure.

This time there was no need to persuade our hero. Just at the mention of beating a fake tiger, Huping got excited, itching to have a go. He declared, "I'm still a tiger-fighter. I'll whip him!"

Because the shooting could be repeated from now on, there wasn't much preparation. We set out for the woods in just one truck. Old Min sat in the cab with a young actress who was allergic to the smog and wore a large gauze mask. On the way, Huping grinned at us, gnashed his teeth, and made hisses through his nose. His eyes radiated a hard light. That spooked me, and I avoided looking at him.

When we arrived at the place and got off the vehicle, he began glaring at Old Min. The look on his face suggested intense malice. It made me feel awful, because he used to be such a good-hearted man, gentle and sweet. That was another reason why the girls had called him Prince.

Old Min changed his mind and refused to play the tiger. Director Yu and Secretary Feng tried to persuade him, but he simply wouldn't do it, saying, "He thinks he's a real tiger-killer and can have his way with me. No, I won't give him the chance."

"Please, he won't hurt you," begged Director Yu.

"Look at his eyes—they give me goose bumps. No, I won't have anything to do with him."

Desperate, Secretary Feng shouted at us, "Who'd like to play the tiger?"

There was no response, only a grasshopper snapping its whitish wings in the air. Then an explosion was heard from the distant mountain, where granite was being quarried.

Director Yu added, "Come on, it will be fun, a great experience." Seeing nobody step forward, he went on, "I'll treat whoever takes the part to an eight-course dinner."

"Where will you take him?" asked the young truck driver, Little Dou.

"Four Seas Garden."

"You really mean it?"

"Of course—on my word of honor."

"Then I'll try. I've never been in a movie, though."

"You know the story *Wu Song Beat the Tiger,* don't you?"

"Yes."

"Just imagine yourself as the tiger being beaten by the hero. Crawl and roll about, keep shaking your head until I say, 'Die.' Then you fall down and begin to die slowly."

"All right, I'll give it a shot."

Huping was already in his outfit, but this time not wearing the cudgel.

They wrapped the small driver in the tiger's skin and tied the strings around his belly. Director Yu said to him, "Don't be scared. Try to be natural. He'll wrestle with you bare-handed. This tiger skin is so thick that nothing can hurt you."

"No problem." The driver spat on the ground, then pulled on the tiger's head.

The director raised his hand, an unlit cigarette between his index and middle fingers. "Action!" he called.

The tiger crawled into the grass, wandering with ease. Its rump swayed a little. Huping leaped on its back and began riding it around, shouting, "Kill!" Gripping its forelock with his left hand, he hit the tiger hard on the head with his right fist.

"Oh, Mama!" the tiger squealed. "He's killing me!"

Huping kept punching until the tiger staggered, then collapsed. Just as we were about to intervene, Director Yu motioned for us not to move. Old Min laughed boisterously, bending forward and holding the swell of his belly with both hands. "Oh my! Oh my!" he kept saying.

Meanwhile, Huping was slapping the tiger's face and spat on it as well. The animal screamed, "Spare me! Spare me, Grandpa!"

"He's hurting him," said Secretary Feng.

"It's all right," Director Yu assured him, then turned to the crew. "Keep the camera rolling."

I said, "If he cripples Little Dou, it'll cost us lots."

"Don't put such a jinx on us!" the director snapped at me. I held my tongue.

Finally, Huping got off the motionless tiger, but then he started in ferociously kicking its flank, head, neck, face. His boots produced muffled thuds as he cursed, "Kill this paper tiger! I'm going to finish him off!"

How frightened we were! The driver wasn't making a sound at this point. Huping stepped aside and, picking up a rock as large as a melon, muttered, "Let me smash this fake."

We ran over and grabbed him.

"Stop it!" the medic yelled at our hero. "You've already beaten the crap out of Little Dou!"

Huping wouldn't listen and struggled to reach the tiger. It took five men to restrain him, wrench the rock from his hands, and haul him away. He shouted, "I killed another tiger! I'm a real tiger-fighter!"

"Shut up!" Director Yu said. "You couldn't handle a tiger, so we gave you a man."

Hurriedly, we removed the animal skin from the driver, who was unconscious. His lips were cut open; his mouth and eyes were bleeding.

Old Min, still unable to stop chuckling, poured some cold

water on Little Dou's face. A moment later Little Dou came to, moaning, "Help . . . save me . . ."

The medic began bandaging him, insisting we had to send him to the hospital without delay. But who could drive the truck? Secretary Feng rubbed his hands and said, "Damn, look at this mess!"

A young man was dispatched to look for a phone in order to call our company to have them send out the other driver. In the meantime, Little Dou's wounds stopped bleeding, and he was able to answer some questions, but he couldn't help groaning every few seconds. Old Min waved a leafy twig over Little Dou's face to keep mosquitoes and flies away. Tired and bored, Huping was alone in the cab, napping. Except for the two leaders, who were in the bushes talking, we all lounged on the grass, drinking soda and smoking cigarettes.

Not until an hour later did the other driver arrive by bicycle. At the sight of him some of us shouted, "Long live Chairman Mao!" although the great leader had passed away five years before.

The moment we arrived at the hospital, we rushed Little Dou to the emergency room. While the doctor was stitching him up, the medic and I escorted Huping back to the mental ward. On the way, Huping said tearfully, "I swear I didn't know Little Dou was in the tiger."

After a good deal of editing, the fake-tiger part matched the rest of the scene, more or less. Many leaders of our prefecture saw the new part and praised it, even though the camera shakes like crazy. Several TV stations in the Northeast have begun rebroadcasting the series. We're told that it will be shown in Beijing soon, and we're hopeful it will win a prize. Director Yu has promised to throw a seafood party if our series makes the finals, and to ask the Municipal Administration to give us all a raise if it receives an award.

Both the driver and Huping are still in the hospital. I was assigned to visit them once a week on behalf of our company. The doctor said that Little Dou, who suffered a concussion, would recuperate soon, but Huping wasn't doing so well. The hospital plans to have him transferred to a mental home when a bed is available there.

Yesterday, after lunch, I went to see our patients with a string bag of Red Jade apples. I found the driver in the ward's recreation room, sitting alone over a chessboard. He looked fine, although the scars on his upper lip, where the stitches were, still seemed to bother him, especially when he opened his mouth.

"How are you today, Little Dou?" I asked.

"I'm all right. Thanks for coming." His voice was smoother, as though it belonged to another man.

"Does your head still hurt?"

"Sometimes it rings like a beehive. My temples ache at night."

"The doc said you could leave the hospital soon."

"Hope they'll let me drive the truck again."

His words filled me with pity, because the other driver had just taken an apprentice who was likely to replace Little Dou eventually. So I gave him all the apples, even though he was supposed to have only half of them. He's a bachelor without any family here, whereas Huping has two elder sisters who live in town.

I found Huping in his room. He looked well physically but no longer possessed any princely charm. He had just returned from kung fu exercises and was panting a little. He wiped his face with a grimy white towel. The backs of his hands were flecked with tiny scars, scabs, and cracks, which must have resulted from hitting sandbags. I told him that we had received over three hundred fan letters addressed to him. I didn't reveal that more than ninety percent of them were from young women and girls, some of whom had mailed him sweetmeats, chocolates, raisins, books, fountain pens, fancy diaries, and even photos of themselves. How come when a man becomes a poor wretch he's all the more splendid to the public?

Huping grinned like an imbecile. "So people still think I'm a tiger-fighter?"

"Yes, they do," I said and turned my head away. Beyond the double-paned window, the yard was clear and white. A group of children were building a snowman, his neck encircled by an orange scarf. Their mouths puffed out warm air, and their shouts rose like sparrows' twitterings. They wore their coats unbuttoned. They looked happy.

Huping stroked his stubbly chin and grinned again. "Well," he said, "I am a tiger-killer."

Broken

During the lunch break, Manjin's colleagues again talked about the typist Tingting. Chang Bofan, the director of the Youth League of the Muji Railroad Company, said, "Who knows? She may already be broken."

"How can you tell?" asked Shuwei, an older clerk.

"Haven't you seen the way she walks?" Bofan picked his flat nose, staring at the chessboard before him.

"No. Tell us how she walks."

"With splayed feet. She must be as broad as a city gate." The office rang with laughter. Bofan slapped a green cannon in front of a red elephant on the chessboard. Then they stopped laughing as the door opened and the director of the Cadre Section, Tan

Na, walked in. She wanted to see a league member's file, which Manjin helped her find in a cabinet.

When talking about Tingting, they rarely failed to mention Benchou, who was a senior clerk in the Security Section at the railroad company's headquarters and could often be found in Tingting's office. Benchou was in his early forties, dark and handsome, but he was married and had two children. "An old bull wants to chew tender grass," people would say behind his back. Both Bofan and Shuwei disliked Benchou, because he had gotten two raises in the past three years, whereas they each had only one.

Shen Manjin was new in the Communist Youth League Section and was too young and too shy to join others in talking about women; but he was also eager to know more about Tingting, the pretty girl who was being courted by several sons of the top officials of the Muji Railroad Company. To him she seemed too flimsy, coquettish, and expensive, like a gorgeous vase only good for viewing. She rode a galvanized Phoenix bicycle, wore a diamond wristwatch, and was dressed in silk in summer and woolens or furs in winter—during which season she changed her scarves every week and sometimes even put on a saffron shawl. Manjin had been to her office a few times to deliver documents that needed typing. She seldom said an unnecessary word to him. When they ran into each other in the building, she would tilt her head a little, just to acknowledge that she saw him.

Most of his colleagues were either married or engaged, and would eat in the dining room of the guesthouse that provided board and lodging for locomotive engineers, stokers, train police, and attendants. Food was inexpensive there and of better quality. You could buy meat and vegetables separately, and a chef would cook them in a wok for you within minutes. The manager of the guesthouse would grant the dining privilege only to some of the cadres who worked at the company's headquarters, which was close by. If he wanted, Manjin could eat there every day; but six days a week he would walk farther east and have lunch and dinner in the Workers Dining Hall, near the company's shopping center. He was interested in the girls who ate at that place, in particular a group of nurses who were on the company's basketball team. They were tall and handsome; of them, he was most attracted to the one who played center. She looked healthy and sturdy, with a thin, white neck, her hair coiled like a pair of earphones. If he were to marry, he would have a tall wife, so that his children would be taller than himself and would have no difficulty in finding a spouse when they grew up.

Before he was promoted to the Youth League Section, few girls had shown any interest in him. He was squat and nondescript, with narrow eyes and a round, pimply chin. These days, however, he found that once in a while a girl would shoot him a glance, but not those tall nurses, whose shoulders he could barely reach when standing in the same line with them to buy food. Yet his recent promotion had boosted his confidence to some extent, because it partly corroborated the prophecy, made by a fortune-teller in his hometown, that eventually he would rise above thousands of people. Indeed, his section was in charge of over a hundred branches of the Youth League, all together more than five thousand young men and women working along the railroads. What's more, the section didn't have a vice director yet. Several times his boss, Chang Bofan, had said to him in private, "You'll have a bright future, Manjin. Work hard, our section will be yours. I shouldn't be here." True, Bofan was already forty-three, too old to run the Youth League.

Bofan also advised him to improve his handwriting, because the Political Department always needed cadres who could write well. Handsome penmanship would give him some leverage in his career; following the director's advice, Manjin often stayed in the office after dinner and practiced his handwriting.

One evening in early July, after a hot bath at the guesthouse, he returned to his office and began copying the pen calligraphy of Chairman Mao. The window overlooked the vast square in front of the train station. The dusk was turning purple, and some automobiles passing by had their lights on. A few food vendors gathered at the roadside, shaking bells and crying for customers.

Manjin hadn't copied half a page when the door opened. In came Bofan, Shuwei, and four other men. One of them wore a pistol and two carried wooden sticks under their arms; they all held long flashlights. "Manjin," Shuwei said, "are you going to join us?"

"For what?" asked Manjin.

"It's already eight o'clock. Liu Benchou and Wang Tingting are still in her office. We're sure they'll do something tonight, and we mean to catch them." Shuwei's mouth bunched up like a snout, his gray mustache spreading fan-shaped.

Manjin took a flashlight out of his desk drawer, but they didn't leave immediately, as they were waiting for the right time. He wondered why on earth Tingting was so attracted to Benchou, a married man who was old enough to be her uncle. How could this dark fellow be superior to those young dandies with powerful fathers?

The door opened again. A slender clerk tiptoed in, reporting with a grin, "They went down to his office."

Two men stood up, about to make for the door. "No rush," Bofan said. "Let them warm their bellies down there for a while."

So they waited another ten minutes.

When they were approaching Benchou's office with their shoes in their hands, they heard half-smothered giggles coming from inside. Shuwei looked through the keyhole, but no light was on in there. Then came Tingting's panting and moaning. "Yes, yes, like this! Oh, my fingers and toes are all tingling."

"Ah, you're so good," Benchou groaned. He chuckled some, then hummed the obscene tune of "Little Girl, Grow Up Quick."

Bofan whispered to Shuwei and Manjin, "Go to the backyard and wait at the window. Don't let them get away."

They left noiselessly along the corridor as Bofan pounded on the door and yelled, "Open the door, open it now!"

Something crashed in there. Bofan shouted again, "If you don't open the door, we'll force it. Comrades Liu Benchou and Wang Tingting, you've made a mistake, but it will be a matter of a different nature if your attitude is so stubborn."

Manjin, Shuwei, and another man hurried out of the building and ran toward the window. The second they arrived there, the window popped open and out jumped a person, who landed on the ground and began crawling away. "Don't move," Shuwei shouted.

Three flashlight shafts were fixed on the person, who was Tingting. She rolled under a Yellow River truck parked nearby. At this moment all the lights in the office were turned on. Manjin heard Bofan, inside, order loudly, "Hold him! Take his belt off."

Tingting was trembling, covering her eyes with one arm, her other hand on the ground supporting her upper body. Apparently she saw the stick in Shuwei's hands and was afraid he would strike her. "You come out," he said. "We won't hit you."

"I, I . . ." Her teeth were chattering and she couldn't speak. They pulled her out while she was sobbing.

"Stinking broken shoe!" the other man cursed.

Manjin felt uneasy, seeing that Tingting had lost all her charm, her permed hair bedraggled. She looked much older, as though in her forties, five or six wrinkles on her forehead.

They took her back to Benchou's office, where a man was busy shooting photographs of the tangled sheets, quilts, and pillows on the cement floor. A used condom was lying beside Benchou's blue cap; the photographer took a picture of that, too. On the tip of a stick held by a man were Tingting's panties, which were decorated with white fringe and a swarm of lavender butterflies. Benchou hung his head, holding his pants with both hands; his face was marked with reddish patches; obviously they had slapped him. As Shuwei was putting the condom and a few pubic hairs into an envelope with a pair of chopsticks, Bofan said, "All right, we have the adulterer and the adulteress and the evidence. Let's take them to the Cadre Section."

Benchou and Tingting were led into different rooms. The interrogation didn't start immediately. Manjin wondered why Bofan and the others wouldn't hurry to interrogate them. They were smoking, reading newspapers, and drinking tea in another office, where three men were playing checkers.

When Director Tan Na arrived an hour later, Manjin was told to join in questioning Tingting. His task was to take notes. Tan Na presided over the interrogation, at which Bofan and Shuwei were also present.

"Comrade Wang Tingting," Tan Na started huskily, "you made a grievous mistake, but don't panic. You still have a chance to redeem yourself."

Tingting nodded, her thin lips bloodless and her eyes dim and sheepish. She dared not look at anybody.

Tan Na went on, "First, tell us how many times you and Benchou had sexual intercourse."

"I'm not sure," she muttered.

"Does this mean more than once?"

Tingting remained silent. Tan Na said again, "Come on, Wang Tingting, the honey season isn't over yet. How can you be so forgetful?"

Seeing that she was too stubborn to answer, Bofan rose to his feet, picked up a sheaf of paper filled with handwriting, and told her, "Look here, Liu Benchou has already confessed everything. Why should you still try to protect him? Now it's up to you to show us a good attitude. We don't have to hear anything from your mouth." He sucked his teeth, two of which, the front ones, were rimmed with stainless steel.

Tingting trembled. Her large eyes turned around, looking from one face to another. Manjin could tell she was terrified by Bofan's words. He was surprised too, because the other group hadn't begun interrogating the adulterer yet.

"That's right," said Director Tan, whose doughy face and slit eyes were absolutely still. "We just want to see your attitude. Now, tell us how many times."

"Four."

"Where did they take place?"

"In his office."

"All four times?"

"No, we were at another place once."

"Where was that?"

"On the train to Changchun."

"You mean in a berth?"

"Yes."

"Weren't you afraid of being caught?"

"It was in the middle of the night."

Tan Na pointed two fingers at her and said sharply, "What I mean is, don't you feel ashamed to do such a thing in a public place?"

Tingting didn't answer but gave a sob instead. Bofan and Shuwei smirked; Tan Na remained expressionless. She went on. "Was that the first time?"

"No, the third time."

"All right, tell us why you had such an abnormal relationship with him. Didn't you know he was married? Didn't you know it was illegal for him to sleep with you?"

"I knew, but . . ." She wiped the tears off her cheeks.

"But what?"

"He said he'd help me know what a man was like."

"When did he say that?"

"Toward the end of May."

"Where?"

"In his office."

"Why did you go to his office alone? To deliver yourself?"

"No. That afternoon we all pulled up grass in the backyard. After the work, I went to his office to return a hoe."

"And that's when he started?"

"Yes."

"How?"

"He explained why the male organ was called a 'cock.' "

"What did he say?"

"He said that by nature it was always restless and about to fly."

For a moment nobody said a word. Tan Na's eyes moved to Shuwei, who was wheezing, trying hard not to laugh. Then she returned to Tingting and asked, "What did he do next?"

"He, he held me, fondled my breasts, and drew up my skirt."

"Why didn't you stop him?"

"How could I? You don't know how much strength he has."

Bofan and Shuwei covered their mouths with their palms. Tan Na asked, "What else did he say?"

"I was scared. He said he wouldn't hurt me. I was afraid his wife might know. He said he didn't go to bed with her very often, and she couldn't know because she was so cold."

"What did he mean by that? What exactly did he say?"

"He said she, she had a cold pussy and couldn't feel anything."

Shuwei chuckled, but stopped at Director Tan's stare. Manjin was shocked by Tingting's words, wondering why she divulged so much. She wouldn't betray Benchou on purpose, would she? Heaven knew why she made a fool of him and his wife like this.

Maybe she did this to protect herself, or maybe she was mad at him.

Tan Na asked again, "How did you two have sexual intercourse the first time?"

"What do you mean?" Tingting's eyes flapped.

"Who was atop whom?"

"He was on me."

"From the front?"

"Yes."

"From the behind?"

"Yes."

"How deep did he get into you?"

"Hmm—I don't know." She blushed, her eyes fixed on the floor.

"Give us a guess."

"Maybe four or five inches."

"How was that for you?"

She answered almost inaudibly, "It was all right."

Tan Na thumped the glass desktop with her palm and stood up. Pointing at Tingting's face, she said, "Your file says clearly that you were a virgin when our company hired you. Didn't you lie to us? You were already a broken thing, weren't you?"

"No. He was my first man," she groaned. "I swear to heaven that I was a virgin then. You can ask him." Her right hand pointed back at the empty office behind her, as though Benchou were in there.

"All right," Bofan put in, "Wang Tingting, you seem pretty honest. You understand the nature of your mistake, don't you?"

"Yes, I think so."

Tan Na said, "I don't understand why you've become such a rotten thing. All right, let's stop here for tonight. You go back and write out your confession about the four times. Write down everything you remember and examine the bourgeois nature of this affair." Beads of sweat dotted Tan Na's puffy cheeks.

"May I ask the Party a favor?" Tingting said timidly.

"What?"

"Please don't let my home village know of this. My younger sister's going to be engaged soon."

"Okay, but you must show us your regret and a sincere attitude."

Manjin felt disgusted with Tingting, who was so gullible and had fallen for a middle-aged man so easily. Was she the same girl who had turned his breath tight whenever he ran into her? According to her own words, Benchou had hardly done anything unusual to seduce her. Why was she so cheap? If this had been just for sex, why hadn't she done it with one of those younger men?

The interrogation of Benchou didn't go smoothly, because he was experienced in this sort of thing. However hard they tried to coax him into confessing the truth, he would insist he had slept with Tingting only once, and he thanked the Party and his comrades for stopping him in time. Finally when they showed him her confession with her signature and thumbprint on the last page, he shuddered in sweat, sniffling and cursing her. "Oh," he moaned, rubbing his temples with both hands, "I should've made the slut bleed, virgin as she was! She swore she wouldn't tell."

Manjin stuffed Tingting's panties into an envelope, sealed it, and put it in her file, together with the confession. He helped Bofan draft a lengthy report on the affair. Within five days, orders were issued regarding the adulterer. Because of his stubborn attitude, Benchou was sent to work as a loader in the Cargo Service at the train station. It was said that his wife was filing for divorce. These days Tingting kept the door of her office shut; the typewriter no longer clicked with a crisp rhythm but with a slow, broken clatter. None of those dandies came to see her anymore.

Three weeks later she was removed from the staff and assigned to the Telegram Station to be an apprentice in telegraphy.

A new typist came, a homely girl, bony and with a mouth like a catfish's. Word went out that the leaders meant to have an unattractive typist in the Political Department from now on, so that no man would fall into the same trap as Benchou and be beguiled by beauty. As a result, the usual gossip about the typist soon disappeared.

Many people were not satisfied with the punishment Tingting had received. In the long run, telegraphy would be a better profession than typing; you could send and transcribe telegrams for thirty or forty years before retirement, whereas you could type well only so long as you were young and had good eyesight. Chang Bofan often said to his clerks, "This is unfair. In our new society, men and women must be equal—equal in work, in pay, and in punishment." Sometimes he insinuated that Tingting must have had unusual connections among the top leaders of the company.

At the dormitory, Manjin's roommates asked him to tell them about Tingting's affair. They had heard he'd taken part in the interrogation. But whenever they tried to make him talk about it, he would either remain silent or change the topic. Dahu, a bricklayer in the Construction Brigade, even proposed to treat him to a lamb dinner if Manjin told him everything, but Manjin refused, saying, "Come on, you're only interested in matters inside the pants. Nothing is so extraordinary as you've imagined." He despised those brazen, uneducated men.

In the Workers Dining Hall he found that more and more girls would glance at him. The tall basketball center once even smiled at him. He noticed she had a good appetite—eating half a pound of rice or steamed bread or corn pancakes at a meal—but he was never brave enough to speak to her. He admired her long fingers, large feet, shapely bust, and strong legs. Whenever her team played on the company's sports ground, he would go and watch. He liked seeing the girls in blue shorts and red T-shirts. He felt attracted to almost every one of them. If only he were four inches taller.

One day in August, when lining up to buy lunch, he overheard some nurses talking about a North Korean movie, *The Village of Blooming Flowers*. One of them assured the others that it was a good movie and was being shown at the company's theater, and a few said they would go see it in the evening. Manjin seldom went to the movies, but that day, out of curiosity, he decided he would go. If lucky, he might meet the tall center and her friends there.

At seven he set out for the theater. In the dusk a swarm of large dragonflies were flitting about to catch gnats and mosquitoes. Old people sat before their homes, chatting and enjoying the cool air, some waving a palm fan. On the sidewalk shaded by maples and drooping willows, a middle-aged man held the carrier of an Everlasting bicycle, on which a child, obviously his daughter, was learning how to pedal. A company of soldiers was marching past, singing a battle song and heading toward the train station. They left behind a thin mist of dust. Assuming the movie would start at seven-thirty, Manjin strolled without hurry.

At the corner near the company's hospital, he saw Wang Tingting walking ahead of him. She wore a white, short-sleeved shirt and a pink skirt. Viewed from behind, she looked thinner, her long braids swaying a little. She reached the front entrance of the theater and then disappeared beyond the gate. He had heard she was engaged to a serviceman in the navy. After the scandal, whenever he ran into her she would lower her head and hurry away.

The movie had already started. The theater was not full, a lot of empty seats on both sides and in the front. Manjin sat down at the back, because he was a little farsighted. Though the audience chuckled and laughed as the movie progressed, he didn't feel it was interesting. Looking around, he couldn't find the nurses. He wondered if he should leave.

A few moments later a female figure appeared, sliding like a cloud along the unoccupied seats on his right. Noiselessly she came close and sat down beside him. He turned to see who she was but couldn't make out her face. She wore light-colored clothes emitting a lilac scent. Strange to say, he clearly saw a bump on an old man's neck five or six feet ahead; why couldn't he see the face of this woman who was so close? Yet he could tell she was young and slim. He felt uncomfortable and kept wondering why she sat here. More than half the seats in the row were free. Why did she want to be so close to him? Was she not afraid of the people behind them?

Hesitantly she placed her hand on his leg, stroking it as though uncertain that he would allow her to do so. He remained motionless, puzzled but eager to see what she wanted.

As she went on caressing his leg, he began to squirm. She then took his hand and pulled it toward her. He, as if in a trance, allowed her to take control of his hand, which landed on her leg. She lifted his wrist and made his fingers caress, back and forth, the soft inside of her thigh. He got the message, and his hand turned bold and went farther inward. She didn't wear underpants, which surprised him. His breathing grew heavy and his heart was thumping. Never had he been so intimate with a woman. He felt dizzy, his temples so tight that he couldn't think of anything except what his hand was touching. How desperately he longed to see what it was like down there. But he dared not move, afraid to attract the attention of the people sitting around.

His fingers opened her fleshy folds, which were surprisingly warm and wet. He wondered why she was sweating so much. One of his knuckles rubbed her stiff kernel; uncertain of what it was, he twisted it gently with the tips of his thumb and forefinger. She began gasping and whining softly, so he let go of it. His hand proceeded to explore around her lips, tracing the valleys, caverns, gullies. How thick and abundant her hair was, like a forest. If only he were able to see everything. If only he could have embraced her and kissed every part of her body, but he dared not budge. Suddenly the human figures, the buffaloes, and the lush paddies on the screen changed, merging and turning into a huge vulva, golden and bushy, throbbing and steaming. Something stirred in his stomach, and, ducking his head below the back of the seat in front of him, he began retching.

This scared the woman. She hurriedly pulled out his hand and wiped it with a handkerchief. She leaned over and whispered, "Sorry. Thank you." Then she stood up, turned, and faded into the darkness.

As he stopped retching, the thought came to him that he must follow her, find out who she was, and do something more. He rose to his feet and moved to the gate.

At the front entrance stood a girl in a white blouse, with her back toward him. There wasn't another person around. It must have been her that he had caressed just now, so without a second thought he hastened toward her. The plaza in front of the theater was lit bright by mercury-vapor lamps. The elm crowns formed a skyline, beyond which stars were blinking.

The girl heard footsteps. She turned around, stared at him with her mouth half open. Although her eyeteeth protruded, she looked rather sweet and delicate, perhaps a college student. He rushed over and threw his arms around her, moaning, "Honey, let's do that again!"

She gave a piercing scream, which almost collapsed him. Two men ran out, shouting, "Hold it there!"

"Help!" she yelled. "Catch the hoodlum, he attacked me!"

Manjin dashed away on shaky legs. "Stop, stop!" the men shouted. They followed him, their leather shoes thumping the cement ramp.

After two turns, Manjin reached the brick wall of the hospital. He scaled it and landed in a flower bed, sending up a cloud of pollen and dust. He jumped to his feet and sprinted away. The men climbed over too and continued pursuing him, shouting to people ahead, "Stop that bastard! Stop him!" Manjin rushed through the cypress bushes and turned toward the front gate.

Seeing a security guard raising a pistol and running toward him, Manjin stopped and put up his hands. The two men grabbed him from behind and pinned him to the ground. One of them kicked him in the face; his nose began bleeding. "It was a mistake!" he moaned. "I mistook her for another person. I meant to do her no harm. Oh, don't, don't beat me, brothers!"

"Shut up!" The taller man chopped his neck with the edge of his hand. "Let's go to the police station."

Manjin knew it was useless to beg, so he made no noise while they were binding his thumbs together from behind with a shoelace. His mind was busy trying to figure out what had actually happened. Heavens, how could he convince the police that he hadn't intended to assault the girl? He was afraid the policemen would beat him too.

Fortunately one of the men on duty at the company's police station knew Manjin, so they unbound his hands and didn't slap and punch him as they would ordinarily do to such a criminal. Instead, they locked him in a small office, whose walls were decorated with framed certificates of merit; then they returned to the girl and the two male witnesses in another room and asked them questions. Looking at the blood on the front of his gray T-shirt, Manjin couldn't help weeping. In his heart he was cursing the unknown woman for getting him into such trouble. If only he hadn't gone to the movies. If only he hadn't been lazy this evening and had stayed in his office to finish his daily handwriting exercise. A few flies buzzed furiously around him, eager to land on the bloodstains on his neck; he went on waving his hand to keep them at bay. Despite his self-disgust, time and again he sniffed his fingertips; a unique smell, something like raw chestnuts, still emanated from his nails.

He heard the girl sobbing in the adjoining office and claiming that he had attempted to attack or kidnap her. Cold sweat broke out on his back, and he began shivering. Looking out, he saw below the window two pairs of power lines stretch along the street. He was on the third floor, impossible to escape.

Half an hour later, the door opened and his boss, Chang Bofan, stepped in. With him were three policemen; one of them was fat with a beer belly, another skinny and bald, and the other so young that he looked like a teenager. They sat down and began interrogating Manjin. Bofan said, "Comrade Shen Manjin, you know this is a very serious charge. I have always believed you to be a good man. You must tell us the truth. If you committed the crime, admit it before it's too late."

Manjin burst into tears and for a minute couldn't say anything. Meanwhile, the bald policeman took a leather flyswatter out of a drawer and, one by one, brought down the droning flies.

The fat man snapped at Manjin, "Stop it! You just pawed the girl, where's your spunk now?"

"No. I didn't do it on purpose."

"All right," Bofan said. "Shen Manjin, explain it to us. You will go to jail if you can't prove your innocence."

Manjin stopped sobbing. Gradually he began to tell them what happened. The boyish man was writing down his words in a large folder. From time to time Manjin was interrupted by the policemen's chuckles. He tried to remain coolheaded so as to convince them of his honesty. To make the unknown woman resemble the girl more, he insisted that she had worn white clothes too, and that he had seen her hurry away to the front gate. But when he finally said, "From behind I thought the girl was the woman in white," all three policemen shook their heads.

"What did the woman look like?" asked the bald man.

"I couldn't see her face in the dark."

"If you can't identify her, how can we believe you?"

"That's true," the fat man chimed in. "The sentence for attempted sexual assault is three years, minimum. We don't believe any woman would do such a thing in a public place. This sounds like a joke."

"Please, I really mistook the girl for the woman." Manjin realized that at any cost he must cling to the story of the mysterious woman, whether he could prove her existence or not. This was his only way out.

"Wait," Bofan broke in, raising a red folder. "Here's what the girl said." He read it out: "He grabbed me and said, 'Honey, let's do that again.' "

"So?" The fat man shrugged.

"It seems something *had* happened in the theater before he approached the girl. Or else why did he use the word 'again'?"

The fat man took the folder from Bofan and looked over the paragraph in question while exhaling a puff of smoke, a jade cigarette-holder clamped between his teeth. Then he said, "He has to tell us who the nymphomaniac is. If not, how do we explain this to the girl's family? She's Vice Mayor Nan's daughter."

The last sentence almost paralyzed Manjin. Things turned foggy before him, and he closed his eyes, too giddy to think or answer their questions.

"Let him rest for a while, all right?" Bofan suggested.

The policemen got up and went into another room for tea. Bofan moved closer and patted Manjin on the shoulder. "Little Shen, you must take this incident seriously. Even if you don't go to jail, your political life will be over if you can't clear your name now. You are lucky they called me. Otherwise, who knows what would happen."

"Director Chang, I really don't know who the woman is."

"Try to remember who you met in the theater."

"I saw nobody but Wang Tingting."

Bofan's eyes lit up. "Did she sit beside you?"

"I don't know where she sat."

"What kind of clothes did she wear?"

"A white shirt and a pink skirt."

"Good. You must tell them this. It's an important clue." Bofan stood up and went into the adjacent office.

Ten minutes later the three policemen returned and resumed the interrogation. "You saw Wang Tingting at the theater?" asked the fat man.

"Yes, but I'm not sure if she was the woman."

Bofan said to the police, "He saw her in a white shirt."

"Yes. It was before she entered the theater," Manjin said.

"Did the woman in white ever speak to you?" asked the fat man.

"Yes."

"She did? What did she say?"

"She said, 'Sorry. Thank you.' That was all."

"Could you tell it was Wang Tingting's voice?"

"I'm not sure."

"Why did she say that?"

"I don't know. She wiped my hand and said that before she left."

"She wiped your hand?"

"Yes."

"With what did she do that?"

"A handkerchief or something."

"Wait," the bald man cut in. "What kind of handkerchief, do you remember?"

"I couldn't see."

"Was it silk?"

"No."

"Dacron?"

"No. It must be cotton, rather crumpled and soft."

That night the police went to Tingting's dormitory and searched her pockets. They found a lavender handkerchief and brought it, along with her, to the police station. She denied having done anything with Manjin in the theater. She wept and claimed he was framing her. To the interrogators she described in detail the second half of the movie; then she challenged, "If I left in the middle of the film, how could I know the entire story."

"Well, you could have seen it before," said Bofan. "And you didn't have to leave the theater afterward."

Manjin was surprised to see that her eyes were so sunken that they appeared larger than they used to be. Blubbering as she was, she couldn't establish an alibi. Nobody would believe what she said. The police let Manjin feel the crumpled handkerchief, which indeed did feel familiar to him. So this was it. Obviously Tingting hadn't reformed and had started seducing men again. What an incorrigible slut!

At about two o'clock in the morning, both Manjin and Tingting, after being ordered to turn in their confessions in two days, were released. Bofan told Manjin that he must show his remorse sincerely, writing out a self-criticism as well. Now it was up to him to decide whether he could remain in the Communist Youth League Section. Bofan's words frightened Manjin, and he couldn't help imagining the terrible life he'd have to live if he was sent back to the Wheel Factory, where he had once worked as an apprentice in its smithy.

The next day, whenever he had a free moment, he would think about how to write the confession. At noon, when others had left the office for lunch, he unlocked the file cabinet, intending to sniff Tingting's panties so as to make sure they had the same smell as the mysterious woman's. But, to his surprise, the envelope was unsealed and the panties had already lost their original scent.

Word came in the evening that Tingting had killed herself with a bottle of DDT. The police went to search through her belongings, looking for her last words, but she hadn't left any.

Her death shook Manjin. He was still unsure whether it was Tingting who had sat beside him in the theater or someone else, or a ghost. When alone, he'd weep and curse himself and his bad luck. To his surprise, the leaders didn't press him for an elaborate self-criticism. The one he had turned in was poorly written, and he had anticipated that they would demand revisions.

He was ready to return to the Wheel Factory, but no such orders ever came. He felt a little relieved when he was informed that the Political Department had issued only a disciplinary warning to him, for such an action wouldn't affect his official career and would be removed from his file at the end of the year if he worked well. It seemed all the leaders were eager to forget this case.

In the Workers Dining Hall girls didn't glance at him anymore; those tall nurses would overlook him as if he were a stranger. Soon he began to eat dinner at the guesthouse with other officials and often got drunk there. He stopped going out in the evenings. If his roommates were not in, he would go to bed early, sometimes with the butterfly panties under his pillow.

The Bridegroom

Before Beina's father died, I promised him that I'd take care of his daughter. He and I had been close friends for twenty years. He left his only child with me because my wife and I had no children of our own. It was easy to keep my word when Beina was still a teenager. As she grew older, it became more difficult, not because she was willful or troublesome, but because no man was interested in her, a short, homely girl. When she turned twenty-three and still had no boyfriend, I began to worry. Where could I find her a husband? Timid and quiet, she didn't know how to get close to a man. I was afraid she'd end up an old maid.

Then, out of the blue, Huang Baowen proposed to her. I found myself at a loss, because they'd hardly known each other. How could he be serious about his offer? I feared he might make a fool of Beina, so I insisted they get engaged if he meant busi-ness. He came to my home with two trussed-up capons, four car-tons of Ginseng cigarettes, two bottles of Five Grains' Sap, and one tall tin of oolong tea. I was pleased, though not very im-pressed by his gifts.

Two months later they got married. My colleagues congratu-lated me, saying, "That was fast, Old Cheng."

What a relief to me. But to many young women in our sewing machine factory, Beina's marriage was a slap in the face. They'd say, "A hen cooped up a peacock." Or, "A fool always lands in the arms of fortune." True, Baowen had been one of the most hand-some unmarried men in the factory, and nobody had expected that Beina, stocky and stout, would win him. What's more, Baowen was good-natured and well educated—a middle school graduate—and he didn't smoke or drink or gamble. He had fine manners and often smiled politely, showing his bright, straight teeth. In a way he resembled a woman, delicate, clear-skinned, and soft-spoken; he even could knit things out of wool. But no men dared bully him because he was skilled at martial arts. Three times in a row he had won the first prize for kung fu at our factory's annual sports meet. He was very good at the long sword and freestyle boxing. When he was in middle school, bigger boys had often picked on him, so his stepfather had sent him to the martial arts school in their hometown. A year later, nobody would bug him again.

Sometimes I couldn't help wondering why Baowen had fallen for Beina. What in her had caught his heart? Did he really like her fleshy face, which often reminded me of a blowfish? Al-though we had our doubts, my wife and I couldn't say anything negative about the marriage. Our only concern was that Baowen might be too good for our adopted daughter. Whenever I heard that somebody had divorced, I'd feel a sudden flutter of panic.

As the head of the Security Section in the factory, I had some pull and did what I could to help the young couple. Soon after their wedding, I secured them a brand-new two-bedroom apartment, which angered some people waiting in line for housing. I wasn't daunted by their criticism. I'd do almost anything to make Beina's marriage a success, because I believed that if it survived the first two years, it might last decades—once Baowen became a father, it would be difficult for him to break loose.

But after they'd been married for eight months, Beina still wasn't pregnant. I was afraid that Baowen would soon grow tired of her and run after another woman, as many young women in the factory were still attracted to him. A brazen one even declared she'd leave her door open for him all night long. Some of them frequently offered him movie tickets and meat coupons. It seemed that they were determined to wreck Beina's marriage. I hated them, and just the thought of them would give me an earache or a sour stomach. Fortunately, Baowen hadn't yet done anything outside the bounds of a decent husband.

One morning in early November, Beina stepped into my office. "Uncle," she said in a tearful voice, "Baowen didn't come home last night."

I tried to remain calm, though my head began to swim. "Do you know where he's been?" I asked.

"I don't know. I looked for him everywhere." She licked her cracked lips and took off her green work cap, her hair in a huge bun.

"When did you see him last?"

"At dinner yesterday evening. He said he was going to see somebody. He has lots of buddies in town."

"Is that so?" I didn't know he had many friends. "Don't worry. Go back to your workshop and don't tell anybody about this. I'll call around and find him."

She dragged herself out of my office. She must have gained at least a dozen pounds since the wedding. Her blue dungarees had become so tight that they seemed about to burst. Viewed from behind, she looked like a giant turnip.

I called the Rainbow Movie Theater, Victory Park, and a few restaurants in town. They all said they had not seen anyone matching Baowen's description. Before I could phone the City Library where Baowen sometimes spent much of his weekends, a call came in. It was from the city's Public Security Bureau. The man on the phone said they'd detained a worker of ours, named Huang Baowen. He wouldn't tell me what had happened. He just said, "Indecent activity. Come as soon as you can."

It was a cold day. As I cycled toward downtown, the shrill north wind kept flipping up the front ends of my overcoat. My knees were sore, and I couldn't help shivering. Soon my asthma tightened my throat and I began moaning. I couldn't stop cursing Baowen. "I knew it. I just knew it," I said to myself. I had sensed that sooner or later he'd seek pleasure with another woman. Now he was in the hands of the police, and the whole factory would talk about him. How would Beina take this blow?

At the Public Security Bureau I was surprised to see that about a dozen officials from other factories, schools, and companies were already there. I knew most of them—they were in charge of security affairs at their workplaces. A policewoman conducted us into a conference room upstairs where green silk curtains hung in the windows. We sat down around a long mahogany table and waited to be briefed about the case. The glass tabletop was brand-new, its edge still sharp. I saw worry and confusion on the other men's faces. I figured Baowen must have been involved in a major crime—either an orgy or a gang rape. On second thought, I was sure he couldn't have been a rapist; by na-

ture he was kindhearted, very gentle. I hoped this was not a political case, which would be absolutely unpardonable. Six or
seven years ago, a half-wit and a high school graduate had started
an association in our city, named the China Liberation Party,
which eventually recruited nine members. Although the sparrow
is small, it has a complete set of organs—their party elected a
chairman, a secretary, and even a prime minister. But before they
could print their manifesto, which expressed their intention to
overthrow the government, the police rounded them up. Two of
the top leaders were executed, and the rest of the members were
jailed.

As I was wondering about the nature of Baowen's crime, a
middle-aged man came in. He had a solemn face, and his eyes
were half-closed. He took off his dark-blue tunic, hung it on
the back of a chair, and sat down at the end of the table. I recognized him; he was Chief Miao of the Investigation Department.
Wearing a sheepskin jerkin, he somehow reminded me of Gen-
ghis Khan, thick-boned and round-faced. His hooded eyes were
shrewd, though they looked sleepy. Without any opening remarks he declared that we had a case of homosexuality on our
hands. At that, the room turned noisy. We'd heard that term before but didn't know what it meant exactly. Seeing many of us
puzzled, Chief Miao explained, "It's a social disease, like gam-
bling, or prostitution, or syphilis." He kept on squirming as if
itchy with hemorrhoids.

A young man from the city's Fifth Middle School raised his
hand. He asked, "What do homosexuals do?"

Miao smiled and his eyes almost disappeared. He said, "People
of the same sex have a sexual relationship."

"Sodomy!" cried someone.

The room turned quiet for at least ten seconds. Then somebody asked what kind of crime this was.

Chief Miao explained, "Homosexuality originated in Western capitalism and bourgeois lifestyle. According to our law it's dealt with as a kind of hooliganism. Therefore, every one of the men we arrested will serve a sentence, from six months to five years, depending on the severity of his crime and his attitude toward it."

A truck blew its horn on the street and made my heart twinge. If Baowen went to prison, Beina would live like a widow, unless she divorced him. Why had he married her to begin with? Why did he ruin her this way?

What had happened was that a group of men, mostly clerks, artists, and schoolteachers, had formed a club called Men's World, a salon of sorts. Every Thursday evening they'd meet in a large room on the third floor of the office building of the Forestry Institute. Since the club admitted only men, the police suspected that it might be a secret association with a leaning toward violence, so they assigned two detectives to mix with the group. True, some of the men appeared to be intimate with one another in the club, but most of the time they talked about movies, books, and current events. Occasionally music was played, and they danced together. According to the detectives' account, it was a bizarre, emotional scene. A few men appeared in pairs, unashamed of necking and cuddling in the presence of others, and some would say with tears, "At last we men have a place for ourselves." A middle-aged painter wearing earrings exclaimed, "Now I feel alive! Only in here can I stop living in hypocrisy." Every week, two or three new faces would show up. When the club grew close to thirty men, the police took action and arrested them all.

After Chief Miao's briefing, we were allowed to meet with the criminals for fifteen minutes. A policeman led me into a small room in the basement and let me read Baowen's confession while he went to fetch him. I glanced through the four pages of interrogation notes, which stated that Baowen had been new to the club, and that he'd joined them only twice, mainly because he was interested in their talks. Yet he didn't deny he was a homosexual.

As it was next to a bathroom, the room smelled of urine. The policeman brought Baowen in and ordered him to sit opposite me at the table. Baowen, in handcuffs, avoided looking at me. His face was bloated, covered with bruises. A broad welt left by a baton, about four inches long, slanted across his forehead. The collar of his jacket was torn open. Yet he didn't appear frightened. His calm manner angered me, though I felt sorry for him.

I kept a hard face and said, "Baowen, do you know you committed a crime?"

"I didn't do anything. I just went there to listen to them talk."

"You mean you didn't do that thing with any man?" I wanted to make sure, so that I could help him.

He looked at me, then lowered his eyes, saying, "I'd thought about doing something, but, to be honest, I didn't."

"What's that supposed to mean?"

"I—I liked a man in the club, a lot. If he'd asked me, I might've agreed." His lips curled upward as if he prided himself on what he had said.

"You're sick!" I struck the table with my knuckles.

To my surprise, he said, "So? I'm a sick man. You think I don't know that?"

I was bewildered. He went on, "Years ago I tried everything to cure myself. I took a lot of herbs and boluses, and even ate baked scorpions, lizards, and toads. Nothing helped me. Still I'm fond of men. I don't know why I'm not interested in women. Whenever I'm with a woman my heart is as calm as a stone."

Outraged by his confession, I asked, "Then why did you marry my Beina? To make fun of her, eh? To throw mud in my face?"

"How could I be that mean? Before we got married, I told her I didn't like women and might not give her a baby."

"She believed you?"

"Yes. She said she wouldn't mind. She just wanted a husband, a home."

"She's an idiot!" I unfolded my hanky and blew my clogged nose into it, then asked, "Why did you choose her if you had no feelings for her at all?"

"What was the difference? For me she was similar to other women."

"You're a scoundrel!"

"If I didn't marry her, who would? The marriage helped us both, covering me and saving face for her. Besides, we could have a good apartment—a home. You see, I tried living like a normal man. I've never been mean to Beina."

"But the marriage is a fake! You lied to your mother too, didn't you?"

"She wanted me to marry."

The policeman signaled that our meeting was over. In spite of my anger, I told Baowen that I'd see what I could do, and that he'd better cooperate with the police and show a sincere attitude.

What should I do? I was sick of him, but he belonged to my family, at least in name, and I was obligated to help him.

On the way home I pedaled slowly, my mind heavy with thoughts. Gradually I realized that I might be able to do something to prevent him from going to jail. There were two steps I must take: first, I would maintain that he had done nothing in the club, so as to isolate him from the real criminals; second, I would present him as a sick man, so that he might receive medical treatment instead of a prison term. Once he became a criminal, he'd be marked forever as an enemy of society, no longer redeemable. Even his children would suffer. I ought to save him.

———

Fortunately both the Party secretary and the director of our factory were willing to accept Baowen as a sick man, particularly Secretary Zhu, who liked Baowen's kung fu style and had once let him teach his youngest son how to use a three-section cudgel. Zhu suggested we make an effort to rescue Baowen from the police. In the men's room inside our office building, he said to me, "Old Cheng, we must not let Baowen end up in prison." I was grateful for his words.

All of a sudden homosexuality became a popular topic in the factory. A few old workers said that some actors of the Beijing Opera had slept together as lovers in the old days, because no women were allowed to perform in any troupe and the actors could associate only with other men. Secretary Zhu, who was well read, said that some emperors in the Han Dynasty had kept male lovers in addition to their large harems. Director Liu had heard that the last emperor, Puyi, had often ordered his eunuchs to suck his penis and caress his testicles. Someone even claimed that homosexuality was an upper-class thing, not something for ordinary people. All this talk sickened me. I felt ashamed of my so-called son-in-law. I wouldn't join them in talking, and just listened, pretending I wasn't bothered.

As I expected, rumors ran wild in the factory, especially in the foundry shop. Some people said Baowen was impotent. Some believed he was a hermaphrodite, otherwise his wife would've been pregnant long ago.

To console Beina, I went to see her one evening. She had a pleasant home, in which everything was in order. Two bookcases, filled with industrial manuals, biographies, novels, and medical books, stood against the whitewashed wall, on each side of the window. In one corner of the living room was a coat tree on which hung the red down parka Baowen had bought her before their wedding, and in another corner sat a floor lamp. At the opposite end of the room two pots of blooming flowers, one of cyclamens and the other of Bengal roses, were placed on a pair of low stools kept at an equal distance from each other and from the walls on both sides. Near the inner wall was a large sofa upholstered in orange imitation leather, and next to it, a yellow enamel spittoon. A black-and-white TV perched on an oak chest against the outer wall.

I was impressed, especially by the floor, inlaid with bricks and coated with bright red paint. Even my wife didn't keep a home so neat. No doubt it was Baowen's work, because Beina couldn't be so tidy. Already the room showed the trace of her sloppy habits—in a corner were scattered an empty flour sack and a pile of soiled laundry. Sipping the tea she had poured me, I said, "Beina, I'm sorry about Baowen. I didn't know he was so bad."

"No, he's a good man." Her round eyes looked at me with a steady light.

"Why do you say that?"

"He's been good to me."

"But he can't be a good husband, can he?"

"What do you mean?"

I said bluntly, "He didn't go to bed with you very often, did he?"

"Oh, he can't do that because he practices kung fu. He said if he slept with a woman, all his many years' work would be gone. From the very beginning his master told him to avoid women."

"So you don't mind?" I was puzzled, saying to myself, What a stupid girl.

"Not really."

"But you two must've shared the bed a couple of times, haven't you?"

"No, we haven't."

"Really? Not even once?"

"No." She blushed a little and looked away, twisting her ear-lobe with her fingertips.

My head was reeling. After eight months' marriage she was still a virgin! And she didn't mind! I lifted the cup and took a large gulp of the jasmine tea.

A lull settled in. We both turned to watch the evening news; my numb mind couldn't take in what the anchorwoman was saying about a border skirmish between Vietnamese and Chinese troops.

A moment later I told Beina, "I'm sorry he has such a problem. If only we had known."

"Don't feel so bad, Uncle. In fact he's better than a normal man."

"How so?"

"Most men can't stay away from pretty women, but Baowen just likes to have a few buddies. What's wrong with that? It's better this way, 'cause I don't have to worry about those shameless bitches in our factory. He doesn't bother to give them a look. He'll never have a lifestyle problem."

I almost laughed, wondering how I should explain to her that he could have a sexual relationship with a man and that he'd been detained precisely because of a lifestyle problem. On second thought, I realized it might be better for her to continue to think that way. She didn't need more stress at the moment.

Then we talked about how to help Baowen. I told her to write a report emphasizing what a good, considerate husband he'd been. Of course she must not mention his celibacy in their marriage. Also, from now on, however vicious her fellow workers' remarks were, she should merely ignore them and never talk back, as if she'd heard nothing.

That night when I told my wife about Beina's silly notions, she smiled, saying, "Compared to most men, Baowen isn't so bad. Beina's not a fool."

I begged Chief Miao and a higher-ranking officer to treat Baowen leniently and even gave each of them two bottles of brandy and a coupon for a Butterfly sewing machine. They seemed willing to help, but wouldn't promise me anything. For days I was so anxious that my wife was afraid my ulcer might recur.

One morning the Public Security Bureau called, saying they had accepted our factory's proposal and would have Baowen transferred to the mental hospital in a western suburb, provided our factory agreed to pay for his hospitalization. I accepted the offer readily, feeling relieved. Later, I learned that there wasn't enough space in the city's prison for twenty-seven gay men, who couldn't be mixed with other inmates and had to be put in solitary cells. So only four of them were jailed; the rest were either hospitalized (if their work units agreed to pay their medical expenses) or sent to some labor farms to be reformed. The two Party members among them didn't go to jail, though they were expelled from the Party, a very severe punishment that ended their political lives.

The moment I put down the phone, I hurried to the assembly shop and found Beina. She broke into tears at the good news. She ran back home and filled a duffel bag with Baowen's clothes. We met at my office, then together set out for the Public Security Bureau. I pedaled my bicycle and she sat behind me, embracing the duffel as if it were a baby. With a strong tailwind, the cycling was easy and fast, so we arrived before Baowen left for the hospital. He was waiting for a van in front of the police station, accompanied by two policemen.

The bruises on his face had healed, and he looked handsome again. He smiled at us and said rather secretively, "I want to ask you a favor." He rolled his eyes as the dark-green van rounded the street corner, coming toward us.

"What?" I said.

"Don't let my mother know the truth. She's too old to take it. Don't tell her, please!"

"What should we say to her, then?" I asked.

"Just say I have a temporary mental disorder."

Beina couldn't hold back her tears anymore, saying loudly, "Don't worry. We won't let her know. Take care of yourself and come back soon." She handed him the duffel, which he accepted without a word.

I nodded to assure him that I wouldn't reveal the truth. He smiled at her, then at me. For some reason his face turned rather sweet—charming and enticing, as though it were a mysterious female face. I blinked my eyes and wondered if he was really a man. It flashed through my mind that if he were a woman, he would've been quite a beauty—tall, slim, muscular, and slightly languid.

My thoughts were cut short by a metallic screech as the van stopped in front of us. Baowen climbed into it; so did the policemen. I walked around the van and shook his hand, saying that I'd visit him the next week, and that meanwhile, if he needed anything, just to give me a ring.

We waved goodbye as the van drew away, its tire chains clattering and flinging up bits of snow. After a blasting toot, it turned left and disappeared from the icy street. I got on my bicycle as a gust of wind blew up and almost threw me down. Beina followed me for about twenty yards, then leaped on the carrier, and together we headed home. She was so heavy. Thank heaven, I was riding a Great Golden Deer, one of the sturdiest makes.

During the following week I heard from Baowen once. He said on the phone that he felt better now and less agitated. Indeed his voice sounded calm and smooth. He asked me to bring him a few books when I came, specifically his *Dictionary of Universal Knowl-*

edge, which was a hefty, rare book translated from the Russian in the late fifties. I had no idea how he had come by it.

I went to see him on Thursday morning. The hospital was on a mountain, six miles southwest of Muji City. As I was cycling on the asphalt road, a few tall smokestacks fumed lazily beyond the larch woods in the west. To my right, the power lines along the roadside curved, heavy with fluffy snow, which would drop in little chunks whenever the wind blew across them. Now and then I overtook a horse cart loaded with earless sheaves of wheat, followed by one or two foals. After I pedaled across a stone bridge and turned in to the mouth of a valley, a group of brick buildings emerged on a gentle slope, connected to one another by straight cement paths. Farther up the hill, past the buildings, there was a cow pen, in which about two dozen milk cows were grazing on dry grass while a few others huddled together to keep warm.

It was so peaceful here that if you hadn't known this was a mental hospital, you might have imagined it was a sanatorium for ranking officials. Entering Building 9, I was stopped by a guard, who then took me to Baowen's room on the ground floor. It happened that the doctor on duty, a tall fortyish man with tapering fingers, was making the morning rounds and examining Baowen. He shook hands with me and said that my son-in-law was doing fine. His surname was Mai; his whiskered face looked very intelligent. When he turned to give a male nurse instructions about Baowen's treatment, I noticed an enormous wart in his ear, almost blocking the earhole like a hearing aid. In a way he looked like a foreigner. I wondered if he had some Mongolian or Tibetan blood.

"We give him the electric bath," Dr. Mai said to me a moment later.

"What?" I asked, wincing.

"We treat him with the electric bath."

I turned to Baowen. "How is it?"

"It's good, really soothing." He smiled, but there was a churlish look in his eyes, and his mouth tightened.

The nurse was ready to take him for the treatment. Never having heard of such a bath, I asked Dr. Mai, "Can I see how it works?"

"All right, you may go with them."

Together we climbed the stairs to the second floor. There was another reason for me to join them. I wanted to find out whether Baowen was a normal man. The rumors in our factory had gotten on my nerves, particularly the one that said he had no penis—that was why he had always avoided bathing in the workers' bathhouse.

After taking off our shoes and putting on plastic slippers, we entered a small room that had pea-green walls and a parquet floor. At its center lay a porcelain bathtub, a ghastly thing, like an instrument of torture. Affixed along the interior wall of the tub were rectangles of black, perforated metal. Three thick rubber cords connected them to a tall machine standing by the wall. A control board full of buttons, gauges, and switches was mounted atop the machine. The young nurse, burly and square-faced, turned on the faucet; steaming water began to tumble into the tub. Then he went over to operate the machine. He seemed good-natured; his name was Long Fuhai. He said he came from the countryside, apparently of peasant stock, and had graduated from Jilin Nursing School.

Baowen smiled at me while unbuttoning his zebra-striped hospital robe. He looked fine now—all the bruises had disappeared from his face, which had become pinkish and smooth. I was frightened by the tub, however. It seemed more suitable for electrocuting a criminal. No matter how sick I might be, I would never lie in it with my back resting against that metal groove. What if there were a problem with the wiring?

"Does it hurt?" I asked Baowen.

"No."

He went behind a khaki screen in a corner and began taking off his clothes. When the water half filled the tub, the nurse took a small bag of white powder out of a drawer, cut it open with scissors, and poured the stuff into the water. It must be salt. He tucked up his shirt sleeves and bent double to agitate the solution with both hands, which were large and sinewy.

To my dismay, Baowen came out in a clean pair of shorts. Without hesitation he got into the tub and lay down, just as one would enter a lukewarm bathing pool. I was amazed. "Have you given him electricity yet?" I asked Nurse Long.

"Yes, some. I'll increase it little by little." He turned to the machine and adjusted a few buttons.

"You know," he said to me, "your son-in-law is a very good patient, always cooperative."

"He should be."

"That's why we give him the bath. Other patients get electric cuffs around their limbs or electric rods on their bodies. Some of them scream like animals every time. We have to tie them up."

"When will he be cured?"

"I'm not sure."

Baowen was noiseless in the electrified water, with his eyes shut and his head resting on a black rubber pad at the end of the tub. He looked fine, rather relaxed.

I drew up a chair and sat down. Baowen seemed reluctant to talk, preferring to concentrate on the treatment, so I remained silent, observing him. His body was wiry, his legs hairless, and the front of his shorts bulged quite a bit. He looked all right physically. Once in a while he breathed a feeble sigh.

As the nurse increased the electric current, Baowen began to squirm in the tub as if smarting from something. "Are you all right?" I asked but dared not touch him.

"Yeah."

He kept his eyes shut. Glistening beads of sweat gathered on his forehead. He looked pale, his lips curling now and again as though he were thirsty.

Then the nurse gave him more electricity. Baowen began writhing and moaning a little. Obviously he was suffering. This bath couldn't be so soothing as he'd claimed. With a white towel Nurse Long wiped the sweat off Baowen's face and whispered, "I'll turn it down in a few minutes."

"No, give me more!" Baowen said resolutely without opening his eyes, his face twisted.

I felt as though he were ashamed of himself. Perhaps my presence made this section of the treatment more uncomfortable for him. His hands gripped the rim of the tub, his arched wrists trembling. For a good three minutes nobody said a word; the room was so quiet that its walls seemed to be ringing.

As the nurse gradually reduced the electricity, Baowen calmed down. His toes stopped wiggling.

Not wanting to bother him further with my presence, I went out to look for Doctor Mai, to thank him and find out when Baowen would be cured. The doctor was not in his office, so I walked out of the building for a breath of air. The sun was high and the snow blazingly white. Once outside, I had to close my eyes for a minute to adjust them. I then sat down on a bench and lit a cigarette. A young woman in an ermine hat and army mittens passed by, holding an empty milk pail and humming the song "Comrade, Please Have a Cup of Tea." She looked handsome, and her crisp voice pleased me. I gazed at the pair of thick braids behind her, which swayed a little in the wind.

My heart was full of pity for Baowen. He was such a fine young man that he ought to be able to love a woman, have a family, and enjoy a normal life.

Twenty minutes later I rejoined him in his room. He looked

tired, still shivering a little. He told me that as the electric currents increased, his skin had begun prickling as though stung by hundreds of mosquitoes. That was why he couldn't stay in the tub for longer than half an hour.

I felt for him and said, "I'll tell our leaders how sincere your attitude is and how cooperative you are."

"Oh, fine." He tilted his damp head. "Thanks for bringing the books."

"Do you need something else?"

"No." He sounded sad.

"Baowen, I hope you can come home before the New Year. Beina needs you."

"I know. I don't want to be locked up here forever."

I told him that Beina had written to his mother, saying he'd been away on a business trip. Then the bell for lunch rang in the building, and outside the loudspeaker began broadcasting the fiery music of "March of the Volunteers." Nurse Long walked in with a pair of chopsticks and a plate containing two corn buns. He said cheerily to Baowen, "I'll bring you the dish in a minute. We have tofu stewed with sauerkraut today, also bean sprout soup."

I stood up and took my leave.

When I reported Baowen's condition to the factory leaders, they seemed impressed. The term "electric bath" must have given their imagination free rein. Secretary Zhu kept shaking his head and said, "I'm sorry Baowen has to go through such a thing."

I didn't explain that the electric bath was a treatment less severe than the other kinds, nor did I describe what the bath was like. I just said, "They steep him in electrified water every day." Let the terror seize their brains, I thought, so that they might be more sympathetic toward Baowen when he is discharged from the hospital.

It was mid-December, and Baowen had been in the hospital for a month already. For days Beina went on saying that she wanted to see how her husband was doing; she was eager to bring him home before the New Year. Among her fellow workers rumors persisted. One said the electric bath had blistered Baowen; another claimed that his genitals had been shriveled up by the treatment; another added that he had become a vegetarian, nauseated at the mere sight of meat. The young woman who had once declared she'd leave her door open for him had just married and proudly told everybody she was pregnant. People began to be kind and considerate to Beina, treating her like an abused wife. The leaders of the assembly shop assigned her only the daytime shift. I was pleased that Finance still paid Baowen his wages as though he were on sick leave. Perhaps they did this because they didn't want to upset me.

On Saturday, Beina and I went to the mental hospital. She couldn't pedal, and it was too far for me to carry her on my bicycle, so we took the bus. She had been there by herself two weeks ago to deliver some socks and a pair of woolen pajamas she'd knitted for Baowen.

We arrived at the hospital early in the afternoon. Baowen looked healthy and in good spirits. It seemed the bath had helped him. He was happy to see Beina and even cuddled her in my presence. He gave her two toffees; knowing I disliked candies, he didn't offer any to me. He poured a large mug of malted milk for both of us, since there was only one mug in the room. I didn't touch the milk, unsure whether homosexuality was communicable. I was glad to see that he treated his wife well. He took a genuine interest in what she said about their comrades in our factory, and now and then laughed heartily. What a wonderful husband he could have been if he were not sick.

Having sat with the couple for a few minutes, I left so that they could be alone. I went to the nurses' office upstairs and found Long Fuhai writing at a desk. The door was open, and I knocked on its frame. Startled, he closed his brown notebook and stood up.

"I didn't mean to scare you," I said.

"No, Uncle, only because I didn't expect anyone to come up here."

I took a carton of Peony cigarettes out of my bag and put it on the desk, saying, "I won't take too much of your time, young man. Please keep this as a token of my regards." I didn't mean to bribe him; I was sincerely grateful to him for treating Baowen well.

"Oh, don't give me this, please."

"You don't smoke?"

"I do. Tell you what, give it to Dr. Mai. He'll help Baowen more."

I was puzzled. Why didn't he want these top-quality cigarettes if he smoked? Seeing that I was confused, he went on, "I'll be nice to Baowen without any gift from you. He's a good man. It's the doctor's wheels that you should grease."

"I have another carton for him."

"One carton's nothing here. You should give him at least two."

I was moved by his thoughtfulness, thanked him, and said goodbye.

Dr. Mai happened to be in his office. When I walked in, he was reading the current issue of *Women's Life,* whose back cover carried a large photo of Madame Mao on trial—she wore black and stood, handcuffed, between two young policewomen. Dr. Mai put the magazine aside and asked me to sit down. In the room, tall shelves loaded with books and files lined the walls. A smell of rotten fruit hung in there. He seemed pleased to see me.

After we exchanged a few words, I took out both cartons of cigarettes and handed them to him. "This is just a small token of my gratitude, for the New Year," I said.

He took the cigarettes and put them away under his desk. "Thanks a lot," he whispered.

"Dr. Mai, do you think Baowen will be cured before the holiday?" I asked.

"What did you say? Cured?" He looked surprised.

"Yes."

He shook his head slowly, then turned to check that the door was shut. It was. He motioned me to move closer. I pulled the chair forward a little and rested my forearms on the edge of his Bakelite desktop.

"To be honest, there's no cure," he said.

"What?"

"Homosexuality isn't an illness, so how can it have a cure? Don't tell anyone I said this."

"Then why torture Baowen like that?"

"The police sent him here and we couldn't refuse. Besides, we ought to make him feel better and hopeful."

"So it isn't a disease?"

"Unfortunately, no. Let me say this again: there's no cure for your son-in-law, Old Cheng. It's not a disease. It's just a sexual preference; it may be congenital, like being left-handed. Got it?"

"Then why give him the electric bath?" Still I wasn't convinced.

"Electrotherapy is prescribed by the book—a standard treatment required by the Department of Public Health. I have no choice but to follow the regulations. That's why I didn't give him any of those harsher treatments. The bath is very mild by comparison. You see, I've done everything in my power to help him. Let me tell you another fact: according to the statistics, so far electrotherapy has cured only one out of a thousand homosexuals. I bet cod liver oil, or chocolate, or fried pork, anything, could produce a better result. All right, enough of this. I've said too much."

At last his words sank in. For a good while I sat there motionless with a numb mind. A flock of sparrows were flitting about in the naked branches outside the window, chasing the one that held a tiny ear of millet in its bill. Another of them dragged a yellow string tied around its leg, unable to fly as nimbly as the others. I rose to my feet and thanked the doctor for his candid words. He stubbed out his cigarette in the ashtray on the windowsill and said, "I'll take special care of your son-in-law. Don't worry."

I rejoined Beina downstairs. Baowen looked quite cheerful, and it seemed they'd had a good time. He said to me, "If I can't come home soon, don't push too hard to get me out. They won't keep me here forever."

"I'll see what I can do."

In my heart I was exasperated, because if Dr. Mai's words were true, there'd be little I could do for Baowen. If homosexuality wasn't a disease, why had he felt sick and tried to have himself cured? Had he been shamming? It was unlikely.

Beina had been busy cleaning their home since her last visit to the hospital. She bought two young drakes and planned to make drunk duck, the dish she said Baowen liked best. My heart was heavy. On the one hand, I'd have loved to have him back for the holiday; on the other hand, I was unsure what would happen if his condition hadn't improved. I dared not reveal my thoughts to anybody, not even to my wife, who had a big mouth. Because of her, the whole factory knew that Beina was still a virgin, and some people called her Virgin Bride.

For days I pondered what to do. I was confused. Everybody said that homosexuality was a disease except for Dr. Mai, whose opinion I dared not mention to others. The factory leaders would be mad at me if they knew there was no cure for homosexuality. We had already spent over three thousand yuan on Baowen. I kept questioning in my mind, If homosexuality is a natural thing, then why are there men and women? Why can't two men get married and make a baby? Why didn't nature give men another hole? I was beset by doubts. If only I could have seen a trustworthy doctor for a second opinion. If only I had a knowledgeable, honest friend to talk with.

I hadn't yet made up my mind about what to do when, five days before the holiday, Chief Miao called from the Public Security Bureau. He informed me that Baowen had repeated his crime, so the police had taken him out of the hospital and sent him to the prison in Tangyuan County. "This time he did it," said the chief.

"Impossible!" I cried.

"We have evidence and witnesses. He doesn't deny it himself."

"Oh." I didn't know how to continue.

"He has to be incarcerated now."

"Are you sure he's not a hermaphrodite?" I mentioned that as a last resort.

Miao chuckled drily. "No, he's not. We had him checked. Physically he's a man, healthy and normal. Obviously it's a mental, moral disease, like an addiction to opium."

Putting down the phone, I felt dizzy, cursing Baowen for having totally ruined himself. What had happened was that he and Long Fuhai had developed a relationship secretly. The nurse often gave him a double amount of meat or fish at dinner. Baowen, in return, unraveled his woolen pajamas and knitted Long a pullover with the wool. One evening when they were lying in each other's arms in the nurses' office, an old cleaner passed by in the corridor and coughed. Long Fuhai was terrified, convinced that the man saw what they had been doing. For days, however hard Baowen tried to talk him out of his conviction, Long wouldn't change his mind, blaming Baowen for having misled him. He said that the old cleaner often smiled at him meaningfully and was sure to turn them in. Finally Long Fuhai went to the hospital leaders and confessed everything. So unlike Baowen, who got three and a half years in jail, Nurse Long was merely put on probation; if he worked harder and criticized himself well, he might keep his current job.

That evening I went to tell Beina about the new development. As I spoke, she sobbed continually. Although she'd been cleaning the apartment for several days, her home was a shambles, most of the flowers half dead, and dishes and pots piled in the sink. Mopping her face with a pink towel, she asked me, "What should I tell my mother-in-law?"

"Tell her the truth."

She made no response. I said again, "You should consider a divorce."

"No!" Her sobbing turned into wailing. "He—he's my husband and I'm his wife. If I die my soul belongs to him. We've sworn never to leave each other. Let others say whatever they want, I know he's a good man."

"Then why did he go to bed with Long Fuhai?"

"He just wanted to have a good time. That was all. It's nothing like adultery or bigamy, is it?"

"But it's a crime that got him put in jail," I said. Although in my heart I admitted that Baowen in every way was a good fellow except for his fondness for men, I had to be adamant about my position. I was in charge of security for our factory; if I had a criminal son-in-law, who would listen to me? Wouldn't I be removed from my office soon? If I lost my job, who would protect Beina? Sooner or later she would be laid off, since a criminal's wife was not supposed to have the same employment opportunities as others. Beina remained silent; I asked again, "What are you going to do?"

"Wait for him."

I took a few spiced pumpkin seeds from a bowl, stood up, and went over to the window. Under the sill the radiator was hissing softly with a tiny steam leak. Outside, in the distance, firecrackers, one after another, scattered clusters of sparks in the indigo dusk. I turned around and said, "He's not worth waiting for. You must divorce him."

"No, I won't," she moaned.

"Well, it's impossible for me to have a criminal as my son-in-law. I've been humiliated enough. If you want to wait for him, don't come to see me again." I put the pumpkin seeds back into the bowl, picked up my fur hat, and dragged myself out the door.

An Entrepreneur's Story

I never thought money could make so much difference. The same children who were often told to avoid me will call me Uncle now whenever they see me. Their parents won't stop asking how things are or whether I have eaten breakfast or lunch or dinner. Many young men in our neighborhood greet me as Lord Liu, and some girls keep throwing glances into my office when they pass by. But at heart I'm disgusted with most of them. They used to treat me like a homeless dog.

The most unexpected changes came from my wife, Manshan, and her mother. Three years ago, when I was a temporary bricklayer in a construction company, I proposed to Manshan through a matchmaker. Her mother, Mrs. Pan, didn't like me, saying she'd rather throw her daughter into a sewer than let me marry her. Her words hurt me. For a whole weekend I didn't go out, sitting on a taboret, drinking black tea and chain-smoking. A friend of mine told me that perhaps Mrs. Pan wouldn't give me her daughter because I didn't have a secure job.

"Look," he said, "that girl works on the train. As long as the iron wheels move in our country, she'll have her rice bowl."

"So I'm a bad match, eh?" I asked.

He nodded and we said no more. It was true my job was temporary and I had no stable income, but I guessed there could be another reason for the Pans to turn down my proposal. In their eyes I must've been a criminal.

What had happened was that two years earlier a fellow worker named Dongping said to me, "Brother Liu, do you want to make money?"

"Of course I do," I answered.

"Well, if you work with me, I guarantee you'll make five hundred yuan a month."

"Tell me how."

He described his plan, which was to buy fancy cigarettes in the South and sell them in our city at a higher price. As his partner, I'd get forty percent of the profit if I provided labor and a tenth of the capital. I agreed to take part in the business, although I knew it was illegal. A month before the Spring Festival, I went to Shanghai and shipped back a thousand cartons of Amber cigarettes, but we didn't sell all the goods before the police arrested us for profiteering. We lost everything—the police confiscated the money we'd made and the remainder of the cigarettes. I was imprisoned for three months, while Dongping got two years because he'd been in the business for a long time and had other partners. I didn't know he was a "professional." Our names appeared in newspapers; our pictures were posted on the streets. So, to the Pans I must've seemed a hoodlum. At times I couldn't help feeling ashamed of myself.

I loved Manshan, but I hated her mother. There was no way to erase my past; what I should do was improve my future. At the time—after the Cultural Revolution—colleges were being re-opened, but I dared not take the entrance exams because I hadn't even finished middle school. I was hopeless. To tell you the truth, my only ambition was to become a decent mason, someone Mrs. Pan wouldn't bother to think of as a potential son-in-law.

The next summer I heard that Manshan had enrolled in the night college, studying modern history in her free time. So I went to the class too, though I couldn't register officially, unable to pass the exams. The class was large, about eighty people gathering in a lecture room; the teacher never knew my name, since I didn't do homework or take tests or ask any questions. I told my class-mates that I was a clerk in a power plant. It looked like they be-lieved me; even Manshan must've taken me for a regular student.

Half a semester passed, and I began to like the textbooks we were reading, especially those chapters on the Opium War. I thought that Manshan might've changed her opinion about me, because she didn't show much dislike of me in the night class. I begged the same old matchmaker to propose to her again, but the hag refused to help me. Only after I bought her a pig's head through the back door, which weighed forty-two pounds and cost me thirty yuan, did she agree to try again.

This time Mrs. Pan said, "Tell Liu Feng to stop thinking of my daughter. He isn't worthy. He's the rooster that dreams of nesting with a swan."

Those words drove me mad, and I swore I'd take revenge on the old bitch. A friend advised me, "Why bother with the mother? Why not go to the girl directly?"

That was a good idea, so I began trying to approach Manshan. She always shunned me at the night college; I'd follow her when-ever I could. Heaven knew how many times I dogged her until she reached home in the small alley. She never bicycled alone, usually together with three or four girls from the railroad company. I had no chance to get close to her.

One evening I stopped her before she entered the classroom building. I asked her to go out with me on Sunday. As I was talking, my legs were shaking. She looked scared, fat snowflakes landing on her pink woolen shawl. She said, "I'm too—too busy this Sunday. How about next week?" Her cheeks reddened. She was panting a little.

"On what day?" I asked.

"I'm not sure yet. I may have to fill in for a comrade on the train."

"Okay, I'll speak with you again."

I waited like a patient donkey the following week, planning to ask her out again, but she didn't show up for the next class. I thought she might've been ill. At the time, flu was spreading in the city and giving red eyes to thousands of people, so I was worried about her. Then my worry turned into disappointment, because three weeks in a row she didn't come to the night college. I realized she had quit. My initial response was to go look for her on the express train. But on second thought I changed my mind, feeling miserable because I'd never meant to frighten her like that.

I quit the night college too, and soon I left the construction company. The job paid too little, only one and a half yuan a day. By that time, things had changed—it was no longer illegal to run a private business, and you could sell merchandise for a profit. The government was encouraging people to find ways to get rich. A peasant who had made a fortune by raising ermines was praised in newspapers as a model citizen and was inducted into the Communist Party. So I started selling clothes at a marketplace downtown. Every two or three weeks I'd go to the South and return with four large suitcases of fashionable clothes, mostly dresses and bell-bottomed jeans. They sold like ice cream on a hot day, even at a doubled price. Each trip would bring me a profit of at least nine hundred yuan. I'd never thought I could make so much money, and so easily. Sometimes I wondered if the banknotes were real, but whenever I took out a sheaf of them at a shop counter, the salesperson's eyes would gleam.

Soon I had a large sum in the bank, but I didn't know what to do with it. My father had been a senior engineer before he died, and I'd inherited from him a decent apartment. There was no way for me to spend so much money. I was worried about my savings, which were known to everybody in the neighborhood and were accumulating rapidly. Every month I'd deposit over a thousand yuan.

Clearly the state can take away my money whenever it likes, just as thirty years ago the government confiscated the wealth of the capitalists and the landowners and redistributed it to the poor. The same thing can happen at any time to us, the newly rich.

Money is a funny thing. It can change your personality. No, not that you actually change inside, but the people around you change their attitudes toward you. This can make you look on yourself differently, as though you were a high official or a celebrity. I haven't lost my senses; inside, I'm the same small man, the same Liu Feng. In our city there's an entrepreneur in the furniture business. Every evening he'll ride a brand-new Yamaha motorcycle to Eight Deities Garden and sit down to a fifty-course dinner alone. He won't speak to anybody and always eats by himself. Behind his back, people call him a spendthrift, a loner, a neo-capitalist, an heirless man. To a degree I feel for him. He must have been maltreated by others. Now he's rich; if he can't hurt them physically, he wants to humiliate them by showing his contempt. People love money, while he doesn't give a damn about what they love. So he squanders cash like trash, eating like an emperor.

That feeling is hard to suppress. Last summer I went to the Central Zoo to see the monkeys. It was a muggy day and I didn't enjoy watching the animals walk lazily in their cages. Some of them looked half dead. At noon I felt hungry. A small crowd was gathering in front of a bakery kiosk, buying cookies, cakes, fruit, and drinks. I waited patiently in the beginning, but the two saleswomen seemed to avoid helping me. A few people who came later than me had already gotten what they wanted; still the women would pay no attention to the banknote I was waving under their eyes, probably because I looked poor and nondescript. I wore a boiler suit, which was clean and quite new.

Finally one of them asked me, "What do you want?"

"Let's see—what's the best stuff you have here?" I said.

"Just tell me what you want."

"What's your most expensive cake?"

The other woman muttered, "As if he could afford it."

That inflamed my temper. I took out a bunch of ten-yuan bills and cried, "Give me all the cakes and cookies you have here!"

They turned pale. Their manager came out and tried to calm me down, saying the shop ought to save some pastry for the afternoon. I wouldn't give in and claimed that I had twenty workers waiting to be fed, so I bought all the cakes and cookies, and hired two boys on the spot to help me carry the stuff to the pit where four bears lived. A crowd watched me dump into the pit all the cakes and cookies, which somehow none of the animals even touched.

The incident was silly. I was upset for days; to some extent I felt ashamed of what I'd done. There were beggars at the train station and at the harbor, and I myself had known hunger pangs. But the incident made me famous in our city. This was ridiculous. Why should a man's name be based on his ability to waste money? Anybody—even a kid—can do that, if he has the money in hand.

People in our neighborhood began to show their respect for me. If they saw me carry something heavy, they'd help me readily. Some older women asked whether I was looking for a fiancée. I said I wasn't interested. Then came a number of matchmakers who tried to convince me of the importance of having an heir before I reached thirty. I told them to forget it; I was in good health, unlikely to die before fifty. A few girls would eye me boldly, as if my face were a blossoming peony. I wasn't interested in any of them, because my heart was still with the girl I loved.

My business had grown too big for me to travel to the South frequently, so I contracted with a garment factory in Dan Yang County, near Shanghai: they would make stylish clothes for me and have them shipped to my company. I stopped retailing and started wholesaling. This was much easier for me, and my profits soon tripled. Five months ago I rented my own office and warehouse and hung a lacquered sign on the front door that says: NEW CLOTHING INC.

Then one day my former matchmaker came and asked if I was still interested in Manshan. Of course I was. This time Mrs. Pan begged the old woman to help her daughter, saying, "I always knew in my heart that Liu Feng is a very able man." I felt overjoyed and confused at the same time. The girl used to treat me like a bedbug, why would she deliver herself this way? Just because I was rich now?

We agreed to meet on the Songhua River that Saturday. On Friday afternoon I took a hot bath in Three Springs Bathhouse and had a haircut in there. I didn't sleep well that night, possessed by a sensation that knotted my chest and stomach, and I couldn't help murmuring the girl's name as if she were with me. Even the air I breathed felt like it was burning me inside.

The riverbank was full of people on Saturday morning, a whole school of children singing their school song and waiting for ferryboats there. I rented a dinghy before Manshan showed up.

She came, almost a different girl, in a black silk dress and a perm. She looked prettier. I was amazed that she didn't seem afraid of me at all, as though we'd been dating for years. She smiled, whispering, "You look like a gentleman."

Her words surprised me, because no one had ever called me that, and I didn't know what to say, wondering if I'd really changed so much. I had on denim shorts, a topee, and a pair of sunglasses. How could I remind her of a gentleman?

We paddled across the main channel and moored at a small island in the middle of the river. I felt dizzy as the sun was blazing on us. Sitting on the white sand, I saw the city across the water appear smaller—the concrete buildings looked like toy houses, as smokestacks at the paper mill were spitting greenish fumes. Along the other shore, parasols were bobbing a little like clusters of mushrooms. The breeze was warm and fishy.

Manshan said timidly, "Do you still hate me?"

I didn't know how to answer, puzzled by the question. My heart was racing. She was so pretty—elegant, I should say. A bang of hair curved on her smooth forehead, and her nose was so straight and so high that it looked like sculpture. Her buckteeth propped up her lip a little, but to me, her teeth were also beautiful. I stretched out my hand, stroking her cheek and small ear, wondering if this slender girl sitting beside me was the same person I'd followed so many times from the night college to the dark alley.

With her toes she pried her white sandals off and buried her feet in a small pile of sand. "Do you still hate me?" she asked again without raising her head.

"Stop that!" I snapped. Somehow the question troubled me. A wind passed by, throwing up waves on the river like endless tiles.

I hooked my arm around her shoulder; to my amazement, she didn't turn away. Instead she was peering at me, her eyes moonstruck and her pointed chin so exquisite that I almost wanted to bite it. As my mouth moved to touch her lips, my heart began jumping and my hands grew bolder.

She didn't resist me and merely said she was afraid of getting pregnant. That was what I wanted. I thought that if she got my baby, she'd never leave me. So I told her, "That will be good. I'll take care of you and the baby. I love kids. Don't be scared."

So on our first date I secured our union, but I wasn't very happy. The whole thing had been too easy, easier than swimming across the river. I was disappointed to some extent. Manshan seemed no longer like the girl who had always made me feel so humble and so unworthy.

A month later we got married. After the wedding the Pans sold their small house and moved into my apartment. I bought a lot of expensive things for my bride, like a ring, a diamond wristwatch, fourteen pairs of leather shoes and boots, a Flying Horse moped, six pairs of earrings, and a gold necklace. In fact, I got thirty gold necklaces, all twenty-four-karat, and put them into a porcelain jar, which I sealed and then buried under a linden in the small park behind our apartment building. I may lose everything at any time; the city can confiscate my business and savings just by issuing an order, so I'd better hide some wealth away. Because nobody is allowed to buy gold bars, which are under the state's control, I bought those expensive necklaces and buried them away, even though I knew I might never be able to sell them if I need money. If I'm turned into a capitalist—a reactionary element of our society—who would dare to buy anything from me?

Manshan has become a business partner of mine. Now that she works on the train to Shanghai, she directly brings back some expensive goods, which can be ruined by the postal service. Also, this saves time and expenses—we don't have to pay for the shipping fee and the insurance. I give her thirty percent of the profits made from what she helps bring back. She seems happy and looks even younger, like a teenager. But her youthful face bothers me, because I want her to be the mother of my children. For some reason I can't get her pregnant, no matter how hard I try. I don't know what to do and dare not go to the hospital to check it out, afraid to lose her if it turns out to be my problem. In our neighborhood there used to be a college teacher whose sperm couldn't crack his wife's eggs, so she left him for a sailor. She desperately wanted to be a mother. Sometimes I can't help wondering whether Manshan is on the pill, but so far I haven't found any evidence.

I still hate my mother-in-law. Her pumpkin face often reminds me of a banker's wife I saw in a movie about the old Shanghai. One night I got drunk and slapped her, but she didn't tell her daughter about it. Since I became her son-in-law, she's been so patient that she never loses her temper. In the morning, when Manshan is not home, I often light a few banknotes in her mother's presence to kindle the kerosene stove, which has twelve wicks. But she's never angry. I feel that her calmness means she despises me.

I read in *Law and Democracy* the other day that an entrepreneur in Henan Province had slept with both his wife and her mother in the same bed to revenge his humiliation—the mother had called him "hooligan" when he was a butcher, but later when he founded his own chicken farms and became a rich man, she had given him her daughter. I wish I could do the same to my old bitch of a mother-in-law, but for the time being I must work harder on giving Manshan a baby.

Flame

A letter was lying on Nimei's desk. She was puzzled because the envelope did not give a return address. The postmark showed the letter came from Harbin, but she knew nobody in that city. She opened the envelope, and the squarish handwriting looked familiar to her. She turned to the end of the letter to see who the sender was. As she saw the name Hsu Peng, her heart began palpitating, and a surge of emotion overcame her. She had not heard from him for seventeen years.

He wrote that through an acquaintance of his he had learned that Nimei worked at the Central Hospital. How glad he was that he had at last found her. He was going to attend a conference at the headquarters of Muji Military Sub-Command at the end of September. "For old time's sake," he said, "I hope you will allow me to visit you and your family." Without mentioning his wife, he told Nimei that he had three children now—two girls and one boy—and that he was the commissar of an armored division garrisoned in the suburbs of Harbin. In the bottom left-hand corner of the second page, he gave her the address of his office.

Nimei locked the letter away in the middle drawer of her desk. She glanced across the office and saw nobody, so she stretched up her arms. Again a pain tightened the small of her back, and she let out a moan.

It was already early September. If she would like to meet Hsu Peng, she should write him back soon, but she was unsure why he wanted to see her.

The door opened and Wanyan, a young nurse, came in. "Nimei," she said, "the patient in Room 3 wants to see you."

"What happened?" she asked in alarm.

"I've no idea. He only wants to see the head nurse."

The patient in Room 3 was the director of the Cadre Department at the Prefecture Administration; he had been operated on for gastric perforation two weeks ago. Although he no longer needed special care, he had to remain on a liquid diet for at least another week. Nimei got up and walked to the door while slipping on her white robe. She stopped to pat her bobbed hair, then went out.

When she arrived at Room 3, the patient was sitting in bed, his shoulders hunched over a magazine, a marking pencil between his fingers. "Director Liao, how are you today?" Nimei asked pleasantly.

"Fine." He put the magazine and the pencil on the bedside cabinet, on which stood two scarlet thermoses and four white teacups with landscapes painted on their sides.

"Did you have a good nap?" she asked, resting her hand on the brass knob of a bedpost.

"Yes, I slept two hours after lunch."

"How is your appetite?"

"My appetite is all right, but I'm tired of the liquid stuff."

She smiled. "Rice porridge and egg-drop soup don't taste very good."

"They're not bad, but it's hard to eat them every day. Can I have something else for a change?"

"What would you like?"

"Fish—a soup or a stew."

Nimei looked at her wristwatch. "It's almost four. It may be too late for today, but I'll go and tell the kitchen manager."

Director Liao thanked her, though he didn't look happy, his thick-lidded eyes glinting as the muscle of his face suddenly hardened. Nimei noticed it, but she pretended she had seen nothing. Although one of the hospital leaders had informed her that the nurses should show special attention to Liao, she didn't bother too much about him. There were too many other patients here. From the sickroom she went directly downstairs to the kitchen and told the manager to have a fish stew made for the patient the next day. Meanwhile, her mind couldn't help thinking of Hsu Peng's letter. She returned to the office, took it out of the drawer, and read it again before she left for home.

Walking along Peace Avenue, she was thinking of Hsu Peng. On the street, dozens of trucks and tractors traveled north or south, transporting lumber, cement, pupils, tomatoes, pumpkins. Even the vehicles' blasting horns and the explosive snarls of their exhaust pipes couldn't interrupt Nimei's thoughts. Her mind had slipped into the quagmire of the past. She and Hsu Peng had been in love once. That was seventeen years ago, in her home village. After her father had died of tetanus, contracted in an accident at the village quarry, many matchmakers came to see her mother, intending to persuade her to marry off Nimei inexpensively. The widow, however, declined their offers, declaring that her daughter had already given her heart to a man. Most people believed her, because they often saw Jiang Bing, a young mess officer from the nearby barracks, visit her house on weekends. Each time, he'd arrive with a parcel under his arm, which the villagers knew must contain tasty stuff from the army's kitchen. Behind dusty windowpanes numerous eyes would observe this small man appear at dusk, as though he were a deity of sorts, knowing the secret of abundance and harvest.

The villagers were hungry. Two years in a row, floods had drowned most of their crops. Dozens of people had died of dropsy in the village, where wails often burst out like cock-a-doodle-doos in broad daylight. So people thought Nimei a lucky girl, as she was going to marry an officer with infinite access to food.

Indeed, Nimei had lost her heart to a man, but he was not the mess officer. In secret she had been meeting Hsu Peng on the bank of Snake Mouth Reservoir on Tuesday afternoons, when she was off work from the commune's clinic. He was a platoon leader and had graduated from high school—much better educated than most of the army men. Later, when her mother urged her to marry Jiang Bing, Nimei opposed her wish, saying she hardly knew him. She revealed to her that she loved another man, also an officer, but her mother was adamant and gruffed, "What's love? You'll learn how to love your man after you marry him. I never even met your father before our wedding."

Nimei showed her mother a photograph of Hsu Peng and begged her to meet the platoon leader in person, hoping his good manners and manly looks might help dissuade her, but her mother refused. Meanwhile, the small mess officer came at least twice a week, as though he had become a part of the family. Every Saturday evening the widow expected to see him and find out what he had brought. Sometimes his parcel contained a braised pig's foot, sometimes a bunch of dried mushrooms, sometimes a string of raw peanuts, sometimes two or three pounds of millet or sorghum. While most cauldrons in the village had rusted because there was little to cook, and while hundreds of people had faces bloated like white lanterns because they had eaten too many locust blossoms, Nimei and her mother never went without. Their chimney puffed out smoke on Sunday mornings, the fragrance of food drifting away from their yard, and children would gather along the high fence to sniff the delicious air.

Fully content, the widow was determined to give her daughter to Jiang Bing. One evening she wept, begging Nimei, "You must marry this man who can save us!" Out of pity and filial duty, the daughter finally yielded.

When she told Hsu Peng that she could not disobey her mother and had to marry the other man, he spat a willow leaf to the ground and said with a ferocious light in his eyes, "I hate you! I'll get my revenge."

She turned and ran away, tears stinging her cheeks in the autumn wind. Those were his last words for her.

Nimei had been married to Jiang Bing for sixteen years, and had left the countryside when he was demobilized, but she had never forgotten Hsu Peng's angry words and his maddened, lozenged eyes. At night, awake and lonesome, she'd wonder where Hsu Peng was and what he was like. Was his wife kindhearted and pretty? Did he still serve in the army? Had he forgotten her?

Despite thinking of him often, she had dreamed of him only twice. Once he appeared in her dream as a farmer raising hundreds of white rabbits; he looked robust and owned a five-room house with a red tiled roof. In her other dream he was graymustached and bald, teaching geography in an elementary school, spinning a huge globe. Afterward she was a little saddened by his aged appearance. But who wouldn't change in seventeen years? Her own body was thick and roundish now, the shape of a giant date stone. There was no trace of her slender waist, admired so much by the girls in her home village. Her chin had grown almost double, and she wore glasses. What hadn't changed was her sighing and murmuring in the small hours when her husband wheezed softly on the other bed in their room. What remained with her were Hsu Peng's last words, which had somehow grown more resonant in her mind each year.

"Want some tea?" Jiang Bing asked Nimei.

"Yes." She was lying on her bed with both hands under her neck. The room still smelled musty, though the windows had been open since she came home two hours ago.

"Here you are." He put a cup of tea on the glass tabletop and walked out with a stoop. He went back to their daughter's room to help her prepare for language and chemistry exams. The girl had not passed the admission test for business school the previous year, so this fall she would take exams for nursing school. In the living room, Nimei's mother and her eleven-year-old son, Songshan, were watching TV, which was showing a kung fu movie made in Hong Kong. Their hearty laughter and the bleating music echoed through the house. Outside, a pair of caged grasshoppers were chirping languidly under the eaves, and the night air smelled of boiled corn and potato.

Why does Hsu Peng want to see me? Nimei wondered. Didn't he hate me? Even if he no longer hates me, surely he must hate my mother and Jiang Bing. It's good that they have never met. Why is he eager to visit me and my family after so many years? Does this mean he still has feelings for me? Eager to fan the old flame? If he knew what I look like now . . .

She turned from side to side, wondering about Hsu Peng's motivation but unable to guess. Then a thought, which had lurked at the back of her mind, came to the fore. Hadn't he said he was a divisional commissar? He must be a general, a VIP. Did this mean he was going to flaunt his high rank in her face? Always so imposing, he hadn't changed.

The image of such an important officer's presence in her shabby house troubled her. In her mind's eye she saw a brand-new jeep parked by their front gate. While the commissar sat inside the house, his chauffeur and bodyguards chatted noisily with the men and children from the neighborhood who gathered around the vehicle. This was awful, too shameful for her to stand. Her own husband was merely a senior clerk in the General Service Section of the hospital, his civilian rank equal at most to a battalion commander's. If only Jiang Bing had held a position one or two ranks higher. Such a useless man.

On the other hand, Hsu Peng's presence in her house could produce a positive effect. After he left, she would reveal to her mother who this general was. His visit would impress the old woman and make her understand what an unforgivable mistake she had made in forcing Nimei to marry Jiang Bing. It was time to teach the crone a lesson, so as to restrain her from nagging incessantly.

Without telling anybody, Nimei wrote Hsu Peng back the next day, saying she and her family would be glad to receive him. She gave him her home address, including the directions, and proposed a tentative date. She even wrote, "For old time's sake, please come to see me. I miss you." On the lavender envelope she pasted a special stamp, issued to celebrate Youth Day, on which a young man tapped a tambourine and kicked the heels of his boots while a girl whirled around, her head thrown back, her numerous braids flying.

At noon, Nimei observed her face in the bathroom mirror on the third floor of the medical building. Gazing at her dim, myopic eyes, she sighed, wiping her glasses with a piece of tissue. Somebody flushed a toilet in a stall, the throaty noise drowning out the mechanic hum of the ventilators. You have to do something about yourself, she thought. Remember to dye your hair. Also, you must lose some weight. You look puffy.

The young nurse, Wanyan, reported that the patient in Room 3 had complained about the fish stew at lunch. She said with a pout, "He's so hard to please. I wonder why his family doesn't come to see him."

"His family's not in town," said Nimei. "I guess his wife must be too busy to care for him. She's an official in Tianjin."

"What should I say if he grumbles at me again?"

"Don't worry. I'll talk with him and see what I can do. By the way, Wanyan, may I ask you a favor?"

"Sure."

"Can you help me buy five hundred bricks from your brother's brickyard?"

"Are you going to build a coal bunker or something?"

"No. My yard always turns muddy when it rains. I want to have it paved before National Day."

"All right, I'll talk to my brother."

"Could you ask him to give me a discount?"

"You can probably use some half-baked bricks. Much cheaper, you know—just four fen apiece."

"Wonderful. Ask him to get me five hundred of those."

Nimei went to Room 3. At the sight of her, Director Liao blew his nose into a crumpled handkerchief and began complaining about the mackerel stew, which he hadn't been able to eat. He disliked saltwater fish except for shrimp and crab. Nimei explained that the kitchen manager said that only mackerel and yellow croaker were available. But she assured Director Liao that she'd try her best to find freshwater fish for him.

Shaking his balding head, the patient snorted, "I can't believe this. Muji City is right on the Songhua River and there are no freshwater fish here."

"I promise I'll find fish for you, Director Liao," Nimei told him.

"Well, I don't mean to claim any special privilege."

"I understand."

That evening Nimei talked with her husband about the patient in Room 3. She wanted him to go to the riverside the next morning and buy a carp, not too big, just a three- or four-pounder. Jiang Bing felt uneasy about her suggestion because carp were expensive these days and few people could afford them. A four-pounder would cost a fifth of his monthly salary. But Nimei said that he shouldn't worry about the money, and that whatever he spent for the fish would come back to him eventually.

"Trust me," she told him. "Go buy a carp. Stew it tomorrow afternoon and take it to my office. It's for yourself, not for me."

He dared not argue more, remembering that she had once burned three ten-yuan notes because he was going to buy her mother an expensive fur coat. He'd had to wrestle with her to rescue the rest of the money. So he promised to get the fish.

The next morning Nimei got up early and went jogging on the playground at the middle school nearby. For the first time she put on the rubber sneakers her husband had bought her three years ago. Jiang Bing was pleased to see that at last she began to take care of her health. Time and again he had advised her to join him in practicing tai chi on the riverbank in the morning with a group of old people, but she disliked "the shadowboxing," which looked silly to her, like catching fish in the air. That morning Jiang Bing went to the riverside with an enamel basin, and he stayed there for almost an hour exercising and chatting with friends, but he didn't find any carp for sale. Instead, he bought a three-pound whitefish, which he carried home and kept alive in a vat of rainwater. Songshan fed the fish a piece of pancake before setting out for school.

Jiang Bing didn't take a break at noon. After lunch he returned to his office immediately and resumed working at account books. He left work an hour and a half early. The moment he reached home, he put on his purple apron and began cooking the fish. He scooped it out of the vat and laid it on the chopping board. It writhed, its tail slapping the board noisily, its mouth wide open, as though it were trying to disgorge its innards. He struck it three times with the side of a cleaver. The fish stopped wiggling.

Having scaled and gutted it, he rinsed it twice with clean water. He heated half a wok of vegetable oil on a kerosene stove and put in the fish to fry for a few minutes. Meanwhile, he chopped its gills and innards to bits for the chickens and then washed clean the knife and the board.

The deep-frying had gotten rid of the fish's earthy smell. Next he boiled it in plain water. As the pot was bubbling, he sliced a chunk of peeled ginger, diced a thick scallion, crushed four large cloves of garlic, poured half a cup of cooking wine, and took out the sugar jar and the sesame oil bottle. He used a scrap of newspaper to get a fire from the stove and lit a cigarette. Sitting on a bench and waving a bamboo fan, he gave a toothy smile to his mother-in-law, who had been watching the boiling pot with bulging eyes. Not until the broth turned milky did he put in the spices and the vegetables, all at once. After adding a touch of salt and a spoon of sesame oil, he turned off the fire, ladled up a bit of the soup, and tasted it. "Yummy," he said and smacked his thin lips.

The old woman asked, "It's not a holiday today, why cook the fish in such a fancy way?"

"My job, Mother. I'm helping Nimei."

"She's forgotten who she is, totally spoiled. She has a princess's heart but a maid's fortune."

At five-thirty Jiang Bing arrived at Nimei's office with a dinner pail. Together the couple went to Room 3. The patient gave them a lukewarm greeting, but at the sight of the fish soup, his eyes brightened. Having tried two spoonfuls, he exclaimed, "I'll be damned, who made this? What a beautiful job!"

"He did." Nimei pointed at her husband. "He used to be a mess officer in the army, so he knows how to cook fish. I'm so glad you like the soup."

"Thank you, Young Jiang." The patient stretched out his right hand while chewing noisily. Gingerly Jiang Bing held Liao's thick thumb and gave it a shake.

Nimei said, "Be careful, Director Liao. Don't eat the head or suck the bones, and don't eat too much for the time being. Your stomach needs time to recover."

"I know—or this wouldn't be enough." The patient gave a belly laugh.

Every morning from then on, Jiang Bing got up early and went to the riverside to buy fish. Sometimes he bought a silver carp, sometimes a pike, sometimes a catfish; once he got a two-pound crucian, which he smoked. Each day he cooked the fish in a different way, and his dishes pleased the director greatly. Soon Jiang Bing ran out of money. When he told Nimei he had spent all their wages, she suggested he withdraw two hundred yuan from their savings account. He did, and day after day he continued to make the fancy dishes. In the meantime, Nimei kept jogging for half an hour every morning. She even borrowed from the hospital's gym (its supervisor was a friend of hers) a pair of small dumbbells, which she exercised with at home. Although she had lost little weight, ten days later her muscles were firmer

and her face less flabby. Her jaw had begun to show a fine con-
tour. She said to herself, You should've started to exercise long
ago. That would've kept you tighter and smaller. A healthy body
surely makes the heart feel younger.

A few times Director Liao wanted to pay Nimei for the fish,
but she refused to accept any money from him, saying, "It's my
job to take care of my patients."

Gradually the director and Jiang Bing got to know each other.
Every day after Liao finished dinner, Jiang would stay an hour or
two, chatting with the leader, who unfailingly turned talkative
after a good meal. The nurses were amazed that the patient in
Room 3 had mellowed so much. When they asked Nimei why
her husband came at dinnertime every day, she said that Liao and
Jiang Bing knew each other from before. Of course
nobody believed her, but the nurses were glad that at last the
patient's manners and attitude became wholesome, and even
avuncular. Nimei claimed Director Liao paid for the fish he ate.

The bricks arrived, a cartful of them, drawn over by three Mongolian ponies. Nimei paid for them promptly and gave the driver
two packs of Great Production cigarettes.

For an entire weekend the couple leveled the ground and laid
the bricks. Nimei wanted the yard to be paved neatly, so Jiang
Bing hammered wooden stakes into the dirt and tied white
threads to them to make sure the bricks would be set in straight
lines. It was an unusually hot day for the fall, and the couple were
soaked with sweat. Nimei's mother cooked a large pot of mung
bean soup for them, to relieve their inner heat and prevent sunstroke. She put white sugar into the soup and ladled it into five
bowls, which were placed on a long bench to cool.

The work was done and Nimei was pleased, despite her
painful back. But her mother tottered around with her bound

feet, muttering, "What a waste of money! We've never used such good bricks for a house."

Nimei ignored her, too exhausted to talk, while Jiang Bing was sipping a bowl of soup, his bony shoulders stooping more than before. A lock of hair, sweaty and gray, stuck to his flat forehead. The sweat-stained back of his shirt looked like an old map. A few maple seeds swirled in the air like helicopter blades while a pair of magpies clamored atop the ridge of the gable roof. Nimei's mother kept saying, "We'll have to spend a lot of money for winter vegetables, and we ought to save for the Spring Festival."

Save your breath, old hag! thought Nimei.

The next day she bought two large pots of wild roses and had them placed on both sides of the front gate. She assigned her daughter to water the flowers every morning.

Director Liao was going to leave the hospital in two days. He was grateful to the couple and even said they had treated him better than his family.

On Tuesday afternoon he had the head nurse called in. He said, "Nimei, I can't thank you enough!"

"It's my job. Please don't mention it."

"I've told the hospital's leaders that they should elect you a model nurse this year. Is there anything I can do for you?"

"No, I don't need anything," she said. "Jiang Bing and I are very happy that you've recovered so soon."

"Ah yes, how about Young Jiang? Can I do something for him?"

She pretended to think for a minute. "Well, maybe. He's worked in the same office for almost ten years. He may want a change. But don't tell him I said this or he'll be mad at me."

"I won't say a word. Do you think he wants to leave the hospital?"

"No, he likes it here. Just moving him to another office would be enough."

"Is there a position open?"

"Yes, there are two—the Personnel and the Security sections haven't had directors for months."

"Good. I'm going to write a note to the hospital leaders. They'll take my suggestion seriously. Tell Young Jiang I'll miss his fish."

They both laughed.

Everything seemed to be going as Nimei had planned. Hsu Peng had written back and said he would be happy to come to her house for tea. She was certain Jiang Bing's promotion would work out, because none of the hospital leaders would dare disobey Director Liao, whose department decided their promotions and demotions. If Jiang Bing became the chief of a section, he'd hold a rank equal to a vice regimental commander's, which, although still several ranks lower than Hsu Peng's, shouldn't be too unpresentable. True, the promotion hadn't materialized yet, but she could be confident it was already in the works. In addition, her daughter had just been notified that a nursing school in Jilin City had admitted her. Nimei felt she could finally meet Hsu Peng without embarrassment.

On the evening of September 29, a Beijing jeep pulled up at the Jiangs' gate. At the sound of the motor, Nimei got up, patting her permed hair, and went out to receive the guest. To her surprise, two soldiers walked in, one shouldering a kraft-paper parcel and the other holding a large, green plastic gasoline can. "Is this Head Nurse Nimei's home?" one of them asked.

"Yes," she said eagerly, her left hand fingering the belt of her chemise, which was flowered and brand-new. Her husband came out and joined her.

The taller soldier declared, "Our commissar cannot come this evening. He's very sorry. He has to accompany Commander Chen of Shenyang Military Region to a party."

"Oh." Nimei was too flustered to say another word.

The man went on, "Commissar Hsu ordered us to deliver the fish and the soy oil to you for National Day." With two thuds they dropped the parcel and the can on a low table in the yard.

"Will he be coming to see us?" she asked.

"No. We're leaving for Harbin on the earliest train tomorrow morning."

"Who's this commissar?" Jiang Bing asked his wife.

"A former patient of mine, as I told you," she managed to reply. She turned to the soldiers. "Tell your leader we thank him."

"How much?" Jiang Bing asked them, still puzzled.

"Our commissar said not to take any money."

The young men turned and went out. Then came a long honk and children's cries—the jeep was drawing away.

The parcel was unwrapped and four salmon appeared, each weighing at least fifteen pounds. One of them still had a three-inch hook stuck through its nostril, with a short piece of fishing line attached to the hook's eye. "Oh my, what sort of fish are these?" asked Nimei's mother, mouthing a long pipe and smiling broadly. The boy and the girl gathered at the table, watching their father spreading the gills to see the scarlet color inside.

"These are salmon, Mother," said Jiang Bing. Then he announced with a thrill in his voice, "They're as fresh as if they were alive! Too bad Director Liao has left the hospital. These are the best fish, but he doesn't have the luck." He asked his wife, "How come I've never met this commissar?"

"He commands an armored division somewhere in Harbin. The fish and the oil probably didn't cost him anything, I guess." She felt like weeping.

"Of course not. If you have power, you can always get the best stuff free." He flicked a bluebottle away with his fingers. "Song-shan, get me the largest basin, quick."

The boy turned, a half-eaten peach in his hand, and ran toward their shack to fetch the washbasin.

Nimei couldn't suppress her tears anymore. She hurried into the house and threw herself on her bed. She broke out sobbing, unsure whether Hsu Peng had ever intended to visit her.

A Bad Joke

At last the two jokers were captured. They didn't know the police were after them, so they had come to town without any suspicion. The instant they entered Everyday Hardware, a group of policemen sprang at them, pinned them to the cement floor, and handcuffed them from behind. With stupefied faces smeared by sawdust, they screamed, "You're making a mistake, Comrade Policemen! We didn't steal anything!"

"Shut up!"

"Ugh . . ."

The police plugged their mouths with washcloths from a bucket and then hauled them out to the white van waiting on the street.

At the city's police station the interrogation started immediately. It didn't go well, though, because the two peasants denied that they had spread any counterrevolutionary slander. The police chief, a bespectacled, pockmarked man, reminded them of the joke they had told. To everyone's astonishment, the tall peasant asked the chief, "Who's Deng Xiaoping? I never met him." He turned to his buddy. "Have you?"

"Uh-uh. I guess he must be a general or a big official," said the short peasant.

"Stop pretending!" the chief shouted. "Comrade Deng Xiaoping is the chairman of our Party and our country."

"Really?" the tall peasant asked. "You mean he's number one now?"

"Yes."

"How about Chairman Mao? We only know Chairman Mao."

"He passed away six years ago. You didn't know?"

"Are you sure?" the short peasant cried. "I didn't know he's dead. He's the Emperor to us—no, more like a granddad. His portrait still hangs in my home."

The police officers tried hard to refrain from laughing. The chief looked thoughtful. Before the interrogation, he had thought he could easily handle this pair of yokels. Now it was obvious they were smart fellows, playing the fool to dodge the charge. He'd better dismiss them for today—it was already late afternoon—so that he could figure out a way to make them admit their crime. He ordered the guards to take the two away and put them in a cell.

Seven weeks ago, the two peasants had gone to Sunlight Department Store on Peace Avenue. "Can we take a look at the rubber loafers?" the tall peasant asked at the counter, drumming his thick fingers on the glass top.

Three salesgirls were sitting on a broad window ledge, silhouetted against the traffic lights on the street. They stopped chatting and one of them got up and came over. "What size?" she asked.

"Forty-two," said the tall man.

She handed him a pair. Pointing at the price tag, she said, "Five-fifty."

"What?" the short peasant exclaimed. "Last month it was five yuan a pair. How come it's five-fifty now? Ten percent inflation in a month? Crazy!"

"Five-fifty," said the girl, annoyed. She twitched her nose, which had the shape of a large garlic clove.

"Too expensive for this old man," said the tall peasant, who was in his mid-thirties. He dropped the shoes on the counter with a thump.

As the two men walked away, the tall one spat on the floor and said loudly to his buddy, "Damn, all the prices go up—only our chairman never grows."

The short man grinned. "Yeah, that dwarf won't change."

Hearing their words, the salesgirls all tittered. The peasants turned around and took off their blue caps, waving and smiling at the girls, their swarthy faces marked with big parentheses.

Within an hour, a joke was circulating in the department store: "All the prices go up, but Deng Xiaoping never grows." Within a day, thousands of people in our city had heard the joke. Like a spook it soon began haunting offices, factories, restaurants, theaters, bathhouses, alleys, neighborhoods, train stations.

The two peasants slept well in the cell, happy for the free dinner of sorghum porridge and stewed pumpkin, but they still had no inkling of what crime they had committed. At 9:00 A.M. the three salesgirls arrived at the police station. One of them was ordered to repeat what she had heard the jokers say. She pointed at the tall man's concave face and testified, "He said, 'All the prices go up, but Deng Xiaoping never grows.' "

"Goddamn it!" the man shouted and slapped his knee, his slanty eyes flashing. "I never heard of him. How could I ever come up with that weird name?"

The short man cut in, "We never mentioned him. We said, 'Our chairman never will change.' "

"What did you say exactly?" asked the bald policeman in charge of the team of detectives.

The tall peasant replied, " 'All the prices go up and only our chairman never grows.' I meant our Chairman Lou—of our commune."

The short peasant added, "Dwarf Lou is an awful man. We all hate him. He wouldn't let us have more than one and a half yuan for a day's work, 'cause he wants to use the money to build a reservoir for catfish and big-headed carp. What can little shrimps like us get from a reservoir? Not even fish droppings. Everybody knows all the fish will end up in the officials' bellies. If you don't believe me, you go check and see if Chairman Lou is a dwarf." He gave a broad grin, displaying his carious teeth.

A few men and women chuckled, but they turned silent at the sight of the interrogators' somber faces.

The chief asked the salesgirls to recall the original words of the joke. To his bewilderment, they remembered that the tall peasant had indeed said "our chairman never grows." In fact, when they relayed the words to others, they hadn't mentioned Deng Xiaoping either. Somehow in the process of dissemination, the joke had changed into its present monstrous form. Could this whole thing have originated from a misinterpretation? Perhaps, and perhaps not.

The interrogators were at a loss now. How could they determine when and where the joke had shed its original ambiguity and acquired its definitive meaning? It was unlikely that their superiors would accept misinterpretation as the explanation for what had happened. The crime was already a fait accompli. And how could there be a crime without a criminal? Even though a deliberate misinterpreter might never be identified, someone had to be responsible for the final version of the joke. So, how should they proceed with the interrogation?

Again the chief had the peasants returned to the cell. He then sent a jeep to their commune to fetch Chairman Lou.

Everybody was impressed by Chairman Lou's good looks: a round forehead, ivory teeth, curved brows, large eyes shaded by miniature fans of lashes. What a handsome and intelligent face he had! If he were not three foot two, you could easily have taken him for a movie star. In addition, he had dignified manners, and his voice sounded so elegant that anyone could tell he was well educated. Small wonder that even with such a deformed physique he could govern a large commune. At noon he met with the police chief and said, "Look, Comrade Chief, you ought to punish the two hooligans, teach them an indelible lesson. Else how can I lead thirty-one thousand people? In the countryside no leader can afford to be the butt of ridicule."

"I can sympathize with that," said the chief. "In fact, last week the provincial governor called our city and asked about this case. Probably Beijing already knows of it too."

At 2:10 P.M. the interrogation resumed. A few minutes after they sat down in the room, the two peasants insisted that they were wronged and should be released. They declared they both came from poor families and always loved the Party and the socialist motherland, though they had not been active in political studies and were ignorant of current affairs. They promised the chief that they would take great pains to educate themselves and would never make trouble again. The first thing they'd do after their release, they said, was buy a radio so that they could keep up with news.

The chief waved his hand to cut them off. "You still refuse responsibility for the slander against Chairman Deng? Then how could I let you go? Your attitude is not right."

"Heavens!" the short peasant wailed. "This is a misunderstanding. Comrade Policeman, please—"

"That's irrelevant," the chief said. "Look at it this way. Say that a sentence in a book can be read in different ways and some people get a reactionary meaning out of it. Now, who should be responsible for the reading—the writer or the reader?"

"Mmm . . . probably the writer," said the tall man.

"Correct. All the evidence shows you two coauthored the slander, so you have to answer for all the consequences."

"Does this mean you won't let us go home?" asked the short man.

"Correct."

"How long are you going to jail us?"

"It depends—a month, maybe life."

"What?" the tall peasant shouted. "I haven't thatched my house for the winter yet. My kids will freeze to death if you keep me in—"

"You still don't get it!" Chairman Lou bellowed and slapped the tabletop with his fleshy hand. "You both should feel lucky that you're still alive. How many people were executed because they spread counterrevolutionary rumors? Keep your butts in prison here, and remold yourselves into new men. I'll have your families informed of where to send your underwear, if you have any."

In amazement, all eyes turned to look at the little man standing on an upholstered chair. Unshod, his large feet were in violet woolen socks.

The chief ordered the guards, "Send them to the City Prison

and put them among the political criminals." He took off his glasses, smirking and wiping the lenses on the sleeve of his shirt. True, he couldn't pass a definite sentence on the jokers, because the length of their imprisonment would depend on how long the Provincial Administration was interested in this case.

"Chairman Lou, have mercy, please," begged the tall man.

Lou said, "It serves you right. See if you dare to be so creative again."

"I do it to your little ancestors, Dwarf Lou!" the short peasant yelled, stamping his feet. Four policemen walked up, grabbed the prisoners, and hauled them away.

An Official Reply

Professor Pan Chendong, Party Secretary
English Department
Beijing Humanities University

Dear Professor Pan:

   Please allow me to express my deep admiration for your
paper on Theodore Dreiser's novels, which you presented at the
Shanghai conference three years ago. My name is Zhao Ningshen, and I have chaired the Foreign Language Department at
Muji Teachers College for two years. You may still remember
me: a man in his mid-thirties, bespectacled, of slender build and
medium height, with slightly hirsute arms and a head of luxuri-
ant hair. After your talk at Splendor Hotel, we conversed for a

few minutes in its lobby, and you gave me your card. Later I wrote you a letter and mailed you under separate cover a paper of mine on Saul Bellow's *Adventures of Augie March*. I assume you received them.

In response to your inquiry about Professor Fang Baichen of my department, I shall refrain from dwelling too much on his character, because he was once my teacher and I can hardly be impartial. Although you may have heard anecdotes and depictions of him—he is a fool, a megalomaniac, an incorrigible lecher, a braggart, a charlatan, an opportunist, and so forth—none of those terms can adequately describe this unusual man. In the following pages, let me provide you with some facts, from which you may draw your own conclusion.

I came to Muji Teachers College as a freshman in the winter of 1977 and met Mr. Fang on the very day of my arrival. At that time he was a lecturer, in charge of the instruction of the freshmen. I had been disappointed by being made to major in English, for I was not interested in any foreign tongue. I had applied for philosophy and Chinese literature in hopes of becoming a scholar of classics. To this day I am still unclear how the hand of fate steered me into the field of English studies. Probably because I was among the few applicants bold enough to tackle the English examination—I mean the written part—some people on the Provincial College Admission Committee had decided to make me specialize in this language. In my heart I resented their decision, though there was no way to express my indignation. On our first evening on campus, all the freshmen were given a listening comprehension test in a lecture hall. Mr. Fang dictated the test.

He read slowly in a vibrant voice: "In the old days, my grandfather was a farmhand hired by a cruel landlord. Day and night he worked like a beast of burden, but still his family did not have enough food and clothes. . . ."

I was impressed by his clear pronunciation, never having met anyone who read English better than this dapper man. But I felt miserable because I couldn't write down a complete sentence and had to turn in my test sheet almost blank. More disappointing was that the result of this test determined our placements in the classes, which were immediately divided into four levels. The freshmen of our year were the first group to take the entrance examinations after the Cultural Revolution. During the previous ten years, colleges had partly or mostly shut down and young talents had accumulated in society, so the student pool now was replete with all kinds of creatures. In our English program, three or four freshmen could read *Jane Eyre, The Gadfly,* and *A Tale of Two Cities* in the original, and they even scored higher than the graduating seniors in a test. On the other hand, many freshmen, like myself, knew only a couple of English words and had been assigned to study the language mainly on the strength of our high scores in the other subjects. A few boys and girls from Inner Mongolia, who had excelled in mathematics and physics, didn't even know a single English word; nonetheless, they had been sent here too, to learn the language because their region needed English teachers.

Naturally I was placed in the lowest class. I was so upset that I began to play truant. Mr. Fang's class was from 7:30 to 9:30 in the morning, so I often skipped it. He was a good teacher, amiable and conscientious, and I bore him no grudge. In truth, I liked his way of running the class—he tried to make every one of us speak loudly, however shy or slow of comprehension we were. He loved the word "apple" because its vowel could force our mouths open. He would drop his roundish jaw and bare his even teeth, saying, "Open your mouth for a big apple." That was his way of building our confidence as English speakers. Later I came to learn that he had been labeled a rightist and banished to the countryside for three years in the late fifties. I also could tell that his English pronunciation was not as impeccable as I had thought. The tip of his tongue often missed the edge of his teeth when he pronounced the interdental *th,* which Chinese does not have. Once in a while he would say "dick" for "thick" or "tree" for "three." In addition, he spoke English with a stiff accent, perhaps because he had studied Russian originally. In the early sixties, when the relationship between China and Russia was deteriorating, Mr. Fang, like thousands of college teachers who responded to the Party's call, had changed his field from Russian to English. (I always wonder who among our national leaders at the time had the foresight to discern the drift of history. How could he, or they, foresee that within twenty years English would replace Russian as the most powerful linguistic instrument for our country?)

One evening I was lying in bed with a pair of earphones on my head, listening to an opera. Someone knocked at the door, but I did not bother to answer. To my surprise, the door opened and Mr. Fang's face emerged. He was panting slightly, with his sheepskin hat under his arm; his left hand held a pale-blue tape recorder that weighed at least thirty pounds (at that time a cassette player was as rare as a unicorn here). On his steaming forehead a large snowflake was still melting, right beside a giant mole. His neck was muffled with a gray woolen scarf, which made him appear shorter than he was. I got up from my bed.

He sat down on a decrepit chair and said to me, "Young Zhao, why didn't you come to class this morning?"

"I'm ill."

"What's wrong?"

"Stomachache."

"You can't walk?"

"Just barely."

"All right, since you still can speak and hear, I'm going to teach you here and now."

I was too shocked to respond. He moved the chair closer, took a mimeographed textbook out of his jacket pocket, and said, "Let's begin with Lesson Four."

Reluctantly I pulled out my textbook from the single-shelf bookcase above the head of my bed.

"Turn to page thirty-one," he said.

I found the lesson. He went on, "Repeat after me, please: This is a bee." The tip of his tongue moistened his heavy upper lip.

I read out the sentence beneath the drawing of the insect, which looked more like a horsefly.

"That is a cabbage," he intoned.

I read out the line under the vegetable. Together we practiced the variation of some simple syntactic patterns—changing statements into questions and vice versa. The whole time I was nervous and couldn't resist wondering why he was so determined to keep me abreast of the class.

After the reading practice, he plugged in the recorder and turned it on to let me hear how a British man pronounced those sentences. As we waited for the machine to produce the genuine English voice, he sighed and said to me, "All your classmates repeat the text after the recording for at least two hours a day, while you don't do a thing. If you continue to be like this, you'll have to drop out soon. You're wasting your talent."

"I've no talent for English," I said.

He raised his long eyebrows and told me calmly, "In fact you don't need talent for learning a foreign language. What you need is endurance and diligence. The more time and effort you put into it, the better your English will be. There's no shortcut."

When the British man's voice finally emerged, I was made to follow it, repeating every sentence in the long pause after it. Meanwhile Mr. Fang was chain-smoking, which soon turned the room foggy. I read out the lesson along with the recording several times. He stayed almost two hours, until one of my roommates came back for bed. How relieved I was after he left. We kept the transom open for a long while.

I did not expect he would come again the next evening. His second appearance disturbed me, because obviously he knew I was not ill. Why did my truancy bother him so much? Despite not showing any temper, he must be exasperated at heart. Was he going to flunk me if I missed more classes? Indeed it was not his fault that I got trapped in the Foreign Language Department. He must take me for a major troublemaker. Burdened with all these worrisome thoughts, I could hardly concentrate on the reading practice.

To my amazement, we ended an hour earlier this time. But before he left, with his hand on the doorknob, he said to me, "I know you don't like English, but think about this: What subject taught in our college can promise you a better career? Last year two of our best students passed the exams and went to Africa to serve as interpreters. They travel between Europe and Africa a lot and eat beef and cheese every day. Another graduate of our department is working as an English editor at *China Times* in Beijing. Every year we'll send some students to the Provincial Administration, where they manage international trade, cultural exchanges, and foreign affairs—all hold important positions. You're still young. All kinds of opportunities may turn up in your life. If you don't get yourself ready, you won't be able to seize any of them. Now, to master English is the only way to prepare yourself, don't you think?"

I didn't answer.

"Think about it. See you tomorrow," he said and went out with the bulky recorder, whose weight bent his legs a little.

His words heartened me to some degree. I had never heard that graduates from this department could enter diplomatic service. That was a wonderful profession and would enable one to travel abroad. I would love to visit some foreign countries in the future. By and by a ray of hope emerged in my mind. There was no way to change my major, so probably I had better not laze around too much. It was not too late to catch up with the class.

So on Mr. Fang's third visit to our dormitory, I told him that I was well enough to go to class the next day.

Gradually I became a diligent student. In the morning I would rise at 4:30, pacing back and forth in corridors and lobbies (it was too cold to stay outside), reading out lessons, and memorizing vocabulary, idioms, expressions, and sentence patterns. Some freshmen got up even earlier than I did. To save time, a few would stay in the classrooms at night and just sleep three or four hours, fully clothed, on the long platforms beneath the blackboards. They would return to the dormitory every other night. On the face of it, we studied feverishly because we cherished the opportunity for a college education, which the majority of our generation dared not dream about; and the department commended us for our dedication. But at bottom there was a stiff competition among us, since better grades might help one get a better job assignment on graduation. I overused my throat so much in practicing English pronunciation that I had to swallow painkillers every day.

Soon Mr. Fang was promoted to professorship. To our dismay, he stopped teaching us. The department at the time had only two associate professors in English, and Mr. Fang was one of them. He was highly respected by the students and the young faculty members, whom he often taught how to waltz or tango. Every Thursday afternoon some teachers would hold a dance party, which we students could only peep at through a keyhole or a door left ajar. By far Mr. Fang was the best male dancer. He didn't have a paunch, but when dancing, he would stick out his belly and make himself somewhat resemble a paunchy business-man, and in this way he also got physically closer to his female partner. We were impressed and thought he was something, truly a man of parts. At our annual conference on foreign literature, he presented a lengthy paper on *For Whom the Bell Tolls,* which was an eye-opener for most of us and was later published in *Modern Literature.* Before that, I had never heard of Hemingway.

I was unhappy during my undergraduate years because I remained in the lowest class all the time. This stung my pride. Twice the students of the lower classes staged a strike, demanding new class placements based on merit. After two years' study, many of us in the lower classes had caught up and knew English as well as some of those in the top class, which had always been taught by a British or Canadian expert. Whereas we had never had a native speaker to teach us. As a result, our spoken English was deplorable. The department refused to consider our demand seriously, but to forestall another strike, Professor Fang, who had been appointed its vice chairman lately, agreed to have a dialogue with us. So we all gathered in a classroom and listened to him explain why the hierarchical order of the classes should remain unchanged. His reason was that we could hire only one foreign expert at a time, and that this person should teach the best students. He mentioned the saying "Give the hardest steel to the blade." We did not disagree about that. What we contended against was the permanency of the top group.

We argued with him tenaciously. Neither side could persuade the other. Gradually Mr. Fang lost his temper, and his face turned the color of pork liver. His voice grew more nasal. He declared with his hand chopping the air, "No, the continuity of instruction must never be disrupted. If we changed the top group constantly, who could teach such a class? Impossible!"

Zhang Mingchen, a willowy fellow with curved eyes and caterpillar brows, who was the monitor of Class Three, stood up and said smilingly, "Professor Fang, this is ludicrous. You've made us feel as if we were all retarded. Why do we have to remain always the same? Why can't we develop? Even you—haven't you added some stature and weight to yourself?"

We exploded into laughter. Glowering at Mingchen, Mr. Fang thumped the lectern and bellowed, "Stop pretending you're Mark Twain! You should know who you're talking to." He turned his head slowly, glaring at us.

More laughter rose from the students. Abruptly Professor Fang wrapped up the meeting and stalked out of the room with a white cotton thread dangling from the hem of his black herringbone blazer. I had not expected he would take so much umbrage. He seemed to have become a different man, no longer the humble, conscientious teacher, as though he had been a high-ranking official all his life. In fact, besides his brand-new vice chairmanship, he had held only one official title—as president of the Regional Bridge Association, which consisted of about two dozen members, mostly old intellectuals.

The next spring Mr. Fang joined the Communist Party. I had some reservations about his induction, but I only represented the students' voice and was among the minority in the Party branch. I couldn't stop wondering whether he had been helpful and considerate to me because I was one of the few student Party members, and so could speak for or against him at Party meetings. In other words, by going to the dormitory to teach me, he might deliberately have curried favor with me so as to earn my support for his Party membership in the future. What a calculating man! But that was just a conjecture without any proof, so I couldn't communicate my doubts to the other Party members.

My suspicion of him was deepened by another occurrence, which unsettled me greatly. At our graduation the next year, Mingchen, an archtroublemaker in Mr. Fang's eyes, was assigned to a coal-mining company in Luomei County; that was the worst job assignment in our department that year. Mingchen got drunk at the graduation banquet and declared he would stab Mr. Fang to death. Lifting the bottom of his jacket, he showed us a bone-handled knife in his belt, which he had bought from an itinerant tinker for fifteen yuan. I turned to look at the table where the departmental leaders were dining. Lucky for Mr. Fang, he was not there, or he would definitely have seen his own blood that evening. When Mingchen collapsed in a stupor, I took the large knife from him. Surely he would have created a disturbance if he had kept the weapon handy. Two days ago his girlfriend, assigned to teach English at a military college in Shenyang City, had insinuated that they should split up. He believed her change of heart was another consequence of Mr. Fang's vengeance.

Fortunately I had done well in the examinations for graduate studies and enrolled in the English Department at Harbin University; it meant I did not have to seek employment upon graduation, so that Mr. Fang could not punish me with a bad job assignment. Otherwise I might have ended in a situation as grim as Mingchen's, for I was positive that Mr. Fang knew I had voted against his admission to the Party. Besides, he must have believed I had masterminded the strikes.

During my three years' graduate work in Harbin, I was well informed about the happenings in this department, because my fiancée, after her graduation, remained here as an instructor in Japanese.

Mr. Fang went on prospering in the meantime. He founded a journal entitled *Narrative Techniques,* which you may have seen, since for several years it maintained a circulation of 90,000 and was quite popular among young people, especially among would-be writers. He lectured at colleges throughout the Northeast, mainly about stream of consciousness as the most advanced narrative technique in the West. He even tried his hand at fiction writing. One of his short stories, "Beyond the Raining Mountain," about a tragic love triangle, won the first prize in a provincial contest. It has been anthologized several times. To be fair, he is a capable fiction writer. In his stories, you often can perceive a kind of primitive passion and peasant cunning that you rarely find in fiction written by academics. In truth, sometimes I cannot help thinking that he might have become an accomplished novelist had he concentrated solely on fiction writing. He spent a great deal of time editing the journal. His energy was dissipated, and he could not sustain the momentum generated by the initial success of his short fiction. Perhaps he has suffered from the absence of an artistic vision, or having misplaced his ambition, satisfied merely with getting ahead of his peers and with temporary fame. He has never planned to follow the masters' way—writing a hefty novel, a monumental chef d'oeuvre, something intended to revise and rejuvenate the genre. Apparently he no longer has the strength for such a book. He always worked on small, minor pieces. In brief, although he was a promising late bloomer, he has not blossomed fully.

My relationship with him began to improve as I contributed to his journal regularly. He treated me well and always published my papers and reviews, often giving me top-rate contribution fees. Besides translations and criticism on foreign literature, *Narrative Techniques* also carried a section of short stories and poems by Chinese authors. I was baffled by this format. Why would such an academic journal publish original poems? Never had Mr. Fang studied poetics. Why did he include a dozen pages of poetry in each issue? No doubt he was aware of the incongruity. He must have been up to something.

In the summer of 1984, I finished my graduate work and returned to my alma mater, where my bride was teaching as a lecturer. I heard that Professor Fang's journal had been suspended because a number of young women, both students and faculty, had accused him of sexual improprieties. A few said he had published their writings in exchange for their favors, while some claimed he had turned their works down because they had resisted his advances. To be frank, I suspect that some of the women might have entered into a relationship with him of their own accord. Of course this is not to deny that he must have taken the initiative. His wife had been ill for years, and sex was out of the question in their marriage. He must have been lonesome and quite concupiscent. Yet one of these affairs was absolutely beyond forgiveness, to wit: he had gotten a student pregnant, which was technically due to the substandard quality of a condom. An old nurse, who had been present at the abortion, spread the scandal, and within a week the student's pregnancy had become a household topic. I knew the girl, who was a fledgling poet and a gracious person, I must say. I had been her older brother's friend for years. She was two grades below me. One of her poems, which she had once recited in our auditorium, had moved me almost to tears and instantly made her the object of numerous young fellows' attentions. It was entitled "The Love I Have Is All You Can Have," such a wonderful poem that our school's radio station broadcast it twice a day for a whole week. In appearance she was demure and blushed easily, with dimmed eyes like a lamb's. I couldn't imagine that such a fine girl would allow an old man like Mr. Fang to explore her carnally, while there were many young men who would be happy to serve her in any way she desired. Later I learned from her brother that Professor Fang had published many of her poems under the pen name Sea Maiden and had promised her that he would help her get accepted, with a scholarship, by the Comparative Literature Department at Indiana University—Bloomington, with which Mr. Fang had claimed to have powerful connections. Oh, a young girl's heart so easily overflowed.

Although Mr. Fang was in disgrace—having received a disciplinary action from the Party Committee and lost his vice chairmanship—I did not shun him. One day I invited him to a simple dinner in my apartment. My bride had left to teach summer school in an oil field south of Tsitsihar. I had just made some money from translating a play by Eugene O'Neill, so I bought a braised chicken, two pounds of beef sausages, tomatoes, a packet of white sugar, salted duck eggs, and ten liters of draft beer. I did not invite anyone else, because other faculty members were reluctant to mix with Mr. Fang at the time. As he and I were drinking and eating, he turned loquacious. He told me that his wife suffered from a cardiovascular disease and that his son had just graduated from Nanjing University, specializing in international trade, and was going to work for a German auto company in Shanghai. His wife was upset by their son's lucrative but faraway job, for she had expected him to come back to Muji City, to marry and settle down near home.

I noticed Mr. Fang had not aged much. His hair was still dark and bushy, and his facial muscles looked quite elastic. Behind the front of his white short-sleeved shirt, his belly seemed firm and flat. You could easily take him to be in his early forties. Half jokingly I asked him how come he was so well preserved. To my amazement, he replied in earnest, pressing his hand on his chest, "First, you must have a large heart and never be depressed by anything, eat well, and sleep well. Second, you must exercise every morning in any kind of weather, hot or cold." He smiled with a shrewd twinkle in his eye. He knew I was a night owl and always went to bed in the wee hours, never bothering about morning exercises. Again I expressed my admiration for his good health.

Soon he was inebriated, and his tongue went unbridled. He sighed and said, "I'm fifty-three already. My life has come to a dead end."

"Don't be so down," I said.

"I'm going to die soon. Ah, to die without achieving any-anything. How sad!"

"Come on, have a larger heart."

He looked tearful and pathetic. I tried to comfort him by pointing out that he was a reputable scholar, at the peak of his powers, and still had a long, bright journey ahead. But the more I said, the more heartbroken he was. "After I graduated from college," he declared as though to a roomful of listeners, "I dreamed about going to Russia to study esthetics. Then Russia became our enemy, and I was made—made to study damned English, which I didn't like until I could read D. H. Lawrence in the original. Now our country is finally o-open, but I'm too old to go abroad to do gra-graduate work. I'm no match for you young people, too old." He dissolved into tears, wiping his cheeks with the back of his short-fingered hand. "Oh I should've had a Ph.D., or at least an M.A., like you!" He patted my forearm.

That was inane. He was already an associate professor. To sidetrack him, I said, lightheartedly, "Stop crying, all right? You've been a lucky old man here, so many girls were around you. Who ever had such luck as you?" I was being slightly ironic, but he took my words as a compliment, or a cue. He grinned and poured another glass of beer.

Then he began talking about the young women he was involved with in recent years. I was surprised that one of my former classmates, who used to be seeded number two in badminton in our province, was among them. She had married an officer, a dog handler, who was often away from home. How could Mr. Fang match that amazon in bed? It made me giddy just to think it. I felt embarrassed by his disordered talk, yet I was fascinated and eager to hear more. What amazed me most was that one of the women had even been willing to marry him, provided he divorced his wife, which he would not do. He explained to me, "I'm not heartless, Young Zhao. I can't abandon my sick wife. When I was in the countryside, she came to see me every two months. Another woman would have divorced me under the circumstances. She alone suffered with me and never complained. Now our son's far away from home, and I'm the only family she has here." His eyes, misty with tears, gazed at me.

I couldn't help wondering what had contributed to his apotheosis in those young women's eyes. His knowledge? His power? His vitality? His pen? His tricks? His optimism? What was the magic wand with which he had held so many of them in thrall? I thought of my friend's younger sister, the lamb-eyed girl, who had been banished to a county town to teach middle school. Before departing for the countryside, she was so distraught that she had almost defenestrated herself, pulled back just in time by her parents. Had Mr. Fang ever felt guilty about her ruin?

"Ah, how I adore those girl poets!" he confessed, rubbing his broad nose.

"Why poets?" I asked.

"You don't know how sweet and innocent girl poets can be. They all have a te-tender heart. Just give them a few words they want to hear, you-you can sweep them off their feet and set their hearts flying like ca-catkins." He giggled.

"So, no fiction writers, only girl poets, eh?"

He grinned. "Yeah. If I come back to this life again, I'll try to be a poet myself. Young Zhao, one of these days you should get to know a girl poet."

"No, I want a nymphet," I said. He reminded me of Nabokov's lecherous Humbert.

"Okay, a nymphet poet then." He burst into laughter.

You see, Professor Pan, that was the advice he gave to me, his former student. I would not try to know a girl poet. My wife is good enough for me, although she is not an extraordinary beauty. Besides, I am in poor health and ought to save my energy and time for completing my book on the Oriental myths in Eugene O'Neill's plays. After that dinner, whenever I ran into Mr. Fang, he seemed evasive and often hurried away as though I were carrying hepatitis, which had broken out in our city that summer. Apparently he regretted having divulged his secrets to me. But I never held that talk against him. Even three years later, when I became the chairman of this department, I wouldn't allude to that talk. No, I did not change my feelings about him because of the secrets he had let slip.

After the suspension of *Narrative Techniques,* our department was pestered by thousands of letters from its subscribers. They demanded a refund. Because the money had been shared out by the faculty as a holiday bonus long ago, all we could do was promise the subscribers that a new issue of the journal would reach them soon. Nobody here was able to edit the journal at the time except for Mr. Fang. So in the fall, *Narrative Techniques* was reinstated, with him as the editor-in-chief again, but now he was ordered to eliminate the section of creative writing. This time the journal turned out to be more focused and more impressive, each issue having a glossy cover and a photograph of a modern master novelist on its back. Gradually, Mr. Fang's fame rose once again. He worked hard and even published a volume of short fiction, *At the Blossoming Bridge,* which he dedicated to Ernest Hemingway as if the American writer were still alive and in correspondence with him. Probably he meant that Hemingway had been a source of inspiration. The book garnered a good deal of critical acclaim and got him ranked among the better contemporary authors for a while. He was promoted to full professor the following year, the first one in our department. He seemed destined to become a minor man of letters, but few people can remain coolheaded on the merry-go-round of success.

His fall occurred on our trip to the United States, in the early summer of 1987. He and I were both chosen for the provincial cultural delegation that was to visit four American cities. I was selected because I could speak English fairly well and was some-what knowledgeable about American literature. Mr. Fang joined the group as a fiction writer and literary scholar. The trip was partly sponsored by Wellington University in Connecticut, which was eager to become our sister school. That was why half the delegates were from our college.

On this trip, I discovered another aspect of Mr. Fang's character which I had not noticed before, namely parsimony. When we had lunch together, he would, if possible, avoid sharing the cost. Twice I paid for him. Despite having a bedridden wife, he was by no means destitute; his son sent him a handsome sum of money every month. Unlike us, he even had a foreign-currency account at the bank. It was less problematic if he took the gratis treatment for granted only among ourselves, the Chinese. What angered me most was that he played the same trick on some Americans, often waiting for them to pay for his coffee or tea or drink, as though everyone in the world owed him a favor or a debt. I could not understand why he acted like a mendicant. Our country had given each of us twenty-two dollars a day for pocket money, which was indeed not much, but a man ought to have his dignity. I could not imagine how a skinflint like Mr. Fang could be a lady-killer. Once, he even wanted an American woman novelist to pay for a cheese strudel he had ordered; he told her, in all insouciance, "I have no money on me." The tall redhead wore a sky-blue bolero and a pair of large Ching Dynasty coins as earrings, apparently for meeting with us. She had an irksome habit: after every sentence, she would add, "See my point?" She was so shocked by Mr. Fang's pointed words that she gave a smile which changed into a sour grimace; then she turned to me, as if questioning me with her green, deep-set eyes to determine whether he was in his right mind. Outraged, I pulled a ten-dollar note out of my pocket and said to him in Chinese, "Take this, but I want my money back tomorrow morning." That, for once, made him open his wallet.

Probably he acted that way because he had misunderstood the

capitalist culture and the so-called American spirit, having confused selfhood with selfishness. A few months before the trip, we
had invited an American professor, Alan Redstone, to our college
to lecture on Faulkner. That florid-faced man from Kentucky
was truly a turkey; he wore a ponytail and a flowered shirt and
played the banjo. He said that in America the self was absolutely
essential, that one had to make every effort to assert one's own
selfhood, that a large ego was fundamental for any individual
success, blah, blah, blah, all that kind of flatus. He even declared
that self-interest was the dynamo of American culture and econ-
omy, and that if you were an American, the center of your life
would have to be yourself. I swear, if he were a Chinese I would
have had him hauled out of the lecture hall before he was done.
But Mr. Fang told me afterwards that he was deeply impressed
by Redstone's talk, which apparently had set his mind spinning.
Now, in Hartford, Mr. Fang asserted himself so aggressively in
front of the American woman that he would not mind smirching
our country's face. It was as though he were altogether immune
to shame. How could he, a well-learned man, be such a credulous
ignoramus? This is still beyond me.

Our American host informed us that there would be a writers' conference at the university on Saturday. The organizers
would love to arrange a special panel for the Chinese writers,
meaning those in our delegation. We agreed to participate, quite
moved by such a friendly invitation. I was asked to talk about
American literature in contemporary China, while the six writers
wouldn't have to speak, just be prepared to answer questions
about their writings and experiences. We were all excited and put
on our best suits or dresses for the occasion. To fortify my spoken
English, I read out articles in *The New York Review of Books* for a
solid hour before we set off.

The university was in a small town, which lay in a wooded
valley. It was clean and eerily quiet, perhaps on account of the

summer break. The roads on the campus were lined with enormous tamaracks and maples. A cream-colored minivan dropped us before a low brick building, wherein several talks were to take place at the same time. Because our panel had not been advertised like the others, most of the conference participants didn't know about it and were heading toward the other rooms. I was nervous, whispering to my comrades, "If we just have a dozen people, that will be good enough."

How we were worried! Ganlan, the woman playwright, kept wringing her fingers and said we should not have agreed to take part in such an ad hoc thing.

Suddenly Mr. Fang shouted in his broken English to the people in the lobby, "Attention, please, ladies and gentlemen, I am Professor Fang Baichen, a great contemporary Chinese fiction writer. Please come to my lecture!" He pointed his index finger at the entrance to our room while his other hand was beckoning every American around us.

People looked puzzled, then some started chortling. We were astounded and had no idea what he was up to. I thought perhaps this was just a last-ditch attempt to fetch an audience. Mr. Fang went on shouting, "Room Elefen. Please. A great writer is going to speak."

If possible, I would have fled through the roof. We stepped aside to make ourselves less conspicuous. But Mr. Fang's performance did attract a sizable audience—about thirty people came to our panel. I made an effort to keep calm so as to talk.

To our astonishment, after the woman moderator introduced us, Mr. Fang grabbed the microphone from me and began delivering a lecture. He was reading loudly from a paper he had written in advance. His voice sounded as domineering as if he were a government official delivering an admonitory speech. My head was tingling and my mouth went numb.

"What's he doing?" whispered Ganlan.

Another writer said, "This is a blitzkrieg."

"Academic hysteria," I added.

Why didn't the moderator stop him? I wondered. Then I saw the woman's oval brown face smiling at me understandingly; she must have assumed he and I had agreed to switch positions.

Mr. Fang was speaking about how he had successfully experimented with the most recent fiction techniques (which were, in fact, all outdated in the West) and how he had inspired the younger generation of Chinese writers to master the technique of stream of consciousness. At first, the audience seemed shocked by the immense volume of his booming voice. Then some of them began chuckling and snickering; many looked amused, as if they were watching a comedian performing a skit. How ashamed we were! He made a fool of all the Chinese in the room! We couldn't help cursing him under our breath.

It took him more than half an hour to finish his lecture. The audience laughed and smirked when he finally stopped. A few young men, who must be students, whistled as Mr. Fang stood up to acknowledge the pitter-patter of applause, which was obviously meant to mock him.

I did not give the talk I had prepared. Completely flustered, I simply couldn't do it. But meanwhile, Mr. Fang kept smiling at us, his compatriots sitting along two folding tables. His broad face was glazed with perspiration, and his eyes glowed complacently. He was engulfed in a rectangle of sunlight falling in through a high window. Again and again he looked at us with a sort of disdain on his face, as if challenging us, "Who among you could deliver a lecture like that in English?" Were I able to reach him, I would have pinched his thigh to restore his senses.

The audience asked us some dull questions. We managed to answer them perfunctorily. Every one of us was somewhat shaken. My English became incoherent, marred by grammatical mistakes, as I struggled to interpret the questions and answers. In fact, I couldn't help stuttering, half throttled by scalding rage. My pulse went at 120 a minute at least.

Finally the whole thing was over, and every one of us felt relieved. Thank heaven, we survived it!

You can imagine how disgusted we were with Mr. Fang after that episode. Nobody would have anything to do with him. We wanted to let him wear the halo of "the great writer" alone. Ganlan even suggested we depart for San Francisco in secret, leaving him behind so that he would have trouble finding money for the return airfare. Of course we could not do that. Even if he had died, we would have had to bring his ashes back; because if he had remained in America, the authorities would have assumed he had defected, and would have criticized us for neglecting to anticipate his motives and, ergo, being the occasion of such an opportunity for him.

When we had returned to China, he was reprimanded by our college's Party Committee, which ordered him to turn in a thorough self-criticism. He did that. Then the Provincial Writers' Association revoked his membership. He became persona non grata again. *Narrative Techniques* was taken out of his hands, this time for good. He was returned to teaching as a regular faculty member and has been barred from attending conferences and giving talks.

Professor Pan, do not assume that this is his end. No, he is very much alive. There is one most remarkable quality in this man, namely that he is simply insuppressible, full of energy and resilience. Recently he has finished translating into English the autobiography of the late Marshal Fu; the book will be published by the International Friendship Press. He has made a tidy sum of money from the work. Rumor has it that he claims he is the best translator of Chinese into English in our country. Maybe that is true, especially after those master translators in Beijing and Shanghai either have passed away or are too old to embark on a large project. It seems Mr. Fang is rising again and will soon tip over. These days he brags that he has numerous connections in the capital, that he is going to teach translation and modern British fiction in your department next year, and that he will edit an English journal for your university.

Professor Pan, please forgive me for this long-winded reply. To be honest, I did not expect to write with such abandon. Actually this is the first time I am composing on a computer. It's quite an experience. The machine has undoubtedly enhanced my eloquence, and perhaps some grandiloquence; I feel as if it could form sentences by itself. Now, I must not digress anymore. Let me conclude by summarizing my opinion of Mr. Fang, though I will withhold my moral judgment: he is a man of vitality, learning, and stratagems; although already in his late fifties, he is still vigorous and may have many years left; as long as you have a way to contain him, he can be very useful and may contribute a great deal to your department. In other words, he can be used but should never be trusted, not unlike the majority of intellectuals, who are no more than petty scoundrels.

My respectful salute!

Zhao Ningshen, Chairman
Department of Foreign Languages
Muji Teachers College
March 29

The Woman from New York

Nobody in our neighborhood expected Chen Jinli would come back. When she was planning to go to America four years ago, many people had tried to dissuade her. What else did she want? She taught math at our city's Teachers College; she had a considerate husband and a lovely daughter, who was about to attend kindergarten; her family had just been allotted a three-bedroom apartment on the ground floor of a new building. We couldn't understand why she was so determined to go abroad. A few people said she wanted to make money. Most of us didn't think so. Although it was rumored that in America banknotes were as abundant as tree leaves, who would believe that? If she were a young girl, we could have guessed her motive, either entering college there or marrying a foreigner—an overseas Chinese or a white man. But she was already in her early thirties and had her family here. In spite of others' admonition, she left early that summer. Soon afterwards, her parents-in-law, both being high-ranking officials in Muji City Administration, told their colleagues and friends that Jinli wouldn't come back anymore. Old people would say, "What a heartless woman. How could she abandon her family like that? What's so good in America?"

Now she was back. She looked like a different woman, wearing a gold necklace, her lips rouged, her eyelashes blackened with ink, and even her toenails dyed red. We wondered why her shoes' heels needed to be four inches high. She could hardly walk on those stilts and often held out her hand for support when walking with others. In a way, her makeup and manners verified the hearsay that she had become the fifteenth concubine of a wealthy Chinese man in New York City.

During the first few months after she left, her husband, Chigan, had told us that she was studying English at a language school there, to get herself ready for a graduate program in math. Then we heard she was ill, unable to move about. A year later, word came that she was running a jewelry store in New York's Chinatown. Some people believed her business must be a gift from the rich old man.

Her last letter to Chigan said she decided to come back and stay with him and their child forever. By her appearance, we doubted that. Yet whenever asked whether she was going back to New York, she'd say, "No, I've lost my job there. The jewelry store was closed." A few relatives of hers were curious about how much money she had made, but she always told them, "I've no money. How could you make lots of money by waiting tables? In America half your income goes to taxes. You earn more, but you spend more, too."

Young people, eager to know of "the Beautiful Land,"

wanted her to talk about New York, but she would shake her head and say, "It's a nice place for rich people."

"Come on, Jinli, aren't most New Yorkers millionaires?"

"No. There're a few millionaires, but most people work harder than us. Some are homeless, sleeping on the streets."

What disappointment her words gave those credulous young ones, who believed Wall Street was paved with gold bricks.

She came back at a bad time. It was midsummer, the best season in the Northeast when the weather is congenial and fresh vegetables and fruits appear on the market, but her daughter, Dandan, had no school and could stay with Chigan's parents day and night. A week before Jinli's return, Dandan had been moved out so as to avoid her. In fact, the child had almost forgotten her mother. Whenever we asked her if she missed her, she would say, "No."

Jinli was disappointed not to see her daughter and got mad at Chigan. He tried to calm her by assuring her that Dandan would be back in a few days.

For a week Jinli was busy cleaning their home, which had been littered by Chigan. He was a clumsy man, though in his work he maintained machines at the Boat Designing Institute. Spoiled in his childhood, he didn't know how to keep things tidy and clean. Jinli found eggshells under the beds and dust cloaking the organ, the chests, and the wardrobe. Cobwebs hung in every corner of the ceilings; the rooms smelled musty, and she had to keep the windows open for days. All the quilts were shiny with grease, and a few had holes in them, burned by cigarettes. She was told that the washer she had sent home from America two years ago was kept at her parents-in-law's. Worst of all, her jasmines and peonies were all dead, standing like skeletons in the flowerpots, and the soil beneath them was covered with cigarette butts and half-burned matches. Within three days, the once-familiar door-slamming and clatter of dishes and pans resounded through the apartment once more—the couple began quarreling again.

"Gather your dirty socks and underwear. Go to your parents' house to wash them," she ordered him.

Without a word he was putting them into a cardboard case. She went on complaining about the cigarette ash in the kitchen and the bathroom. "This is like inside a crematorium," she kept saying.

He pushed up his wire-rimmed glasses with his fingertips and said finally, "If you don't like this home, why did you bother to come back?"

"You think I came back for you?" She bit her lower lip, her teeth showing neat and white. That was another miracle about her: before going to America she'd had compressed teeth, but now they were all regular and pearly, and her upper lip looked normal, no longer protruding. For sure, American dentists know how to straighten out teeth.

Indeed, she didn't return for Chigan. She missed their daughter. That was why Chigan's parents had prevented Dandan from meeting her. They despised Jinli, declaring they had no such daughter-in-law, even calling her "hussy" in the presence of others. Naturally, when Jinli stood at their doorstep one evening and begged them to allow her to say a word to Dandan, her mother-in-law refused to let her in, saying, "She doesn't want to see you. She has no such mother as you. Get away with your penciled eyes."

Chigan's father was standing in the living room, holding a fly-swatter and shaking his gray head. His back toward the door, he pretended he hadn't seen his daughter-in-law.

"When—when will she come home?" Jinli asked.

"This is her home," said Chigan's mother.

"Please, let me have a look at her." Tears were gathering in her eyes, but she tried suppressing them.

"No. She doesn't want to be disturbed by you."

"Mother, forgive me just this once, please!"

"Don't call me that. You're not my daughter-in-law anymore."

The door was shut. Jinli realized they'd never allow her to see her child. Hard as she tried, she couldn't get in touch with Dandan, who was kept from coming out of that brick house, a Russian bungalow. She didn't beg Chigan, knowing he dared not oppose his parents' will, and he might prefer such an arrangement as well.

When we heard she couldn't see her daughter, some of us thought it served her right, because hadn't she abandoned the child in the first place? But a few felt for her and said that since she couldn't see her daughter, she shouldn't stay for Chigan, who didn't deserve that kind of devotion. We were all eager to see what she would do next.

Two years after she left for America, her name had been removed from the payroll of the Teachers College, so now she no longer had a work unit and belonged to the army of the unemployed. How can she live without a job? we wondered. This is China, a socialist country, not like in New York where she could get along just by pleasing an old man. She didn't know she had lost her teaching position for good, assuming the removal of her name was temporary. She was shocked when they told her that because of her lifestyle in America, she was no longer suitable for teaching.

Somehow she found out that it was Professor Fan Ling who had spread the concubinary story. A few people urged her to go slap Fan Ling. Nobody liked Professor Fan, who was a smart tigress and had earned a master's degree in education from Moscow University in the early 1950s. According to Jinli, Fan Ling had slandered her because she wouldn't agree to be the sponsor of Professor Fan's nephew, who wanted to go to college in the U.S. "You see," Jinli told others, spreading her slim hands, revealing a chased gold ring on her third finger, "I'm not an American citizen and it's illegal for me to do that." Her words might be true, but we were not fully convinced.

She was informed that Fan Ling was going to attend the faculty and staff meeting on Tuesday afternoon. This would be a good opportunity for her to catch the professor and disgrace her publicly. We were eager to witness the scene, though also ready to intervene in time so that she wouldn't rough her up too much. Fan Ling was old, suffering from high blood pressure and kidney disease.

To our dismay, Jinli didn't show up in the auditorium on Tuesday afternoon. Professor Fan sat there in the back, dozing away peacefully, while the principal spoke about how we should welcome a group of heroes coming from the Chinese-Vietnamese border to give speeches on campus.

Later Jinli declared she would "sue" Fan Ling for calumny and make her "pay." That was an odd thing for her to say. Who had ever heard of a court that would handle such a trifle? Besides, there was no lawyer available for a personal case like this, which should be resolved either through the help of the school leaders or by the victim herself. Some people thought Jinli must have lost her nerve; this might prove that she had indeed led a promiscuous life abroad. Also, why on earth would she think of "pay" as a solution? This was a matter of name and honor, which no money could buy. She ought to have fought for herself, that is, to combat poison with poison.

One morning she went to the city's Bureau of Foreign Affairs to look for a job. She had heard there was a need for English interpreters. Our city was just opening to foreigners. To attract tourists, an amusement park was being constructed on one of those islands in the middle of the Songhua River. Jinli filled out six forms, but no official in charge of personnel received her. A young woman, a secretary, told her to come back next Thursday; in the meantime, the bureau would look into her file. Jinli pinned to the forms a copy of the certificate that confirmed she had studied English at an American language school and passed the standard exams, her spoken English rated "Excellent." She told the secretary that ideally she'd like to be a tourist guide.

"We need nine of them according to what I heard," the young woman whispered, her eyes still fixed on the applicant's lips, rouged so heavily they looked purple.

Jinli thought she would be asked to take an English test for the job, so she began listening to the BBC and Voice of America for at least three hours a day and reviewing a volume on TOEFL. Even when she was washing laundry, she'd keep the radio on. She returned to the bureau on Thursday afternoon and was referred to a section director. The official was a large man, fiftyish, with a bald patch on his crown. He listened attentively to her describing herself and her qualifications for working with foreigners. She grew excited, a bit carried away in her enthusiasm, and even said, "I lived in New York for four years and visited many places in America. As a matter of fact, I have lots of connections there and can help our city in some ways. I have an international driver's license."

The man cleared his throat and said, "Miss Chen, we appreciate your interest in the job." She was taken aback by his way of addressing her, not as a "Comrade," as though she were a foreigner or a Taiwanese. He went on, "We studied your file the day before yesterday. I'm afraid I have to disappoint you. That's to say, we can't hire you."

"Why?" She was puzzled, knowing there couldn't be enough applicants for the nine positions.

"I don't want to be rude. If you insist on knowing why, let me just say that we have to use people we can trust."

"Why? Am I not a Chinese?"

"You're already a permanent resident in the United States, aren't you?"

"Yes, but I'm still a Chinese citizen."

"This has nothing to do with citizenship. We don't know what you did in New York, or how you lived in the past few years. How can we trust you? We're responsible for protecting our country's name."

She understood now and didn't argue further. They had gotten her file from the college and must have been notified of her lifestyle in New York. Anger was flushing her face.

"Don't be too emotional, Miss Chen. I didn't mean to hurt your feelings. I am just passing the bureau's decision on to you." On the desk a shiny ant was scampering toward the inkstand; he crushed it with his thumbnail and wiped the dead ant off on his thigh.

"I understand." She stood up and turned to the door without saying goodbye.

Waiting for the bus outside the office building, she couldn't stop her tears. Now and again she wiped her cheeks with pinkish tissue. She fished her makeup kit out of her handbag and with the help of the mirror removed the smudges from her cheeks. The leatherette case in her hand attracted the eyes of a teenage girl, whose gaze roved between Jinli's necklace and the glossy case.

Having failed to get the job, she came up with another idea, which surprised us. She began trying to persuade Chigan to go to America with her. This terrified him. He didn't know English except for a few phrases like "Good morning," "Long live China!" "Friendship." For three decades, no family in our city had moved that far—clear across the Pacific Ocean—though a few had left for Hong Kong and Japan. One young woman, we were told, had been sold by her husband to a whorehouse in Hong Kong the moment they landed there. Understandably Chigan was frightened by his wife's suggestion. He believed that once they were in New York she'd sell him as a laborer or a gigolo. Physically he looked all right, a bit short but solid, with a flat face and round shoulders, but he would perish in America in no time if he did that kind of work. So, he resolutely refused to go with her, saying, "I'm a Chinese, I don't want to be a foreign devil!"

"You know," she said, "New York has a big Chinatown. You don't have to speak English there. There're so many Chinese around. Books, newspapers, TV, and movies are all in Chinese. You don't have to become an American devil at all."

"I won't go!" His beady eyes glittered and his nostrils were flaring.

"Come on, we'll make lots of money. Life's better there than here. You can eat meat and fish every day."

"Then why did you come back?"

"I came back to take you with me." Her apricot eyes winked at him, the long lashes flapping. "Did I go abroad just for myself? Didn't I say I was leaving to look for a new life for our family four years ago?"

"Yes, you did."

"You see, now I'm back to fetch you and our child. If we work hard, we'll get rich there and have a big house and two cars. Don't you want to drive a brand-new Ford?"

"No, I don't know how to drive."

"You can always learn. I can drive, it's much easier than riding a bicycle." Her hands gripped an imaginary wheel, turning it left and right, while her head tilted back, her eyes half shut.

He swallowed. "No. Even if you give me a gold mountain, I won't go."

"You know, Chigan, we can have more kids there." She winked again and smiled with a dimple on her chin.

This seemed to sink in, because he always wanted a son but wasn't allowed to have another child here. Yet after a moment's silence, he said, "Dandan is enough for me. I don't want another kid."

"Come on, will you be happy to remain a mechanic in the boatyard for the rest of your life?"

"Happy is the man who's content."

"All right, if you don't want to leave, let Dandan go with me. She'll have a good future there. She will go to Harvard."

"What's that?"

"The best university in the world."

"No, it can't be better than Oxford."

"Please, let her go with me." She tried to smile again, but her face twisted.

Of course he wouldn't trust her with the child. She couldn't bear his refusal anymore and burst into tears, begging him to let her see Dandan just once. Her crying softened him a little, and he agreed to talk to their daughter and see what the child thought.

The next afternoon he pedaled to his parents'. Onto the carrier of his Flying Pigeon bicycle was tied a long carton containing an electronic keyboard, a gift Jinli had brought back for her daughter.

Chigan's father scolded him and called him a thickhead, saying that if Jinli saw the child she could easily talk her into leaving
with her. "Why can't you see through such a simple trick?" the
old man asked, pointing a half-eaten tomato at his son.

The keyboard was put away; they would give it to Dandan at
the right time. The grandparents then asked the child, who was
upstairs watching the TV program "Baby Science," to write to
her mother. Chigan returned with the short letter before night-
fall. After reading it, Jinli was heartbroken and locked herself
in her room, weeping quietly. The letter said: "Go away, bad
woman. I don't want a mother like you!"

That stopped her from attempting to take the family abroad.
What was she going to do next? Probably she would return to
New York soon. But when asked about that, she said she would
stay, since neither her husband nor their child wanted to leave.

To our surprise, a week later Chigan filed for divorce. Who could
have imagined this feckless man was capable of taking such a
step? It must have been his parents who planned it and used their
connections to make the court give priority to the case, for without delay the divorce was granted. Jinli didn't seem to mind los-
ing her husband, though she did fight in court for custody of her
daughter. The judge said she was an irresponsible parent, then
announced to her, "Out of our concern for the child's physical
and mental health, this court declines your request." She was,
however, ordered to pay thirty-yuan in child support a month.
Strange to say, she insisted on paying a hundred instead. This
puzzled us. People began to wonder how much money she actually had. Perhaps she was a lady of wealth.

Then word went about that Jinli had a lot of money. Some
people said she was small-minded and stingy. If she was so rich,
why not buy her parents-in-law a twenty-seven-inch color TV—

either a Sony or a Sanyo? Had she done that, surely they'd have let go of the child. Yet some people didn't believe she was rich. They proved to be wrong.

On a windy afternoon Jinli arrived at Five Continents Commons to buy a new apartment. Recently our city had put up a few residential buildings on the riverbank to attract foreign customers, mainly overseas Chinese from Southeast Asia and businesspeople form Taiwan. Jinli seemed still set on staying in Muji, or at least spending a few months a year here.

"Your passport, please," said a slender young man, the manager of the estate.

Having handed him her passport, she felt something was wrong and wiggled slightly in the chair.

The man looked through the maroon-covered passport and said without raising his eyes, "This was issued by the People's Republic of China. You're a Chinese citizen?"

"Yes."

"Well, I can't help you. These apartments are only for foreign customers. We want hard currencies."

"I'll pay you U.S. dollars." She blushed a little and clasped her hands. Her interlaced fingers made the ring invisible.

A gleam crossed his dark eyes, but he shook his head and said, "No. I'm allowed to do business with foreigners only."

"What's the difference if I pay the same money and the same price?"

"I'm sorry, Comrade. This is a rule I have to follow or I'll lose my job." He combed back his soft hair with his fingers.

So she gave up the idea of buying an ultramodern apartment, which would cost twenty thousand dollars—about a quarter-million yuan according to the exchange rate on the black market at the time. None of us would dare dream of having so much money! Not even a medium-sized factory here would have that amount of cash. Finally we realized we might have a millionairess among us. Some people began to suck up to Jinli, saying they would help her find a job or a place to stay. But she didn't seem interested anymore. Whenever people condemned Chigan and his parents in front of her, she would say drily, "When I left I thought I could always come back." And she began to avoid others.

Nobody knows when she disappeared from Muji City. It's said that she left for Shenzhen or Hong Kong. Professor Fan, however, claims Jinli returned to New York to rejoin the old man and has changed her name. Chigan refuses to comment; maybe he doesn't know her whereabouts either.

A month after the divorce, he got married again. The bride, who was a young widow with a four-year-old boy, works in the same institute with him. She's a decent woman, loves her new husband, and takes good care of him and their home. We often see the newlyweds walking hand in hand in the evening. Never has Chigan looked so happy and healthy. His stomach has begun growing into a potbelly like a general's.

More amazing is that Dandan adores her stepbrother. She tells others she always wanted a younger brother and now she finally has one. The boy is attached to her, too; together they read picture-storybooks and recite nursery rhymes every day after school. Asked whether her stepmother is kind to her, Dandan will say, "My dad found me a good mommy." Sometimes she plays hopscotch with other children in front of the apartment building. A pair of huge butterflies, made of yellow ribbons, dangles at the ends of her braids as she capers around. Smiles widen her gazelle eyes.

After Cowboy Chicken
Came to Town

"I want my money back!" the customer said, dropped his plate on the counter, and handed me his receipt. He was a fiftyish man, of stout girth. A large crumb hung on the corner of his oily mouth. He had bought four pieces of chicken just now, but only a drumstick and a wing were left on the plate.

"Where are the breast and the thigh?" I asked.

"You can't take people in like this." The man's bulbous eyes flashed with rage. This time I recognized him; he was a worker in the nearby motor factory.

"How did we take you in?" the tall Baisha asked sharply, brandishing a pair of long tongs. She glared at the man, whose crown barely reached the level of her nose.

He said, "This Cowboy Chicken only sounds good and looks tasty. In fact it's just a name—it's more batter than meat. After two pieces I still don't feel a thing in here." He slapped his flabby side. "I don't want to eat this fluffy stuff anymore. Give me my money back."

"No way," Baisha said and swung her permed hair, which looked like a magpies' nest. "If you hadn't touched the chicken, we'd refund you the money. But—"

"Excuse me," Peter Jiao said, coming out of the kitchen together with Mr. Shapiro.

We explained to him the customer's demand, which Peter translated for our American boss. Then we all remained silent to see how Peter, our manager, would handle this.

After a brief exchange with Mr. Shapiro in English, Peter said in Chinese to the man, "You've eaten two pieces already, so we can only refund half your money. But don't take this as a precedent. Once you've touched the food, it's yours."

The man looked unhappy but accepted the offer. Still he muttered, "American dogs." He was referring to us, the Chinese employed by Cowboy Chicken.

That angered us. We began arguing with Peter and Mr. Shapiro that we shouldn't have let him take advantage of us this way. Otherwise all kinds of people would come in to sample our food for free. We didn't need a cheap customer like this one and should throw him out. Mr. Shapiro said we ought to follow the American way of doing business—you must try to satisfy your customers. "The customer is always right," he had instructed us when we were hired. But he had no idea who he was dealing with. You let a devil into your house, he'll get into your bed. If Mr. Shapiro continued to play the merciful Buddha, this place would be a mess soon. We had already heard a lot of complaints about our restaurant. People in town would say, "Cowboy Chicken is just for spendthrifts." True, our product was more expensive and far greasier than the local braised chicken, which was cooked so well that you could eat even the bones.

Sponge in hand, I went over to clean the table littered by that man. The scarlet Formica tabletop smelled like castor oil when greased with chicken bones. The odor always nauseated me. As I was about to move to another table, I saw a hole on the seat the size of a soybean burned by a cigarette. It must have been the work of that son of a dog; instead of refunding his money, we should've detained him until he paid for the damage.

I hated Mr. Shapiro's hypocrisy. He always appeared good-hearted and considerate to customers, but was cruel to us, his employees. The previous month he had deducted forty yuan from my pay. It hurt like having a rib taken out of my chest. What had happened was that I had given eight chicken breasts to a girl from my brother's electricity station. She came in to buy some chicken. By the company's regulations I was supposed to give her two drumsticks, two thighs, two wings, and two breasts. She said to me, "Be a good man, Hongwen. Give me more meat." Somehow I couldn't resist her charming smile, so I yielded to her request. My boss caught me stuffing the paper box with the meatiest pieces, but he remained silent until the girl was out of earshot. Then he dumped on me all his piss and crap. "If you do that again," he said, "I'll fire you." I was so frightened! Later, he fined me, as an example to the seven other Chinese employees.

Mr. Shapiro was an old fox, good at sweet-talking. When we asked him why he had chosen to do business in our Muji City, he said he wanted to help the Chinese people, because in the late thirties his parents had fled Red Russia and lived here for three years before moving on to Australia; they had been treated decently, though they were Jews. With an earnest look on his round, whiskery face, Mr. Shapiro explained, "The Jews and the Chinese had a similar fate, so I feel close to you. We all have dark hair." He chuckled as if he had said something funny. In fact that was capitalist baloney. We don't need to eat Cowboy Chicken here, or appreciate his stout red nose and his balding crown, or wince at the thick black hair on his arms. His company exploited not just us but also thousands of country people. A few villages in Hebei Province grew potatoes for Cowboy Chicken, because the soil and climate there produced potatoes similar to Idaho's. In addition, the company had set up a few chicken farms in Anhui Province to provide meat for its chain in China. It used Chinese produce and labor and made money out of Chinese customers, then shipped its profits back to the U.S. How could Mr. Shapiro have the barefaced gall to claim he had come to help us? We have no need for a savior like him. As for his parents' stay in our city half a century ago, it's true that the citizens here had treated Jews without discrimination. That was because to us a Jew was just another foreigner, no different from any other white devil. We still cannot tell the difference.

We nicknamed Mr. Shapiro "Party Secretary," because just like a Party boss anywhere he did little work. The only difference was that he didn't organize political studies or demand we report to him our inner thoughts. Peter Jiao, his manager, ran the business for him. I had known Peter since middle school, when his name was Peihai—an anemic, studious boy with few friends to play with. Boys often made fun of him because he had four tourbillions on his head. His father had served as a platoon commander in the Korean War and had been captured by the American army. Unlike some of the POWs, who chose to go to Canada or Taiwan after the war, Peihai's father, out of his love for our motherland, decided to come back. But when he returned, he was discharged from the army and sent down to a farm in a northern suburb of our city. In reality, all those captives who had come back were classified as suspected traitors. A lot of them were jailed again. Peihai's father worked under surveillance on the farm, but people rarely maltreated him, and he had his own home in a nearby village. He was quiet most of the time; so was his wife, a woman who never knew her dad's name because she had been fathered by some Japanese officer. Their only son, Peihai, had to walk three miles to town for school every weekday. That was why we called him Country Boy.

Unlike us, he always got good grades. In 1977, when colleges reopened, he passed the entrance exams and enrolled at Tianjin Foreign Language Institute to study English. We had all sat for the exams, but only two out of the three hundred seniors from our high school had passed the admission standard. After college, Peihai went to America, studying history at the University of Iowa. Later he changed his field and earned a degree in business from that school. Then he came back, a completely different man, robust and wealthy, with curly hair and a new name. He looked energetic, cheerful, and younger than his age. At work he was always dressed formally, in a Western suit and a bright-colored necktie. He once joked with us, saying he had over fifty pounds of American flesh. To tell the truth, I liked Peter better than Peihai. I often wondered what in America had made him change so much—in just six years from an awkward boy to a capable, confident man. Was it American water? American milk and beef? The American climate? The American way of life? I don't know for sure. More impressive, Peter spoke English beautifully, much better than those professors and lecturers in the City College who had never gone abroad and had learned their English mainly from textbooks written by the Russians. He had hired me probably because I had never bugged him in our school days and because I had a slightly lame foot. Out of gratitude I never spoke about his past to my fellow workers.

On the day Cowboy Chicken opened, about forty officials from the City Hall came to celebrate. At the opening ceremony, a vice mayor cut the red silk ribbon with a pair of scissors two feet long. He then presented Mr. Shapiro with a brass key the size of a small poker. What's that for? we wondered. Our city didn't have a gate with a colossal lock for it to open. The attendees at the ceremony sampled our chicken, fries, coleslaw, salad, biscuits. Coca-Cola, ginger ale, and orange soda were poured free like water. People touched the vinyl seats, the Formica tables, the dishwasher, the microwave, the cash register, the linoleum tile on the kitchen floor, and poked their heads into the freezer and the brand-new rest rooms. They were impressed by the whole package, shipped directly from the U.S. A white-bearded official said, "We must learn from the Americans. See how they have managed to meet every need of their customers, taking care of not only what goes in but also what comes out. Everything was thought out beforehand." Some of them watched us frying chicken in the stainless-steel troughs, which were safe and clean, nothing like a soot-bottomed cauldron or a noisy, unsteady wok. The vice mayor shook hands with every employee and told us to work hard and cooperatively with our American boss. The next day the city's newspaper, the *Muji Herald,* published a lengthy article about Cowboy Chicken, describing its appearance here as a significant breakthrough in the city's campaign to attract foreign investors.

During the first few weeks we had a lot of customers, especially young people, who, eager to taste something American, came in droves. We got so much business that the cooked-meat stands on the streets had to move farther and farther away from our restaurant. Sometimes when we passed those stands, their owners would spit on the ground and curse without looking at us, "Foreign lackeys!"

We'd cry back, "I eat Cowboy Chicken every day and gained lots of weight."

At first Mr. Shapiro worked hard, often staying around until we closed at ten-thirty. But as the business was flourishing, he hung back more and stayed in his office for hours on end, reading newspapers and sometimes chewing a skinny sausage wrapped in cellophane. He rested so well in the daytime and had so much energy to spare that he began to date the girls working for him. There were four of them, two full-timers and two part-timers, all around twenty, healthy and lively, though not dazzlingly pretty. Imagine, once a week, on Thursday night, a man of over fifty went out with a young girl who was happy to go anywhere he took her. This made us, the three men hired by him, feel useless, like a bunch of eunuchs, particularly myself because I'd never had a girlfriend, though I was almost thirty. Most girls were nice to me, but for them I was merely a good fellow, deserving more pity than affection, as if my crippled foot made me less than a man. For me, Mr. Shapiro was just a dirty old man, but the girls here were no better, always ready to sell something—a smile, a few sweet words, and perhaps their flesh.

The day after Mr. Shapiro had taken Baisha out, I asked her about the date, curious to see what else besides money made this paunchy man so attractive to girls. What's more, I was eager to find out whether he had bedded them in his apartment after dinner. That was illegal. If he had done it, we'd have something on him and could turn him in when it was necessary. I asked Baisha casually, "How many rooms does he have?" My hands were busy pulling plates out of the dishwasher and piling them up on a table.

"How should I know?" she said and gave me a suspicious stare. I must admit, she was smart and had a mind quick like a lizard.

"Didn't you spend some time with him yesterday evening?"

"Yes, we had dinner. That was all."

"Was it good?" I had heard he had taken the girls to Lucky House, a third-rate restaurant near the marketplace.

"So-so."

"What did you eat?"

"Fried noodles and sautéed beef tripe."

"Well, I wish somebody would give me a treat like that."

"What made you think it was his treat?"

"It wasn't?" I put the last plate on the pile.

"I paid for what I ate. I won't go out with him again. He's such a cheapskate."

"If he didn't plan to spend money, why did he invite you out?"

"He said this was the American way. He gave the waitress a big tip, though, a ten, but the girl wouldn't take it."

"So afterwards you just went home?"

"Yes. I thought he'd take me to the movies or a karaoke bar. He just picked up his big butt and said he had a good time. Before we parted on the street, he yawned and said he missed his wife and kids."

"That was strange."

Manyou, Jinglin, and I—the three male employees—talked among ourselves about Mr. Shapiro's way of taking the girls out. We couldn't see what he was up to. How could he have a good time just eating a meal with a girl? This puzzled us. We asked Peter whether all American men were so stingy, but he said that like us they would generally pay the bill in such a case. He explained, "Probably Mr. Shapiro wants to make it clear to the girls that this isn't a date, but a working dinner."

Who would buy that? Why didn't he have a working dinner with one of us, the male employees? We guessed he might have used the girls, because if he had gone to a fancy place like Four Seas Garden or the North Star Palace, which had special menus for foreigners, he'd have had to pay at least five times more than a Chinese customer. We checked with the girls, and they admitted that Mr. Shapiro had asked them to order everything. So he had indeed paid the Chinese prices. No wonder he had a good time. What an old fox. Still, why wouldn't he take the girls to his apartment? Though none of them was a beauty, just the smell of the youthful flesh should have turned his old head, shouldn't it? Especially the two part-timers, the college students, who had fine figures and educated voices; they worked only twenty hours a week and wouldn't condescend to talk with us very often. Probably Mr. Shapiro was no good in bed, a true eunuch.

Our business didn't boom for long. Several handcarts had appeared on Peace Avenue selling spiced chicken on the roadside near our restaurant. They each carried a sign that declared: PATRIOTIC CHICKEN — CRISPY, TENDER, DELICIOUS, 30% CHEAPER THAN C.C.! Those were not false claims. Yet whenever we saw their signs, we couldn't help calling the vendors names. Most citizens here, especially old people, were accustomed to the price and taste of the Patriotic Chicken, so they preferred it to ours. Some of them had tried our product, but they'd complain afterwards, "What a sham! So expensive, this Cowboy thing isn't for a Chinese stomach." And they wouldn't come again. As a result, our steady clientele were mainly fashionable young people.

One day Mr. Shapiro came up with the idea of starting a buffet. We had never heard that word before. "What does it mean?" we asked.

Peter said, "You pay a small amount of money and eat all you can."

Good, a buffet would be great! We were all ears. Our boss suggested nineteen yuan and ninety-five fen as the price for the buffet, which should include every kind of Cowboy Chicken, mashed potato, fries, salad, and canned fruit. Why didn't he price it twenty yuan even? we wondered. That would sound more honest and also make it easier for us to handle the change. Peter explained this was the American way of pricing a product. "You don't add the last straw to collapse the camel," he said. We couldn't understand the logic of a camel or a horse or an ox. Anyway, Mr. Shapiro fell in love with his idea, saying even if it didn't fetch us enough customers, the buffet would help spread our name.

Peter wasn't enthusiastic about it, but we all said it was a brilliant idea and would definitely make us famous. Of course we knew it wouldn't work. We supported it because we wanted to eat Cowboy Chicken. Mr. Shapiro was such a skinflint that he would never give us a discount when we bought chicken for ourselves. He said the company's policy didn't allow any discount for its employees. On the other hand, our friends, when buying chicken here, often asked us to do them a favor—give them either some choice pieces or a discount—but we dared not break the rules for them. Now came an opportunity, so without delay we put out notices and spread the word about the buffet, which was to start the following week. For a whole weekend, we biked around town in our free time to make sure the news would reach our relatives, friends, and whoever might benefit from it.

Two feet of snow fell on Sunday night, and traffic was paralyzed the next morning, but we all arrived at work on time. Mr. Shapiro was worried, fearing the severe weather would keep people indoors. We assured him that they were not hibernating bears and would definitely show up. Still anxious, he stood outside the front door with the fur earflaps of his hat tied around his jaw, smoking and looking up and down the street at the people shoveling snow. Whisps of smoke and breath hung around his head. We all had on dogskin or quilted trousers in such weather, but he wore only woolen pajamas underneath jeans. It was glitteringly cold outside; the wind tossed the phone lines, which whistled like crazy.

With his protruding mouth pointed at Mr. Shapiro, Manyou

said to us, "See how hard it is to be a boss in America. You have to worry about your business all the time."

"Boy, he's scared," I said.

"For once he's working," added Feilan, who, though a plump girl, had a pleasant apple face with two dimples on it. Unlike us, she hadn't gone to high school because she had flunked two of the entrance exams.

We set the buffet stand in a corner and fried piles of chicken. Gradually people arrived. When about a dozen customers had sat down to their meals, Mr. Shapiro looked relieved, though he couldn't stop rubbing his cheeks and ears, which must have frozen numb. He retreated into his office for coffee, having no idea that this was just the first skirmish of a mighty battle. As the morning went by, more and more people came in, and we could hardly cook enough chicken and fries for them. The room grew noisy and crowded, undoubtedly reaching its maximum capacity, but still our boss was happy. Encouraged by the bustling scene, he even whistled in his office, where he, through bifocal lenses, was reading the *China Daily*.

My father and uncle were among the first dozen customers. Both could hardly walk when done with eating. After they left, my brother brought over six young men from his electricity station; they all had a soda or a beer in their pockets so that they wouldn't have to buy a drink. Without delay they began to attack the buffet; they ate as though this were their last supper on earth. I kept count of their accomplishment—on average they each finished at least a dozen pieces of chicken. Even when they were done and leaving, every one of them held a leg or a wing in his hand. Baisha's family had come too, including her father, uncles, and aunts. So had the folks of Manyou, Jinglin, and Feilan. The two part-timers had no family in town, but more than ten of their schoolmates turned up. In the back corner a table was occupied by five people, whose catlike faces showed that they belonged to Peter's clan. Among them was a young woman at least seven months pregnant; she was Peter's sister, and surely her unborn baby needed nutrition.

We all knew the buffet was headed for disaster, but we didn't care very much and just continued deep-frying chicken and re-filling the salad and mashed-potato bowls. Once in a while we also went over to the buffet stand and picked a piece of chicken for ourselves, because today nobody could keep a record. At last we too could eat our fill. I liked the chicken better with soy sauce and slapped plenty on. The employees shared a bottle of soy sauce, which we kept under the counter.

By midday some people in the marketplace had heard of this rare bargain, and they came in, all eating like starved wolves. Most of them were from the countryside, in town selling and buying stuff; surely they had never dreamed that any restaurant would offer such an abundant meal.

Peter wasn't around most of the time. He had to be at the Tax Bureau in the morning, and in the afternoon he went to the bank to fetch our wages. When he returned at four o'clock, his face darkened at the amount of food consumed by the buffet. Twenty boxes of chicken and eighteen sacks of fries were gone—which should have lasted three days. He went to inform Mr. Shapiro, who came out of his office and looked disconcerted. Peter suggested we stop the buffet immediately. Our boss's face reddened, his Adam's apple going up and down as though he were guzzling something. He said, "Let's offer it a little while longer. We're not sure if we lost money or not."

We closed twenty minutes early that night in order to count the money. The result didn't surprise us: we lost seven hundred yuan, exclusive of our wages.

In spite of his misshapen face, Mr. Shapiro insisted on trying the buffet for another day. Perhaps he meant to show who was in command, reluctant to admit the buffet was a flop. This suited us fine, since not all of our people had come yet.

The next day, Mr. Shapiro sat on a chair outside his office and watched the customers stuffing themselves. He looked like a giant bulldog, vigilant and sulky, now shaking his head, now smiling exaggeratedly. At times his face turned grim, his eyelids trembling a little. A few men from my father's office showed up, and two of them even attempted to chat with me in front of my boss. This scared me. I responded to their greetings and questions cursorily, for fear that Mr. Shapiro might detect my connection with them. Fortunately he didn't understand our language, so he noticed nothing.

After my father's colleagues left, a tall, thirtyish man in a buff corduroy jacket turned up. After paying for the buffet, he left his fur hat on a table, then walked across to the stand and filled a plate with drumsticks and breasts. As he was about to return to his seat, Mr. Shapiro stopped him and asked, "Why did you come again?"

The man happened to know some English and said with a friendly grin, "First-time customer."

"You ate tons of chicken and mashed potato just now. How come you're hungry again so soon?"

"What's this about?" The man's face changed.

Peter came over, but he wasn't sure if the man had been here before. He turned to us and asked, "Is this his second time?"

Before we could answer, the man flared up, "This is my hundredth time. So what? I paid."

Manyou laughed and told Peter, "There was a fella here just now in the same kind of jacket, but that was a different man."

"That's true," I piped in. I knew the other man—he was an accountant in my father's bureau. This fellow fuming in front of us was a genuine stranger, with a beeper on his belt. He must be a cabdriver or an entrepreneur.

Peter apologized to the man, told him to go ahead and eat, then he explained the truth to Mr. Shapiro, who had become so edgy that some customers began to look identical to him. "How the hell could I tell the difference?" our boss said. "To me they all look alike—they're all real Chinese, with appetites like alligators." He laughed heartily, like a young boy.

Peter interpreted his words to us, and we all cracked up.

On the second day, we lost about six hundred yuan, so that was the end of the buffet. Lucky for us, Mr. Shapiro didn't withhold our wages, which we all received the next day. This was the beauty of working for Cowboy Chicken—it was never late in paying us, unlike many Chinese companies, especially those owned by the state, which simply didn't have enough cash to pay employees their full wages. My mother often got only sixty percent of her salary from her weather station, which could not increase its clientele, or run a night school, or have any power over other companies. She'd sigh and say, "The longer I work, the more I lose."

At the sight of my monthly wages—468 yuan—my father became heartbroken. He'd had a drop too much that night, full of self-pity, and, waving a half-smoked cigarette, he said to me, "Hongwen, I've joined the Revolution for almost forty years, and I earn only three hundred yuan a month. But you just started working and you draw a larger salary. This makes me feel duped, duped by the Communist Party I've served."

My youngest brother butted in, "It's never too late to quit, Dad."

"Shut up!" I snapped. He was such an idiot, he couldn't see the old man was really suffering. I said to my father, "You shouldn't think that way. True, you're not paid a lot, but your job is secure, like a rubber rice bowl that nobody can take away from you or smash—even a tank cannot crush it. Every day you just sit at your desk drinking tea and reading newspapers, or chatting away, and at the end of each month you take home a full salary. But I have to work my ass off for a capitalist who pays me by the hour."

"You make so much and always eat high-protein food. What else do you want?"

I didn't answer. In my heart I said, I want a job that pays a salary. I want to be like some people who go to their offices every morning for an eight-hour rest. My father kept on: "Cowboy Chicken is so delicious. If I could eat it and drink Coke every day, I'd have no need for socialism."

I wouldn't argue with him. He was beside himself that night. Indeed, I did often have some tidbits at the restaurant, mainly fries and biscuits. As a result, I seldom ate dinner when I came home, but mainly it was because I wanted to save food for my family. My father, of course, assumed I was stuffing myself with chicken every day.

After the disastrous buffet, Mr. Shapiro depended more on Peter, who in fact ran the place single-handedly. To be fair, Peter was an able man and had put his heart into the restaurant. He began to make a lot of connections in town and persuaded people to have business lunches at our place. This made a huge difference. Because their companies would foot the bill, the business-people would order table loads of food to treat their guests to hearty American meals, and then they'd take the leftovers home for their families. By and by our restaurant gained a reputation in the business world, and we established a stable clientele. So once again Mr. Shapiro could stay in his office in the morning drinking coffee, reading magazines, and even listening to a tape to learn the ABCs of Chinese.

———————

One afternoon the second son of the president of Muji Teachers College phoned Peter, saying he'd like to hold his wedding feast at our restaurant. I knew of this dandy, who had divorced his hardworking wife the year before; his current bride used to be a young widow who had given up her managerial position in a theater four years ago in order to go to Russia. Now they had decided to marry, and he wanted something exotic for their wedding dinner, so he picked Cowboy Chicken.

Uneasy about this request, Mr. Shapiro said to Peter, "We're just a fast-food place. We're not equipped to cater a wedding banquet."

"We must not miss this opportunity," said Peter. "A Chinese man would spend all his savings on his wedding." His owlish eyes glittered.

"Well, we'll have to serve alcoholic beverages, won't we? We have no license."

"Forget that. Nobody has ever heard of such a thing in China. Even a baby can drink alcohol here." Peter grew impatient.

Manyou, who could speak a few words of English, broke in, "Mr. Shapiro, Peter is right. Men of China use all moneys for wedding, big money." He seemed embarrassed by his accent and went back to biting his cuticles.

So our boss yielded. From the next day on, we began to prepare the place for the wedding feast. Mr. Shapiro called Cowboy Chicken's headquarters in Beijing to have some cheesecakes, ice cream, and California wines shipped to us by the express mail. Peter hired two temps and had the room decked out with colorful ribbons and strings of tiny lightbulbs. Since it was already mid-December, he had a dwarf juniper and candlesticks set up in a corner. We even hung up a pair of large bunny lanterns at the front door, as the Year of Rabbit was almost here. Peter ordered us to wear clean uniforms for the occasion—red sweaters, black pants, and maroon aprons.

The wedding banquet took place on a Thursday evening. It went smoothly, since most of the guests were from the college, urbane and sober-minded. The bride, a small woman in her mid-thirties, wore a sky-blue silk dress, her hair was permed, and her lips were rouged scarlet. She smiled without stopping. It was too bad that her parents hadn't given her beautiful eyes; she must have been altered by cosmetic surgery, which had produced her tight, thick double lids. Baisha said the woman owned two gift shops in Moscow. Small wonder she wore six fancy rings and a tiny wristwatch in the shape of a heart. With so many diamonds and so much gold on her fingers, she must be lazy, not doing any housework. From her manners we could tell she had seen the world. By comparison, her tall groom looked like a bumpkin despite his fancy outfit—a dark-blue Western suit, a yellow tie studded with tiny magpies, and patent-leather boots with brass buckles. He had a hoarse voice, often laughing with a bubbling sound in his throat. When he laughed, you could hardly see anything on his face except his mouth, which reminded me of a crocodile's. His gray-haired parents sat opposite him, quiet and reserved, both of them senior officials.

The man officiating at the banquet spoke briefly about the auspicious union of the couple. Next, he praised the simple wedding ceremony, which had taken place two hours ago. After a round of applause, he turned to our boss and said, "We thank our American friend, Mr. Ken Shapiro, for providing us with such a clean, beautiful place and the delicious food. This is a perfect example of adapting foreign things to Chinese needs."

People clapped again. All our boss could say in Chinese was "Thank you." He looked a little shy, his cheeks pink and his hazel eyes gleaming happily.

As people were making the first toast, we began to serve chicken, every kind we had—crispy, spicy, barbecued, Cajun, and Cowboy original. An old woman opened a large paper napkin with a flowered pattern on it, and studied it for a long time as though it were a piece of needlework on lavender silk which she was reluctant to spoil. A bottle of champagne popped and scared the bridesmaid into screaming. Laughter followed.

"Boy, this is hot!" the groom said, chewing a Cajun wing and exhaling noisily.

They all enjoyed the chicken, but except for the champagne they didn't like the American wines, which were too mild for them. Most women wouldn't drink wine; they wanted beer, Coca-Cola, and other soft drinks. Fortunately Peter had stocked some Green Bamboo Leaves and Tsingtao beer, which we brought out without delay. We had also heated a basin of water, in which we warmed the liquor for them. Mr. Shapiro raved to his manager, "Fabulous job, Peter!" He went on flashing a broad smile at everyone, revealing his white teeth. He even patted some of us on the back.

I liked the red wine, and whenever I could, I'd sip some from a glass I had poured myself. But I dared not drink too much for fear my face might change color. When the guests were done with chicken, fries, and salad, we began to serve cheesecake and ice cream, which turned out to be a big success. Everybody loved the dessert. An old scholarly-looking man said loudly, "Ah, here's the best American stuff!" His tone of voice suggested he had been to the U.S. He forked a chunk of cheesecake into his mouth and smacked his thin lips. He was among the few who could use a fork skillfully; most of them ate with chopsticks and spoons.

That was the first time we offered cheesecake and ice cream, so all of us—the employees—would take a bite whenever we could. Before that day, I had never heard of cheesecake, which I loved so much I ate two wedges. I hid my glass and plate in a cabinet so that our boss couldn't see them. As long as we did the work well, Peter would shut his eyes to our eating and drinking.

For me the best part of this wedding feast was that it was subdued, peaceful, and short, lasting only two hours, perhaps because both the bride and the groom had been married before. It differed from a standard wedding banquet, which is always raucous and messy, drags on for seven or eight hours, and often gets out of hand since quarrels and fights are commonplace once enough alcohol is consumed. None of these educated men and women drank to excess. The only loudmouth was the bridegroom, who looked slightly retarded. I couldn't help wondering how come that wealthy lady would marry such a heartless ass, who had abandoned his two small daughters. Probably because his parents had power, or maybe he was just good at tricking women. He must have wanted to live in Moscow for a while and have another baby, hopefully a boy. Feilan shook her head, saying about him, "Disgusting!"

When the feast was over, both Mr. Shapiro and Peter were excited, their faces flushed. They knew we had just opened a new page in Cowboy Chicken's history; our boss said he was going to report our success to the headquarters in Dallas. We were happy too, though sleepy and tired. If business was better, we might get a bigger raise the next summer, Mr. Shapiro had told us.

That night I didn't sleep well and had to go to the bathroom continually. I figured my stomach wasn't used to American food yet. I had eaten fries and biscuits every day, but had never taken in ice cream, cheesecake, red wine, and champagne. Without doubt my stomach couldn't digest so much rich stuff all at once. I was so weakened that I wondered if I should stay home the next morning.

Not wanting to dampen our spirit of success, I hauled myself to the restaurant at nine o'clock, half an hour late. As we were cutting vegetables and coating chicken with spiced flour, I asked my fellow workers if they had slept well the night before.

"What do you mean?" Baisha's small eyes stared at me like a pair of tiny daggers.

"I had diarrhea."

"That's because you stole too much food, and it serves you right," she said with a straight face, which was slightly swollen with pimples.

"So you didn't have any problem?"

"What makes you think I have the same kind of bowels as you?"

Manyou said he had slept like a corpse, perhaps having drunk too much champagne. To my satisfaction, both Jinglin and Feilan admitted they too had suffered from diarrhea. Feilan said, "I thought I was going to die last night. My mother made me drink two kettles of hot water. Otherwise I'd sure be dehydrated today." She held her sides with both hands as if about to run for the ladies' room.

Jinglin added, "I thought I was going to poop my guts out." Indeed, his chubby face looked smaller than yesterday.

As we were talking, the phone rang. Peter answered it. He sounded nervous, and his face turned bloodless and tiny beads of sweat were oozing out on his stubby nose. The caller was a woman complaining about the previous evening's food. She claimed she had been poisoned. Peter apologized and assured her that we had been very careful about food hygiene, but he would investigate the matter thoroughly.

The instant he put down the phone, another call came in. Then another. From ten o'clock on, every few minutes the phone would ring. People were lodging the same kind of complaint against our restaurant. Mr. Shapiro was shaken, saying, "Jesus, they're going to sue us!"

What did this mean? we asked him, unsure how suing us could do the complainers any good. He said the company might have to pay them a lot of money. "In America that's a way to make a living for some people," he told us. So we worried too.

At noon the college called to officially inform Peter that about a third of the wedding guests had suffered from food poisoning, and that more than a dozen faculty members were unable to teach that day. The bridegroom's mother was still in Central Hospital, taking an intravenous drip. The caller suspected the food must have been unclean, or past its expiration dates, or perhaps the ice cream had been too cold. Mr. Shapiro paced back and forth like an ant in a heated pan, while Peter remained quiet, his thick eyebrows knitted together.

"I told you we couldn't handle a wedding banquet," our boss said with his nostrils expanding.

Peter muttered, "It must be the cheesecake and the ice cream that upset their stomachs. I'm positive our food was clean and fresh."

"Maybe I shouldn't have gone the extra mile to get the stuff from Beijing. Now what should we do?"

"Don't worry. I'll explain to them."

From then on, whenever a complainer phoned, Peter would answer personally. He said that our food had been absolutely fresh and clean but that some Chinese stomachs couldn't tolerate dairy products. That was why more than two thirds of the previous night's diners had not felt anything unusual.

His theory of Chinese stomachs was sheer nonsense. We had all drunk milk before and had never been poisoned like this. Three days later, a 1,200-word article appeared in the *Muji Herald*. Peter was its author. He wrote that there was this substance called lactose, to which many Chinese stomachs were allergic because our traditional diet included very little dairy food. He even quoted from a scientific journal to prove that the Chinese had different stomachs from the Westerners. He urged people to make sure they could endure lactose before they ate our dairy items. From now on, he declared, our restaurant would continue to offer ice cream, but also a variety of non-milk desserts, like Jell-O, apple pie, pecan pie, and canned fruit.

I was unhappy about the article, because I had thought the company might compensate us for the suffering we'd gone through. Even a couple of yuan would help. Now Peter had blown that possibility. When I expressed my dissatisfaction to my fellow workers, Feilan said to me, "You're small-minded like a housewife, Hongwen. As long as this place does well, we'll make more money."

Bitch! I cursed to myself. But I gave some thought to what she said, and she did have a point. The restaurant had almost become our work unit now; we'd all suffer if it lost money. Besides, to file for compensation, I'd first have to admit I had pilfered the ice cream and cheesecake. That would amount to asking for a fine and ridicule.

Soon Peter had Cowboy Chicken completely in his clutches. This was fine with us. We all agreed he could take care of the place better than Mr. Shapiro. We nicknamed him Number-Two Boss. Since the publication of his article, which had quieted all complaints, more and more people ate here, and some came especially for our desserts. Young women were partial to Jell-O and canned fruit, while children loved our ice cream. Again we began to cater for wedding banquets, which gradually became an important source of our profits. From time to time people called and asked whether we'd serve a "white feast"—the dinner after a funeral. We wouldn't, because it was much plainer fare than a wedding banquet and there wasn't much money to be made. Besides, it might bring bad luck.

———

When the snow and ice had melted away from the streets and branches began sprouting yellowish buds, Mr. Shapiro stopped going out with the girls as often as before. By now most restaurants in town treated him as a regular customer, charging him the Chinese prices. One day, Juju, the younger part-timer, said our boss had gotten fresh with her the previous evening when he was tipsy at Eight Deities Garden. He had grasped her wrist and called her "Honey." She declared she wouldn't go out with him anymore. We told the girls that if he did anything like that again, they should report him to the police or sue him.

In late April, Mr. Shapiro went back to Texas for a week to attend his stepdaughter's wedding. After he returned, he stopped dating the girls altogether. Perhaps he was scared. He was wise to stop, because he couldn't possibly contain himself all the time. If he did something indecent to one of the girls again and she reported him to the authorities, he would find himself in trouble, at least be fined. Another reason for the change might be that by now he had befriended an American woman named Susanna, from Raleigh, North Carolina, who was teaching English at Muji Teachers College. This black woman was truly amazing, in her early thirties, five foot ten, with long muscular limbs, and a behind like a small cauldron. She had bobbed hair, and most of the time wore jeans and earrings the size of bracelets. We often speculated about those gorgeous hoop earrings. Were they made of fourteen-karat gold? Or eighteen-karat? Or twenty-karat? At any rate, they must have been worth a fortune. Later, in the summer, she took part in our city's marathon and almost beat the professional runners. She did, however, win the Friendship Cup, which resembled a small brass bucket. She was also a wonderful singer, with a manly voice. Every week she brought four or five students over to teach them how to eat American food with forks and knives. When they were here, they often sang American songs she had taught them, such as "Pretty Paper," "Winter Wonderland," and "Silent Night, Holy Night." Their singing would attract some pedestrians, which was good for business, so we were pleased to have her here. Mr. Shapiro gave them a twenty-percent discount, which outraged us. We wondered why he kept a double standard. We had a company policy against discounts, but it must apply only to Chinese employees. Still, we all agreed Susanna was a good woman. Unlike other customers, she gave us tips; also, she paid for her students' meals.

One afternoon in late May, Susanna and four students were eating here. In came a monkey-like man, who had half-gray hair and flat cheeks. With a twitching face he went up to Peter, his fist clutching a ball of paper. He announced in a squeaky voice, "I'm going to sue your company for ten thousand yuan."

This was the first time I ever had heard a Chinese say he would sue somebody for money. We gathered around him as he unfolded the paper ball to display a fat greenhead. "I found this fly in the chicken I bought here," he said firmly, his right hand massaging his side.

"When did you buy the chicken?" Peter asked.

"Last week."

"Show me the receipt."

The man took a slip of paper out of his trouser pocket and handed it to Peter.

About twenty people formed a half-circle to watch. As the man and Peter were arguing, Mr. Shapiro and Susanna stepped out of his office. Seeing the two Americans, the man wailed at Peter, "Don't dodge your responsibility. I've hated flies all my life. At the sight of this one I puked, then dropped to the floor and fainted. I thought I'd recover soon. No, the next evening I threw up again and again. That gave me a head-splitting migraine and a stomach disorder. My ears are still ringing inside, and I've lost my appetite completely. Since last Wednesday I haven't gone to work and have suffered from insomnia every night." He turned to the spectators. "Comrades, I'm a true victim of this capitalist Cowboy Chicken. See how skinny I am."

"Like a starved cock," I said. People laughed.

"Stop blustering," Peter said to him. "Show us your medical records."

"I have them in the hospital. If you don't pay me the damages I'll come again and again and again until I'm fully compensated."

We were all angry. Feilan pointed at the man's sunken mouth and said, "Shameless! You're not Chinese."

Baisha said, "Ten thousand yuan for a fly? How could you dream of that? Even your life isn't worth that much."

When a student had interpreted the man's accusation to Mr. Shapiro and Susanna, our boss turned pale. He moved closer and managed a smile, saying, "Sir, if you have concrete evidence, we'll be willing to consider your demand."

The student interpreted those words to the man, on whose face a vile smile appeared. We were angry at Mr. Shapiro, who again was acting like a number-one Buddha. If you run into an evil man, you have to adopt uncivil measures. Our boss's hypocrisy would only indulge this crook.

"Excuse me," Manyou cried and arrived with a bowl of warm water. He put it on the counter and said to the man, "I'm going give your fly a hot bath, to see if it's from our place." He picked up the insect with a pair of chopsticks and dropped it into the bowl. We were all puzzled.

A few seconds later, Manyou announced, "This fly is not from Cowboy Chicken because, see, there isn't any oil on the water. You all know we only sell fried chicken."

Some spectators booed the man, but he wouldn't give way. He fished out the fly with his hand and wrapped it up, saying, "I'm going take you to court no matter what. If you don't offer a settlement, there'll be no end of this."

With a false smile Jinglin said to him, "Uncle, we're one family and shouldn't be so mean to each other. Let's find a quiet place to talk this out, all right? We can't negotiate in front of such a crowd."

The man looked puzzled, flapping his round eyes. Jinglin hooked his heavy arm around the man's neck while his eyes signaled at me. Reluctantly the crook moved away with him.

I followed them out the front door. It was slightly chilly outside, and the street was noisy with bicycle bells, vendors' cries, and automobile horns. A few neon lights flickered in the north. After about fifty paces, we turned in to a small alley and then stopped. Jinglin smiled again, revealing his rotten teeth, and he took out a small pocketknife and a ten-yuan note. He opened the knife and said to the man, "I can pay you the damages now. You have a choice between these two."

"Don't make fun of me! I asked for ten thousand yuan."

"Then I'll let you taste this knife."

The man wasn't frightened by the two-inch blade. He grinned and asked, "Brothers, why help the foreign devils?"

"Because Cowboy Chicken is our company, and our livelihood depends on it," I answered.

Jinglin said to him, "You're the scum of the Chinese! Come on, choose one."

The man didn't lift his hand. Jinglin said again, "I know what you're thinking. I can't stab you with such a small thing, eh? Tell you what—I know your grandson who goes to the Second Elementary School, and I can catch him and cut off his little pecker with this knife. Then your family line will be gone. I mean it. Now, pick one."

The crook was flabbergasted, looking at me and then at

Jinglin, whose fat face became as hard as though made of copper sheet. With a trembling hand he took the money and mumbled, "Foreign dogs." He turned and hurried away. In no time he disappeared in a swarm of pedestrians.

We both laughed and walked back to the restaurant. Across the street, three disheveled Russian beggars were playing the violin and the bandora. Unlike most Chinese beggars, who would cry woefully and accost people, those foreign musicians were reserved, with just a porkpie hat on the ground to collect money, as though they didn't care whether you gave or not.

We didn't tell our boss what we had done; we just said the man was satisfied with a ten-yuan note and wouldn't come again. Susanna and her students applauded when they heard the news. Peter reimbursed Jinglin the money on the spot. Still, Mr. Shapiro looked suspicious and was afraid the man would return.

"He won't trouble us anymore," Peter said, smiling.

"Why are you so sure?" asked our boss.

"I have this." With two fingers Peter pulled the crook's receipt out of his breast pocket.

We all laughed. Actually, even with the receipt in hand, that old bastard wouldn't have dared come again. He wasn't afraid of Jinglin exactly but feared his four brothers, who were all stevedores on the riverbank, good at fighting and never hesitant to use a club or a dagger or a crowbar. That was why Jinglin, unlike the rest of us, could get rid of him without fear of retaliation.

Later we revealed to Peter what we had done in the alley. He smiled and promised he would not breathe a word to Mr. Shapiro.

As our business became stable, Peter grew into a local power of sorts. For months he had been building a house in the countryside. We wondered why he wanted his home to be four miles away from town. It would be costly to ride a motorcycle back and forth every day. One Sunday morning, Baisha, Feilan, Manyou, Jinglin, and I set out to see Peter's new home. We pedaled abreast on the wide embankment along the Songhua River, humming movie songs and cracking jokes. Birds were crying furiously in the willow copses below the embankment, while on a distant jetty a team of men sang a work song as they unloaded timber from a barge. Their voices were faltering but explosive. It hadn't rained for weeks, so the river was rather narrow, displaying a broad whitish beach. A few boys fishing there lay on their backs; around them stood some short bamboo poles planted deep into the sand. When a fish bit, a brass bell on one of the poles would jingle. On the other shore, toward the horizon, four or five windmills were turning, full like sails; above them the gray clouds floated lazily by, like a school of turtles.

We knew Peter had a few American dollars in the bank, but we were unsure how rich he really was. His house, though unfinished, staggered us. It was a three-story building with a garage in its back; it sat in the middle of two acres of sloping land, facing a gentle bend in the river and commanding a panorama that included two islands and the vast landscape on the other shore.

Peter wasn't around. Six or seven workers were busy, rhythmically hammering something inside the house. We asked an older man, who looked like a supervisor, how much the house would cost.

"At least a quarter of a million yuan," he said.

"So expensive?" Manyou gasped, his large lashless eyes blazing.

"You know what? It could be even more than that. We've never seen a home like this before."

"What kind of house is this?" asked Feilan.

"It's called Victorian. Mr. and Mrs. Jiao designed it themselves. It has two marble fireplaces, both imported from Hong Kong."

"Damn! Where did he get so much money?" Baisha said and kicked a beer bottle with her white leather sandal.

We were all pondering the same question, and it weighed down our hearts like a millstone. But we didn't stay long, fearing Peter might turn up. On the way back we spoke little to one another, unable to take our minds off Peter's house. Obviously he made much more than we did, or he wouldn't have had the money for such a mansion, which was larger even than the mayor's. Before setting out, we had planned to have brunch together at a beer house, but now none of us had an appetite anymore. We parted company the moment we turned away from the quay.

After that trip, I noticed that my fellow workers often looked suspiciously at Peter, as though he were a hybrid creature. Their eyes showed envy and anger. They began learning English more diligently. Manyou attended the night college, working with a textbook called *English for Today,* while Baisha and Feilan got up early in the morning to listen to the study program on the radio and memorize English words and expressions. Jinglin wanted to learn genuine American English, which he said was more natural, so he was studying *English 900.* I was also learning English, but I was older than the others and didn't have a strong memory, so I made little progress.

At work, they appeared friendlier to Mr. Shapiro and often poured coffee for him. Once Baisha even let him try some scallion pancake from her own lunch.

One morning, when we were not busy, I overheard Baisha talking with Mr. Shapiro in English. "Have you a house in U.S.A.?" she asked.

"Yes, I have a brick ranch, not very big." He had a cold, his voice was nasal and thick.

"How many childs in house?"

"You mean children?"

"Yes."

"I have two, and my wife has three."

"Ah, you have five jildren?"

"You can say that."

Mr. Shapiro turned away to fill out a form with a ballpoint pen, while Baisha's narrow eyes squinted at his heavy cheek and then at the black hair on his wrist. She was such a flirt, but I was impressed. She was brave enough to converse with our boss in English!—whereas I could never open my mouth in front of him.

Because we had seen Peter's mansion, our eyes were all focused on him. We were eager to find fault with him and ready to start a quarrel. But he was a careful man, knowing how to cope with us and how to maintain our boss's trust. He avoided arguing with us. If we didn't listen to him, he'd go into Mr. Shapiro's office and stay in there for a good while. That unnerved us, because we couldn't tell if he was reporting us to the boss. So we dared not be too disobedient. Every night Peter was the last to leave. He'd close the shutters, lock the cash register, wrap up the unsold chicken, tie the package to the back of his Honda motorcycle, and ride away.

Ever since the beginning, the daily leftovers had been a bone of contention between Mr. Shapiro and us. We had asked him many times to let us have the unsold chicken at the end of the day, but he refused, saying the company's policy forbade its employees to have leftovers. We even offered to buy them at half price, but he still wouldn't let us. He assigned Peter alone to take care of the leftovers.

It occurred to us that Peter must have been taking the leftovers home for the construction workers. He had to feed them well, or else they might jerry-build his mansion. Damn him, he not only earned more but also got all the perks. The more we thought about this, the more resentful we became. So one night, after he closed up the place and rode away, we came out of the nearby alley and pedaled behind him. Manyou was at the night college, and Jinglin had to look after his younger brother in the hospital who had just been operated on for a hernia, so they couldn't join us. Only Feilan, Baisha, and I followed Peter. He was going much faster than we were, but we knew where he was headed, so we bicycled without hurry, chatting and laughing now and then.

In the distance Peter's motorcycle was flitting along the embankment like a will-o'-the-wisp. The night was cool, and a few men were chanting folk songs from their boat anchored in the river. We were eager to prove Peter had shipped the leftovers home, so that we could report him to Mr. Shapiro the next morning.

For a long while the light of Peter's motorcycle disappeared. We stopped, at a loss. Apparently he had turned off the embankment, but where had he gone? Should we continue to ride toward his home, or should we mark time?

As we were discussing what to do, a burst of flames emerged in the north, about two hundred yards away, at the waterside. We went down the embankment, locked our bicycles in a willow copse, and walked stealthily toward the fire.

When we approached it, we saw Peter stirring something in the fire with a trimmed branch. It was a pile of chicken, about twenty pieces. The air smelled of gasoline and burned meat. Beyond him, the waves were lapping the sand softly. The water was sprinkled with stars, rippling with the fishy breeze. On the other shore everything was buried in darkness except for three or four clusters of lights, almost indistinguishable from the stars in the cloudless sky. Speechlessly we watched. If there had been another man with us, we might have sprung out and beaten Peter up. But I was no fighter, so we couldn't do anything, merely crouch in the tall grass and curse him under our breath.

"If only we had a gun!" Baisha whispered through her teeth.

Peter was in a happy mood. With a ruddy face he began singing a song, which must have been made up by some overseas Chinese:

> *I'm not so carefree as you think,*
> *My feelings never unclear.*
> *If you can't see through me,*
> *That's because again you waste*
> *Your love on a worthless man.*
>
> *Oh my heart won't wander alone.*
> *Let me take you along.*
> *Together we'll reach a quiet place*
> *Where you can realize*
> *Your sweetest dream. . . .*

For some reason I was touched by the song. Never had I known he had such a gorgeous baritone voice, which seemed to come a long way from the other shore. A flock of ducks quacked in the darkness, their wings splashing the water lustily. A loon let out a cry like a wild laugh. Then all the waterfowl turned quiet, and Peter's voice alone was vibrating the tangy air chilled by the night.

Feilan whispered, "What a good time he's having here, that asshole."

"He must miss his American sweetheart," Baisha said.

Feilan shook her chin. "Makes no sense. He's not the romantic type."

"Doesn't he often say American girls are better than Chinese girls?"

"Shh—" I stopped them.

When the fire almost went out, Peter unzipped his fly, pulled out his dick, and peed on the embers, which hissed and sent up a puff of steam. The arc of his urine gleamed for a few seconds, then disappeared. He yawned, and with his feet pushed some sand over the ashes.

"Gross!" said Feilan.

Peter leaped on his motorcycle and dashed away, the exhaust pipe hiccuping explosively. I realized he didn't mind riding four miles to work because he could use some of the gasoline provided by our boss for burning the leftovers with.

"If only I could scratch and bite that bastard!" Feilan said breathlessly.

"Depends on what part of him," I said.

Baisha laughed. Feilan scowled at me, saying, "You have a dirty mind."

The next day we told all the other workers about our discovery. Everyone was infuriated, and even the two part-timers couldn't stop cursing capitalism. There were children begging on the streets, there were homeless people at the train station and the ferry house, there were hungry cats and dogs everywhere, why did Mr. Shapiro want Peter to burn good meat like garbage? Manyou said he had read in a restricted journal several years ago that some American capitalists would dump milk into a river instead of giving it to the poor. But that was in the U.S.; here in China, this kind of wasteful practice had to be condemned. I told my fellow workers that I was going to write an article to expose Ken Shapiro and Peter Jiao.

In the afternoon we confronted Peter. "Why do you burn the leftovers every night?" Manyou asked, looking him right in the eye.

Peter was taken aback, then replied, "It's my job."

"That's despicable," I snapped. "You not only burned them but also peed on them." My stomach suddenly rumbled.

Feilan giggled. Baisha pointed at Peter's nose and said sharply, "Peter Jiao, remember you're a Chinese. There are people here who don't have enough corn flour to eat while you burn chicken every night. You've forgotten your ancestors and who you are."

Peter looked rattled, protesting, "I don't feel comfortable about it either. But somebody has to do it. I'm paid to burn them, just like you're paid to fry them."

"Don't give me that crap!" Jinglin cut in. "You're a capitalist's henchman."

Peter retorted, "So are you. You work for this capitalist company too."

"Hold on," Manyou said. "We just want to reason you out of this shameful thing. Why do you waste chicken that way? Why not give the leftovers to the poor?"

"You think I enjoy burning them? If I gave them away, I'd be fired. This is the American way of doing business."

"But you're a Chinese running a restaurant in a socialist country," said Jinglin.

As we were wrangling, Mr. Shapiro came out of his office with coffee stains around his lips. Peter explained to him what we quarreled about. Our boss waved his hand to dismiss us, as though this were such a trifle that it didn't deserve his attention. He just said, "It's company's policy, we can't do anything about it. If you're really concerned about the waste, don't fry too many pieces, and sell everything you've fried." He walked to the front door to have a smoke outside.

Peter said, "That's true. He can't change a thing. From now on we'd better not fry more than we can sell."

I was still angry and said, "I'm going to write to the *Herald* to expose this policy."

"There's no need to be so emotional, Hongwen," Peter said with a complacent smile, raising his squarish chin a little. "There have been several articles on this subject. For example, the *Beijing Evening News* carried a long piece last week about our company.

The author praised our policy on leftovers and believed it would reduce waste eventually. He said we Chinese should adopt the American way of running business. In any case, this policy cannot be exposed anymore. People already know about it."

That silenced us all. Originally we had planned that if Mr. Shapiro continued to have the leftovers burned, we'd go on strike for a few days. Peter's words deflated us all at once.

Still, Jinglin wouldn't let Peter off so easily. When it turned dark, he pressed a thumbtack into the rear tire of the Honda motorcycle parked in the backyard. Peter called home, and his wife came driving a white Toyota truck to carry back the motorcycle and him. This dealt us another blow, because we hadn't expected he owned a brand-new pickup as well. No one else in our city could afford such a vehicle. We asked ourselves, "Heavens, how much money does Peter actually have?"

We were all anxious to find that out. On payday, somehow Mr. Shapiro mixed Peter's wages in with ours. We each received an envelope stuffed with a bundle of cash, but Peter's was always empty. Juju said Peter got only a slip of paper in his envelope, which was called a check. He could exchange that thing for money at the bank, where he had an account as if he were a company himself. In Juju's words, "Every month our boss just writes Peter lots of money." That fascinated us. How much did he get from Mr. Shapiro? This question had remained an enigma ever since we worked here. Now his pay was in our hands, and at last we could find it out.

Manyou steamed the envelope over a cup of hot tea and opened it without difficulty. The figure on the check astounded us: $1,683.75. For a good moment nobody said a word, never having imagined that Peter received an American salary, being paid dollars instead of yuan. That's to say, he made twenty times more than each of us! No wonder he worked so hard, taking care of

Cowboy Chicken as if it were his home, and tried every trick to please Mr. Shapiro.

That night after work, we gathered at Baisha's home for an emergency meeting. Her mother was a doctor, so their apartment was spacious and Baisha had her own room. She took out a packet of spiced pumpkin seeds, and we began chatting while drinking tea.

"God, just think of the money Peter's raking in," Jinglin said, and pulled his brushy hair, sighing continually. He looked wretched, as if ten years older than the day before. His chubby face had lost its luster.

I said, "Peter can afford to eat at the best restaurants every day. There's no way he can spend that amount of money."

Feilan spat the shells of a pumpkin seed into her fist, her eyes turning triangular. She said, "We must protest. This isn't fair."

Baisha agreed with a sigh, "Now I know what exploitation feels like."

"Peter has done a lot for Cowboy Chicken," Manyou said, "but there's no justification for him to make that much." He seemed still in a daze and kept stroking his receding chin.

"We must figure out a countermeasure," said Jinglin.

I suggested, "Perhaps we should talk with our boss."

"You think he'll pay each of us a thousand dollars?" Baisha asked scornfully.

"Of course not," I said.

"Then what's the point of talking with him?"

Manyou put in, "I don't know. What do you think we should do, Baisha?"

I was surprised that he should be at a loss too, because he was known as a man of strategies. Baisha answered, "I think we must unite as one and demand our boss fire Peter."

Silence fell in the room, in which stood a double bed covered with a pink sheet. A folded floral blanket sat atop a pair of eider-down pillows stacked together. I wondered why Baisha needed such a large bed for herself. She must have slept with her boy-friends on it quite often. She was such a slut.

"That's a good idea. I say let's get rid of Peter," Manyou said, nodding at her admiringly.

Still perplexed, I asked, "Suppose Mr. Shapiro does fire him, then what?"

"One of us may take Peter's job," said Manyou.

Feilan picked up, "Are you sure he'll fire Peter?"

To our surprise, Baisha said, "Of course he will. It'll save him fifteen hundred dollars a month."

"I don't get it," said Jinglin. "What's the purpose of doing this? Even if he fires Peter, he won't pay us more, will he?"

"Then he'll have to depend on us and may give us each a raise," answered Baisha.

Unconvinced, I said, "What if the new manager gets paid more and just ignores the rest of us?"

Manyou frowned, because he knew that only Baisha and he could be candidates for that position, which required the ability to use English. Feilan, Jinglin, and I couldn't speak a complete sentence yet.

"Let's draw up a contract," Feilan said. "Whoever becomes the new manager must share his wages with the rest of us."

We all supported the idea and signed a brief statement which said that if the new manager didn't share his earnings with the rest of us, he'd be childless and we could get our revenge in any way we chose. After that, Baisha went about composing a letter addressed to Mr. Shapiro. She didn't know enough English words for the letter, so she fetched a bulky dictionary from her parents' study. She began to write with a felt-tip pen, now and again consulting the dictionary. She was sleepy and yawned in-cessantly, covering her mouth with her left palm and disclosing her hairy armpit. Meanwhile, we cracked pumpkin seeds and chatted away.

The letter was short, but it seemed to the point. Even Manyou said it was good after he looked it over. It stated:

> Our Respected Mr. Kenneth Shapiro:
>   We are writing to demand you to fire Peter Jiao immediately. This is our united will. You must respect our will. We do not want a leader like him. That is all.
>   Sincerely,
>
>   Your Employees

We all signed our names and felt that at last we had stood up to that capitalist. Since I'd pass our restaurant on my way home, I took charge of delivering the letter. Before we left, Baisha brought out a bottle of apricot wine, and together we drank to our solidarity.

I dropped the letter into the slot on the front door of Cowboy Chicken. After I got home, for a while I was light-headed and kept imagining the shock on Mr. Shapiro's pudgy face. I also thought of Peter, who, without his current job, might never be able to complete his outrageous mansion. But soon I began to worry, fearing Baisha might become the new manager. Compared with Peter, she had a volatile temper and was more selfish. Besides, she couldn't possibly maintain the connections and clientele Peter had carefully built up, not to mention develop the business. Manyou wasn't as capable as Peter either. Sometimes he could be very clever about trivial matters, but he had no depth. He didn't look steady and couldn't inspire trust in customers. To be fair, Peter seemed indispensable to Cowboy Chicken. I wouldn't have minded if Mr. Shapiro had paid him five times more than me.

We all showed up at work at eight-thirty the next morning. To our surprise, neither Mr. Shapiro nor Peter betrayed any anxiety. They acted as if nothing had happened, and treated us the same as the day before. We were baffled, wondering what they had planned for us. Peter seemed to avoid us, but he was polite and quiet. Apparently he had read the letter.

We expected that our boss would talk with us one by one. Even if he wouldn't fire Peter, he might make some concessions. But for a whole morning he stayed in his office as if he had forgotten us altogether. He was reading a book about the Jews who had lived in China hundreds of years ago. His calm appearance agitated us. If only we could have had an inkling of what he had up his sleeve.

When the day was at last over, we met briefly at a street corner. We were confused, but all agreed to wait and see. Feilan sighed and said, "I feel like we're in a tug-of-war."

"Yes, we're in a mental war, so we must be tough-minded and patient," Manyou told us.

I went home with a stomachache. Again my father was drunk that night, singing revolutionary songs and saying I was lucky to have my fill of American chicken every day. I couldn't get to sleep until the wee hours.

The next day turned out the same. Peter assigned each of us some work, and Mr. Shapiro still wouldn't say an unnecessary word to us. I couldn't help picturing his office as a giant snail shell into which he had shut himself. What should we do? They must have devised a trap or something for us. What was it? We had to do something, not just wait like this, or they would undo us one by one.

That night we gathered at Baisha's home again. After a lengthy discussion, we agreed to go on strike. Baisha wrote a note, which read:

Mr. Shapiro:

Because you do not consider our demand, we decide to
strike at Cowboy Chicken. Begin tomorrow.

We didn't sign our names this time, since he knew who we
were and what we were referring to. I was unsure of the phrase
"strike at Cowboy Chicken," but I didn't say anything, guessing
that probably she just meant we'd leave the place unmanned.
Again I delivered the letter. None of us went to work the next
morning. We wanted the restaurant to lose some business and
our boss to worry a little so that he'd be willing to cooperate with
his workers. But we had agreed to meet at one o'clock in front of
Everyday Hardware, near Cowboy Chicken; then together we'd
go to our workplace and start to negotiate with Mr. Shapiro. In
other words, we planned to strike only for half a day.

After lunch we all arrived at the hardware store. To our astonishment, a squad of police was standing in front of Cowboy
Chicken as if a fire or a riot had broken out. They wouldn't allow
people to enter the restaurant unless they searched them. What
was going on? Why had Mr. Shapiro called in the police? We
were puzzled. Together we walked over as if we had just returned from a lunch break. The front of the restaurant was cor-
doned off, and three police were stationed at the door. A tall
policeman stretched out his arm to stop us. Baisha asked loudly,
"Hey, Big Wan, you don't remember me?" She was all smiles.

"Yes, I saw you," Wan said with a grin.

"We all work here. Let us go in, all right? We have tons of
work to do."

"We have to search you before letting you in."

"I've nothing on me. How do you search?" She spread her
arms, then lifted her long skirt a little with one hand, to show she
didn't even have a pocket.

"Stand still, all of you," said Wan. A policewoman waved a black wand over Baisha, a gadget like a miniature badminton racket without strings.

"Is this a mine detector or something?" Jinglin asked the policewoman.

"A metal detector," she said.

"What's going on here?" Baisha asked Wan.

"Someone threatened to blow this place up."

We were all horrified by that, hoping it had nothing to do with us.

The police let us in. The moment we entered we saw an old couple standing behind the counter taking care of orders. Damn it, Peter had brought his parents in to work! How come he wasn't afraid a bomb might blow them to pieces? In a corner, Susanna and two student-looking girls were wiping tables and placing silver. They were humming "We Shall Overcome," but stopped at the sight of us. In the kitchen the two part-timers were frying chicken. Dumbfounded, we didn't know how to respond to this scene.

Mr. Shapiro came over. He looked furious, his face almost purple. He said to us, his spit flying about, "You think you can frighten me into obeying you? Let me tell you, you are all terminated!"

I didn't know what his last word meant, though I was sure it had a negative meaning. Manyou seemed to understand, his lips twitching as if he were about to cry. He gulped and couldn't say a word.

Peter said to us, "We can't use you anymore. You're fired."

"You can't do this to us," Baisha said to Mr. Shapiro and stepped forward. "We are founders of this place."

Mr. Shapiro laughed. "What are you talking about? How much stock do you have in this company?"

What did he mean? We looked at one another, unable to

fathom his meaning. He said, "Go home, don't come anymore. You'll receive this month's pay by the mail." He turned and walked off to the men's room, shaking his head and muttering, "I don't want any terrorists here."

Peter smiled at us with contempt. "Well, the earth won't stop spinning without the five of you."

I felt the room swaying like a lumbering bus. I never thought I could be fired so easily: Mr. Shapiro just said a word and my job was no more. The previous fall I had quit my position in a coal yard in order to work here. Now I was a total loser, and people would laugh at me.

The five of us were terribly distressed. Before we parted company on the street, I asked Manyou to spell for me the word Mr. Shapiro had used. With his fountain pen he wrote on my forearm, "Terminated!" There was no need for an exclamation mark.

At home I looked up the word in my pocket dictionary; it says "finished." My anger flamed up. That damned capitalist believed he was finished with us, but he was mistaken. We were far from terminated—the struggle was still going on. I would ask my elder brother to cut the restaurant's electricity first thing the next morning. Baisha said she'd have one of her boyfriends create some problems in Cowboy Chicken's mail delivery. Manyou would visit his friends at the garbage center and ask them not to pick up trash at the restaurant. Jinglin declared, "I'll blow up Peter's Victorian!" Feilan hadn't decided what to do yet.

This was just the beginning.